SHATTERED Vows

CHRISTINA SOL

Shattered Vows

By: Christina Sol

Published by: Sol Media LLC

Cover Design: Mayhem Cover Creations

Paperback ISBN: 979-8-9855935-7-0

❀ Created with Vellum

CONTENTS

Chapter 1   1
Chapter 2   7
Chapter 3   15
Chapter 4   27
Chapter 5   33
Chapter 6   35
Chapter 7   41
Chapter 8   51
Chapter 9   57
Chapter 10   61
Chapter 11   75
Chapter 12   79
Chapter 13   95
Chapter 14   101
Chapter 15   109
Chapter 16   119
Chapter 17   129
Chapter 18   141
Chapter 19   145
Chapter 20   151
Chapter 21   155
Chapter 22   163
Chapter 23   173
Chapter 24   183
Chapter 25   195
Chapter 26   207
Chapter 27   211
Chapter 28   219
Chapter 29   229
Chapter 30   239
Chapter 31   243
Chapter 32   249
Chapter 33   261

Chapter 34   265

Chapter 35   279

Chapter 36   283

Chapter 37   295

Chapter 38   305

Chapter 39   311

Chapter 40   315

Epilogue   321

Enjoy this Book?   325

Also By Christina Sol   327

About the Author   329

Acknowledgments   331

For the 2005 NaNoWriMo crew.
Who would have thought it would lead to this?

CHAPTER ONE

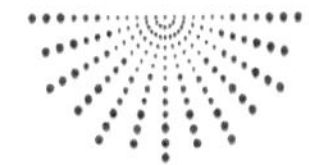

The heat in the car was stifling. The air conditioning had conked out somewhere in Middle America. But after six grueling days of driving, Alexandra Garcia had finally reached her destination: Hudson Island, Washington.

She stared at the large two-story Craftsman house with its wraparound porch. Two wooden rockers and a couple potted plants with pink and purple blooms gave it a warm, homey ambiance. Still, nerves and trepidation swirled in her stomach.

She let out a shaky breath. She'd be safe here. She had to be.

A wave of nausea hit, and her mouth filled with saliva. She shoved open the car door and, with her seatbelt cutting into her neck and shoulder, retched onto the driveway.

When her stomach stopped heaving, she eased back into the car and grimaced at the bitter taste lingering in her mouth.

With a tired sigh, she began to lower the vanity mirror, then thought better of it. She didn't want to know what she looked like. She imagined she looked a lot worse than she felt —and she felt like absolute crap.

Readjusting her oversized sunglasses, she got out of the car, carefully avoided her vomit, and gingerly climbed the steps to the house. Her entire body ached as she made her way to the far side of the porch and tried to recall Joe's instructions. Unsure if her memory was correct—the last couple weeks had been one giant blur—she reached behind the planter that sat between the two well-loved rocking chairs. A groan of relief escaped her lips when her fingers found the key.

She trudged to the door and slipped the key into the lock. But before she could turn the handle, the door swung open, and a large, solid man came to an abrupt halt in the threshold.

She swallowed a scream, and her pulse raced as she staggered backward. She nearly tumbled down the front steps, but strong hands caught her arms, righted her, and then promptly released her. The man stepped away and back into the doorway. His arms crossed over his broad chest, and he quickly looked her over. From the way his jaw tensed and his eyes narrowed, it was obvious he didn't like what he saw.

"Alex Garcia, I assume?"

Her heart pounded in her ears. All she could do was nod.

"I'm Quinn," he said.

The two words were spoken as if she should know who he was. She didn't. He let out a sigh that sounded exasperated.

She opened her mouth to respond, but nothing came out.

"I'm a friend of Joe's." He spoke in a quiet baritone, his gray eyes never leaving hers. "He told me you were coming so I could open up the house. Our friend Roxie will be over later tonight to make it livable for you. I'm in the house next door, and Roxie's in the guest house behind mine. Want a tour of the place?"

Somewhere along the line, her heartbeat had almost returned to normal. She found her voice, shaky as it was, and said, "Yes, thank you."

Quinn stepped aside to allow her to enter. Her gaze flickered between him and the floor as she hurried past, and she was thankful when he didn't close the front door behind her.

Pausing in the entryway, she turned to face him. "Um, Joe didn't mention you, but he did mention someone named Conner or Connie . . . someone he used to work with, I think. Does he . . . er, she . . . live nearby as well?"

The stern look on Quinn's face eased, and the corners of his lips lifted.

Her breath caught, and she blinked. The man's smile changed him completely. In one second flat, he'd gone from serious-and-a-little-bit-scary to charming-twinkling-eyes-whoa.

She frowned, diverting her attention to her feet. The *last* thing she needed right now was more trouble in her life, and nothing said "trouble" better than a disarming grin. God knew she'd learned that the hard way.

"One and the same. Quinn O'Conner. My annoying friends sometimes call me Connie." He stuck out his hand, the somber expression back. "And sorry for almost barreling over you a few minutes ago. We weren't expecting you until tonight."

"Um, I'm Na—" She stopped, catching herself. Then, stammering, she said, "Alexandra. Alexandra Garcia, but feel free to call me Alex. But yeah . . . you, uh, knew that already."

Good god, she wanted to kick herself. When had it become so hard to form a sentence? Mortified, she cleared her throat and pushed her sunglasses to the top of her head, then shook his hand. And froze.

Until she'd touched him, until her hand had completely disappeared in his, she hadn't realized just how much larger he was. He could easily break her in two if he wanted. And she knew from experience there would be nothing she could do about it. She'd tried to defend herself against Preston . . . and that obviously hadn't turned out well.

She startled when Quinn softly squeezed her hand. The gesture pulled her from her ruminations as he let go.

"Can I get your things from your car? Give you a minute to wander around by yourself?" She nodded, and he motioned down the hallway. "The bathroom's the first door on the right." A muscle in his jaw clenched, and he didn't wait for a reply. Just took the keys from her hand and silently walked out.

Once the door shut behind him, she let out a breath she hadn't realized she'd been holding. She wandered down the hall and into the bathroom. Glancing at the mirror, she groaned.

Her stomach dropped at the reflection that stared back at her. "Holy crap," she muttered, resting her hands on the counter. "No wonder he was looking at you like you're a freak. You should have left the sunglasses on."

Her long black hair was pulled into a messy bun, unruly strands sticking out haphazardly around her head. And her face? A complete disaster.

Her left cheek and jaw had taken on a new color. They were a bluish-purple tint, a drastic improvement over the raw, reddish black of a week ago. The left side of her forehead was still a little puffy, but the swelling had gone down enough that it no longer hurt every time her expression shifted. She could also open her left eye now. Not all the way, but she'd take any progress as a win.

The right side of her face had fared better, relatively

speaking. Still, there was considerable bruising toward her ear and six tiny stitches on the edge of her lower lip.

Preston's eyes flashed in her mind. Tropical blue and spotted by flecks of green, they were the first part of him she had fallen in love with. They were also the last thing she remembered seeing before losing consciousness. In those final moments, they'd been anything but beautiful. The calm blues had transformed, raging at her with the fury of an ocean storm.

Somewhere in the background of her memories, a familiar song played softly, mocking her.

"Take my hand. Take my whole life, too. For I can't help falling in love with you."

While his eyes had raged, so had his fists. The hands that had once held her close had instead rained down upon her. She'd tried to fight back, but it had quickly become too much. When he'd kicked her, her breath had seized in her lungs, and she hadn't been able to move. The intensity of his rage had convinced her he was actually going to do it this time. Her husband was really going to kill her.

And he nearly had.

The sound of the front door opening brought Alex back to the present. She squared her shoulders, ignoring the uncomfortable pull of her tender muscles.

"You're safe here," she murmured to her reflection. She placed a protective hand over her abdomen. "We're both safe here."

If only she believed it.

CHAPTER TWO

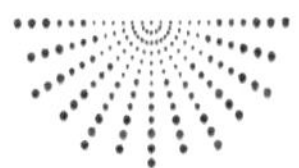

Quinn O'Conner sat in his usual corner booth at Ray's Diner and stared out the window, watching the boats at the marina across the street bob up and down with the tide. The smell of bacon and fried food should have comforted him, but it didn't. His jaw was beginning to ache from grinding his teeth, but he didn't care. He was brooding, the meal in front of him forgotten.

No. He was beyond brooding. He was thoroughly pissed.

Joe had done it again. The fucker.

When his childhood best friend had called him a few days earlier and said he was sending over a friend to crash at his place, Quinn had assumed that Joe was being straight with him. But after one look at Alex, he'd realized Joe had purposely withheld details about this particular "friend." He'd bet his life on it. And to Quinn, lying by omission was still lying.

As if he didn't already have enough to deal with, now he had Alex Garcia to worry about. Because something had his gut screaming that trouble was coming.

Well, he wasn't going to be swayed by her broken and

bruised appearance. He was done playing the hero to alleged damsels in distress. No matter how badly his first instinct was to throw a protective bubble around her—and then beat the living piss out of whoever had knocked her around. He'd been deceived before. And he *hated* that damn fool-me-once saying.

Should he keep an eye out to protect Alex from whatever trouble she'd come here to escape? Or was *she* the trouble?

He didn't fucking know. And though he'd tried to convince himself that he didn't *want* to know, he couldn't lie to himself. He was curious. And that seriously pissed him off.

Letting out a deep breath, he slowly worked his jaw side to side. If Joe were in front of him, he would have said some choice words. He loved the guy like a brother, but still . . .

Quinn's foul mood further soured when an auburn-haired blur noisily plopped down onto the seat across from him, then yanked the menu out from under his elbow.

"Dude, what's with the scowl? And gee, thanks for waiting for me to order," the woman grumbled as she flipped through the menu. She absently nodded to the entrance. "In case you care, your face is not at all pretty right now, and it *might* scare off those tourists that just walked in. If they leave because of your ugly mug, I can guarantee you Ray will be more than happy to kick your ass. I'd even hold you down for him. In fact, I would pay good money for the privilege and—"

"Take a breath, Roxie. You're giving me a headache," he interrupted, even though he knew it was useless.

"You know, Quinn, that mumbling, I'm-the-strong-but-silent-type thing you do gets really annoying." She glanced up from the menu. "Didn't your mom ever tell you that if you keep frowning like that, your face will stay that way forever? You're what, thirty-seven, thirty-eight now? It's a little too early for you to look like a constant sourpuss."

He stared at the woman across from him. Roxanne Elizabeth Jameson. They'd known each other their entire lives—and she'd been a pain in his ass the whole time. Along with Joe, they'd grown up in each other's homes, experiencing their happiest and darkest days together. They knew one another better than they knew themselves.

So, as he studied Roxie's expression, he recognized that she wouldn't let up until she got her way. He shook his head, and the corners of his lips curved up.

She raised her arms in victory. "Aha, half a smile! Success!" After a moment, she grew somber, pinning him with her green eyes. It was only years of practice that had him not squirming under her scrutiny. "Seriously, what's with the face? You look like you want to slug someone."

"You volunteering, Roxie?" He could deflect all damn day.

"Don't be a smart-ass, Quinn. It's not attractive." With a roll of her eyes, she reached across the table and stole a handful of fries. "Spill it."

"Smart-ass? Pot, meet kettle." He held up a hand to prevent her response. As much as he wanted to redirect the conversation, his friend truly was like a dog with a bone. Or whatever the hell that saying was. And besides, she would find out, anyway. For better or worse, gossip spread like wildfire on Hudson Island. "I was over at Joe's earlier, opening up the house like the shithead asked, when his mystery houseguest arrived."

Roxie paused mid-chew, her eyes widening. "Ooh, the mysterious Alex," she said with her mouth full. "What's he like?"

"Hard to tell." He didn't bother to correct her, didn't bother telling her that *he* was, in fact, a *she*. Because that revelation still floored him.

"Well, what does he look like?"

"Again, hard to tell." His earlier tension returned.

He wasn't a violent person. He honestly believed almost everything could be resolved without force. But the mere thought of Alex's battered face made him see red. Made him want to howl. Made him want to put his own fist through the face of whoever had assaulted her.

"Really, Quinn? Did you not look at him? Was there a friggin' paper bag over his head?"

He blew out his breath and tried to relax his jaw. Again. "There may as well have been."

Roxie slammed her hand down on the table, and his silverware rattled. "Enough with the cryptic replies already! Would it kill you to talk in sentences that consist of more than six words?" She examined him with narrowed eyes. "What exactly did this Alex guy do to get your panties in a wad, Sheriff?"

"Cute, Roxie, real cute." He shook his head and leaned forward, elbows on the table, and clasped his hands under his chin. What he wouldn't give to be at the gym with a heavy bag in front of him to pound on. "First, Alex is a *she*. Alexandra Garcia. Second, there's more to the story than Joe told us. I don't know how she and Joe know each other, but they have to be tight. I mean, we both know Joe. He'd do anything to avoid this place. And he sends her here? With barely any warning? That's huge for him."

"Maybe she and Joe are together, and he wanted her to see where he grew up . . ." Her nose scrunched. "Who am I kidding? When Joe left, he was pretty damn adamant about not coming back. Ever. So, why send his girlfriend here?"

Why, indeed.

"Well, what's she like?"

"Like I said, I'm not really sure." He hurried on before she could interject with a sarcastic comment. "Really, Roxie. Her face is a mess of bruises and cuts and stitches. I'm not sure what's swollen and what's her actual face."

Like a deflating balloon, Roxie's shoulders slumped. "Oh, shit. I feel like an ass."

"What pisses me off is that Joe didn't say a damn thing. He said he had a friend named Alex who'd be staying at his place indefinitely and that he'd be in touch. That's it. So, after I met her, I ran her—"

"Naturally," she scoffed.

He raised an eyebrow, and she went quiet. "Anyway, she has a fairly common name, so there was a lot to sort through, but I came up with absolutely nothing to match this particular Alexandra Garcia. No driver's license, social, last known address—nothing."

And that was *never* a good thing. His stomach turned.

"Roxie, you should've seen her. She looks like she's barely old enough to drink. She's fucking tiny. And you know what?" He paused, and the sour ball rolling in his gut grew. "It's been a long time since I've seen someone worked over like that."

Roxie's brow furrowed. "Do you think she's hiding or on the run?"

"Is there really a difference?"

"You know what I mean. Do you think it's a domestic abuse thing, or was she part of a bank robbery gone wrong?"

"Considering Joe sent her, I'm leaning toward her being on Team Good Guy. But you never know." And that not knowing bothered him. "It's probably an asshole boyfriend, but then that begs the question of whether the asshole is still a threat. Did he, or is he going to, follow her? I think Joe knows, but he's not talking." Roxie tried to look away, but Quinn caught her gaze. "I told her you'd be stopping by tonight to drop off some food and stuff. Maybe she'll talk to you."

Roxie shook her head, disbelief etched on her face. "Do you honestly think she's just going to spill her guts at the sight of me? I assume, after what you've described, the girl's going to have some serious trust issues. Besides, I'm not going to befriend her just so I can pump her for answers that are, frankly, none of our business."

"You do recall that I'm the sheriff, right?" As old-fashioned as it sounded, this was *his* town, and he was in charge of protecting it and its people. "Everything's my business."

"Then ask her yourself. Or call Joe and demand answers from him," Roxie said. "I'm not going to schmooze Alex into talking just because you say so. Really, Quinn, that's plain mean. Even for you."

"Look, Rox. I'm not saying you need to become best friends with her, just . . ." He searched for his next words. "Like you said, she's been through a lot. I'm sure she could use a friend. And for whatever reason, people find it easy to open up to you. You've got that you-can-completely-trust-me-so-please-tell-me-your-deepest-darkest-secret-and-I'll-be-there-for-you thing going on. So, if you spend some time together, and she naturally opens up, what's the harm?"

He flashed his most charming grin and went in for the kill. "Besides, you told Joe you'd go over there and help with the place. Regardless of the hostility between you two, I assume you'll keep your word since you gave it in the first place. You know you'll run into Alex while you're over there, and you know you can't help but be your usual friendly self."

She sighed. Loudly. "If I didn't know you so well, I'd think you actually had a heart and wanted to help this poor girl. But I do know you, Quinn O'Conner. And. You. Are. An. Ass. So, save your cute little grin for someone else. You just want to know if Little Miss Alex is going to bring trouble to your peaceful little town."

He smothered a smirk when Roxie started fidgeting with the corner of the menu. She was going to cave. Beneath the smart-ass facade, Roxie was a sucker for helping anyone in trouble.

"Fine," she spat. "I'll go over there. Not for you, but because I foolishly told Joe I would. If Alex and I so happen to develop a friendship, what she tells me is between me and her. Not you. Agreed?"

He gave her his sweetest smile. "Of course, darlin'. But you know you can't keep anything from me."

Roxie glared. "You. Are. A. Jackass."

"Yeah, but you still love me." He chuckled. "Let me buy you lunch."

CHAPTER THREE

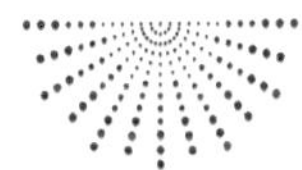

The grandfather clock downstairs chimed six o'clock, startling Alex out of her trance. She slowly turned away from the window, shaking her head. Too much time alone. Too much time to think.

She looked around the bedroom at the antique mahogany furniture and smiled. It was the kind of room she'd once dreamed of having. Classic, fancy, and romantic. Featuring a giant four-poster bed with matching side tables, an armoire fit for a queen, and a delicate vanity with a matching mirror, anyone who'd ever fantasized about being a princess would have been thrilled to call it theirs.

Sitting at the edge of the bed was her suitcase. A single, lonely, carry-on-size suitcase. She glanced at the unzipped bag and knew its contents were generic possessions that were as foreign to her as the house she stood in. All the clothes and toiletries—even the suitcase itself—had been purchased over the past six days.

She leaned against the wall, frowning. The bedroom was a beautiful space, and it should have felt like a haven. But it was too much.

Everything was too much. The past two weeks . . .

Her chest squeezed, and she fought for air.

Inhale for four. Hold for four. Exhale for four. Hold for four. Repeat.

Her therapist's soothing voice echoed in her mind, and the panic receded.

Slipping down the wall until she was sitting on the floor, she dropped her head to her knees, wincing as her bruised skin protested the contact. How the hell had she ended up here?

"Five years ago," she murmured as she closed her eyes.

That's when it had all started. She remembered every detail of that miserable winter day. She had been so excited and happy. If only she'd known that it was the day her life would go to hell. If only it hadn't taken her the next four years to realize it.

She'd been on her way to a job interview with Mayor Downing. Her umbrella had lost its battle with the wind and flipped inside out, yanking her in the opposite direction with each gust. She'd struggled to use her briefcase as a rain shield while also juggling her purse, coffee, and renegade umbrella. With her attention elsewhere, she had run directly into him.

She'd watched in slow motion as his eyes had widened in shock and her steaming, creamy latte had spilled across the entire front of his very expensive suit. She wasn't what anyone would call graceful. But that had been ridiculous. Even for her.

Completely mortified, she'd glanced up at the stranger, worried about what she would see. Reality had been worse than she'd feared: she'd known the man. Well, known *of* him.

The guy she'd spilled her coffee on? The mayor's right-hand man. She'd been horrified. But to her surprise—and to her deep regret much later on—he'd laughed it off, and his tropical-blue eyes smiled at her. It had been on that sidewalk, soaked by the rain and shivering from the wind, that she'd fallen blindly—and stupidly—in love.

A loud bang sounded downstairs. Her eyes darted across the room, looking for a place to hide. The noise came again. She sprang up, back flush against the wall, and froze. Then she remembered where she was.

Her shoulder slumped, and she let out a breath. "Idiot," she cursed herself, willing her heartbeat to return to normal.

She made her way down the stairs. As the front door and its side windows came into view, she startled at the silhouette of a woman.

Holy crap, get a grip, Nat—

She took in a deep breath. Held for four, then exhaled. *Alex. You're* Alex *now.*

She flipped on the porch light and cautiously cracked open the door to peek through. "Can I help you?"

Silence. A woman, arms full of grocery bags, stared at her in what looked like stunned shock. Then, "Hi! I'm Roxie." Her voice was cheerful—overly cheerful—and she had a bright and friendly smile on her face. "Alex, right?"

She inwardly cringed. She'd employed that just-keep-smiling-and-no-one-will-notice-how-awkward-this-is tactic herself. Countless times.

Roxie rushed on, "Joe or Quinn may have mentioned I'd be by?" The woman's smile remained in place, though she shifted awkwardly on her feet.

"Um, they both did, actually." Alex hesitated, then wanted to kick herself. *He's behind bars, and you're safe here. Now pull it together!* She straightened her spine and stepped aside, holding the door open. "And yes, I'm Alex. It's nice to meet you. Please come in."

She shoved her hands into the pockets of her oversized sweatshirt as Roxie entered, heading straight for the kitchen.

"I brought over a couple pies, some quiches, a couple

casseroles, and some other stuff," Roxie said over her shoulder. "I wasn't sure what you'd like."

Alex waited a moment before following the other woman into the kitchen.

Whirlwind. The woman was an absolute whirlwind.

She found Roxie unloading prepared food and groceries onto the island. The bags reminded her of Mary Poppins: they didn't seem all that big, but she was amazed by the amount of food Roxie pulled from them.

"I figure that everyone loves a good quiche. I hope you're not a vegetarian or anything because there's ham in this one. The other two have turkey and chicken. But if you are vegetarian, then no problem at all because I'm sure Quinn will eat these and I'll just whip up some new, non-meaty ones for you. The casseroles freeze really well, so there's no worries about eating them right away. I also figured apple and blueberry were probably the safest bets for the pies. And I got you some vanilla ice cream, of course."

Alex blinked, her mind attempting to process the woman's rapid-fire chatter. It had all sounded like one giant, continuous sentence with zero breaths between words.

Roxie went to open the freezer, then paused. She shot Alex an apologetic look before grabbing the handle.

"I'm so sorry," she said, shoving the ice cream and casseroles into the freezer. "I shouldn't have barged in like this. It's just that I pretty much grew up in this house, so it's comfortable for me, you know? Sorry, I have this horrible habit of thinking everyone needs food to make them feel better and"—Roxie's eyes widened, panic flashing over her face—"not that you feel bad or anything or have a reason to feel bad. I just, uh, figured that . . ."

Roxie's gaze shifted to the floor.

"Hey, no worries at all," Alex said, trying to sound confident. "Truly. Thank you for all this delicious food. Would you, uh, care to join me for some apple pie à la mode?"

She wasn't sure she remembered how to be good company, but she knew she was making Roxie uncomfortable. Hell, if she were faced with someone who looked like she did, she'd be uncomfortable, too. The least she could do to reassure the woman was share some dessert with her.

Roxie met her gaze and smiled, visibly relaxing. "Sounds like a plan." She turned back to the freezer. "You sit, and I'll dish it up. Fork or spoon?"

"Spoon, please." She settled her aching body onto a stool at the island and watched the woman move about, completely at home in Joe's kitchen.

Roxie was easily one of the most gorgeous people Alex had ever laid eyes on. The woman was exceptionally tall and athletically lean, a build that she—at a whopping five foot one—had always envied. Her bright-green eyes contrasted beautifully with her fair skin and dark-auburn hair. Add in her high cheekbones and perfectly symmetrical features, and her face was magazine-cover pretty.

"Quinn mentioned you lived next door," Alex said, searching for something to talk about. She could do this. She was an expert at small talk.

"Yup. Well, in his guest house. It's kind of a long and boring story, though. Not sure you want to hear it," Roxie said, opening the ice cream container.

"Sure I do. Joe warned me about you already."

Roxie froze mid-scoop, one of her perfectly groomed eyebrows arching.

Alex didn't know whether to laugh or hide. Instead, she backpedaled. "Um, what I meant to say is that Joe *told* me about you."

She took her plate of pie and ice cream from Roxie and shoveled a spoonful into her mouth. After another quiet moment passed, she peeked up at Roxie's still-raised eyebrow, swallowed, and cleared her throat.

"All he said was that you like a good story and that if I ever need anyone to talk to, or listen to, then I should give you a call. Great pie, by the way. It's absolutely delicious. You really are an expert baker." She proved the point by stuffing her trap with more pie and ice cream.

Roxie jabbed her spoon into her own slice. "Nice recovery, Alex," she grumbled. "Did Joe mention that, too? 'Tell her she talks too much, but buffer it by saying she's a damn fine baker.'"

She nodded, chuckling.

Roxie let out an exaggerated sigh, then held up a spoonful of ice cream. "To Joe," she toasted. "I guess even after all this time, the guy still knows me pretty well."

She tapped her spoon against Roxie's with a soft clink. "To Joe."

Her mind drifted to the last time she had seen him. He'd given her keys to a car, an envelope of cash, and directions to his childhood home clear across the country. He'd told her he would take care of everything and be in touch. He'd promised she would be safe.

Prior to these last two chaotic weeks, she could count on one hand the number of times they'd spoken. Yet there he'd been. Saving her life. Again.

Her throat tightened, and her chest squeezed. She blinked away the tears that threatened to fall. The pie, delectable moments ago, lost all flavor. "So, are you going to tell me that story or what?"

Sensing her need for distraction, Roxie launched into her story with gusto. "Well, it's actually not that exciting, so I'll give you the short version. As you probably know, Joe grew up in this house. Quinn next door, and me"—she gestured with her head in the opposite direction—"two doors down.

When Quinn's folks died a few years ago, they left him the house."

Roxie paused for a split second, and if Alex hadn't been watching, she would have missed the flash of grief over the woman's face. "So when he came back to town, he moved right in. Joe's dad still owns this place and rents it out from time to time. Mostly, it sits empty, and Joe uses it when he's in town, which is pretty damn rare these days. My folks retired a couple years ago and moved to the complete opposite corner of the country to God's Little Waiting Room. So I—"

"What?" Alex's brow furrowed. She couldn't have heard that right. "Where?"

"Oh, sorry. Florida."

Smiling, she wiped her mouth with a napkin.

"So I, being their only child, moved in. I couldn't have them selling my childhood home, now could I?" Roxie shrugged, the picture of innocence. "I was living there happily for the last couple years, blah, blah, blah, then I got the call that my folks had had enough. They were sick and tired of dealing with a bunch of *old* people."

Roxie rolled her eyes as she took another bite of pie. "Can you believe that? I think the sun fried their brains when they were down there. Truly. So anyway, they moved back into the house with me and—hold on, I can't actually eat when I say this." She swallowed dramatically and frowned. "They moved back in and started acting like they were on their freaking honeymoon! I'd walk into a room and there they were, making out on the couch or groping each other in the kitchen! I'd walk in to find my dad's hands up my mom's shirt! It was traumatizing!"

Alex choked on a laugh.

"No," Roxie said, shaking her head furiously while Alex alternated between laughing and coughing. "Not funny at all!

It was sick! Disturbing! No child should ever witness that kind of horror!" Roxie shuddered. "So, I moved out. Fast. And being lazy, I just moved into Quinn's guesthouse. My folks ended up getting a fancy RV, so their house mostly sits empty now, but . . ." She cringed. "I don't want any part of that. Now here we are. Short version complete."

As their amusement settled, they fell into a comfortable silence. Alex couldn't remember the last time she had felt so at ease. Something warm bloomed in her gut. Something she didn't fully recognize but knew she didn't want to jinx. "Thanks, Roxie."

"For what?"

Staring down at her plate, she pushed the remaining apple pie around. How did you tell someone—who was basically a stranger—that they were the first person in years that you had relaxed with? How did you say that without sounding like a complete headcase?

"I don't want this to sound like a pity party or anything, but I can't even tell you how long it's been since I've had a good, real laugh." There. That hadn't been so awkward. Right? She felt her face flushing. "So, thank you."

"You're welcome. That's what I'm here for." The jovial look on Roxie's face sobered. "Look, considering we've just met, I don't want to overstep any lines—please feel free to tell me to shut the hell up if I do—but I'm obviously not blind, and I can see what that monster, whoever he is, did to you."

Her gaze dropped to her plate.

"No," Roxie said, that one word fierce. "Please don't do that. Don't shy away like you're embarrassed. You have absolutely no reason to be. Look." She waited until Alex met her gaze. "I don't know what went on or what led you here. All I do know is that Joe sent you. And even though we've just met, I want you to know that you can talk to me. About anything. Pies, exes, movies, puppies. Anything. I know this probably sounds strange, but I promise you I'm not saying this because I'm some sort of do-gooder. I'm not. What I am is someone who helps my friends."

She didn't know what to say. *Overwhelmed* didn't begin to describe her ricocheting emotions. The last thing she'd ever expected on her first day in town was this show of support from a virtual stranger.

For the second time that evening, her throat tightened. And for the millionth time that evening, she thought it was just all too much.

"I've known Joe all my life," Roxie said. "We have our differences and all, but knowing him the way I do, if he sent you here, then he cares about you. If he cares about you, then I care about you. Same goes for Quinn. He and I will do whatever we can to help you out."

"Easy as that?" She couldn't hide the skepticism in her voice.

"Yeah, easy as that."

"Why?"

Roxie shrugged. "It's what friends do." She rose and cleared the dishes while Alex mulled over that one simple sentence.

Simple, yet so foreign.

"I'm sure you'll figure this out pretty quickly," Roxie continued, "but with Quinn being the sheriff around here and—"

Her breath caught, and her lips parted in shock.

Roxie continued to speak but Alex didn't hear a word. Her heart pounded an unsteady rhythm as she tried to suppress her rising panic.

Of course Quinn was the town's sheriff. Of course.

Dread turned her belly.

She tried to quiet the voice in her head. The one that

whispered it was only a matter of time now. That reminded her of Preston's endless connections. That behind bars or not, he was going to find her. But it was no use. The voice grew until it was achingly loud.

She mentally shook her head, desperate to quell her anxiety.

It'd be okay. She'd be okay.

All she had to do was steer clear of the sheriff and—

"Alex?"

She jerked, and her hands flew to her chest, clasping tight over her racing heart. "Sorry. I, uh . . ." She racked her brain for any recollection of what Roxie had been saying. And came up blank.

"No problem at all." Roxie plastered the cheery, overbright smile from earlier back on her face. She quickly gathered her now-empty grocery bags, then eyed Alex with obvious concern before making her way to the front door. She hesitated in the hallway and turned back. "So that works for you, then?"

What? "Um, sure." She cleared her throat and nodded. "That works great."

"Excellent. I'll give you a call in the next couple days. In the meantime, feel free to swing by the café any time. Good night!" With a wave, Roxie shut the front door behind her.

Alex sat rooted in place. Her mind was a mess. What just happened? Better yet, what the hell had she just agreed to?

She replayed what she could remember of their conversation over and over in her head. And each time, her memory went blank the moment Roxie had dropped the bomb that Quinn, her handsome neighbor, was the sheriff.

Whoa. *Handsome?* Where had *that* come from?

Uncomfortable with the direction of her thoughts, she busied herself at the sink, loading the dishwasher and reflecting on the evening.

She had never met anyone like Roxie before. The woman was definitely a bundle of energy, but she seemed kind. Caring. Alex couldn't help but like her. She wasn't sure exactly why, but there was something she instinctively trusted about Roxie.

She caught her reflection in the kitchen window and scoffed, shaking her head in self-disgust. "Like that means anything. You have absolute crap for instincts."

She used to be so open, so trusting . . . so damn naïve. But time had a way of changing things. *Preston* had a way of changing things. Putting her faith in others was now something she just didn't do.

Shutting the dishwasher door, she continued to tidy the already tidy kitchen and questioned why—and how—Roxie had snuck past her defenses.

What was it about the woman that tempted Alex to trust her? Was it her unguarded personality? Her friendship with Joe? Or the simple fact that Alex hadn't had an actual friend in years?

Holy crap, wow. Let the pity party begin.

Closing her eyes, she let out a breath. And then another. Then one more.

She replaced the negative voice in her mind with the calming, soothing words of her therapist.

You have nothing to be ashamed of. Nothing. It's time to let go of the guilt and allow yourself to move on.

Baby steps.

A friendship with Roxie could be the first step. Joe trusted Roxie, so in friend math, that meant she could trust Roxie, too. But . . .

Quinn.

He was also Joe's friend. And he was the sheriff.

Her heartbeat accelerated. And not in a good way.

Stop! They're not all the same. You know *that. Preston's in jail. He can't find you.*

With trembling hands, she tossed the kitchen towel she'd been using next to the sink and rushed from the room. She needed to shut her brain down, to stop thinking, to quit over-analyzing and second-guessing every. Damn. Thing.

She tossed and turned in bed. Her body was beyond exhausted, and she desperately needed rest. But her mind refused to settle. To drown out her thoughts, she repeated her mantra: *You're safe here. He can't find you.*

However, as Alex drifted off to sleep, curled into a tight ball, her doubts crept back in.

But what if he does? What are you going to do then?

CHAPTER FOUR

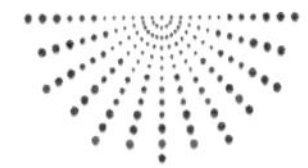

Lulled by the song of chirping birds and the warm sunshine coming through the window, Alex snuggled deeper into the duvet. She rolled onto her side, anticipating another final few minutes of sleep, but winced as her body made its discomfort known. She peeked her eyes open to check the time.

Her forehead crinkled in confusion. Where was her alarm clock?

She took in the strange lamp sitting atop the bedside table —a table she didn't recognize—and her heart tripped. She shot up in bed, frantic. Her gaze tore around the room, and her breath caught in her chest.

A heartbeat later, her mind cleared.

Joe's house.

Her breath released in a slow wheeze, and the tension eased from her muscles. She flopped back down on the mattress.

She counted her breaths and willed her heartbeat to steady. She was staring at the dome light fixture on the ceiling when it suddenly swayed to the right. A wave of nausea engulfed her, and she slapped both hands over her mouth. Stomach heaving, she scrambled out of the bed and flung open the adjoining bathroom door.

Her entire body cramped, and the contents of her stomach emptied into the toilet.

Leaning against the bathtub, she found herself soothed by the cool edge against her clammy face. She swallowed, then cringed. The bitter taste of bile brought back the nausea. She stilled, waiting it out.

Once she was relatively sure she wasn't going to puke again, she scraped herself up off the bathroom floor and made her way to the sink with tentative steps. After washing her face and brushing her teeth twice, she studied herself in the mirror, her hands moving over her flat stomach.

Morning sickness.

She was barely a month into her pregnancy. While she *knew* she was pregnant—after all, it had been confirmed by multiple doctors, not to mention the symptoms—she was having a *really* hard time believing it.

On one hand, she was thrilled. She'd always wanted to be a mother. In theory.

On the other hand, she was nervous. And if she thought about it too much, she was absolutely petrified.

Nope. Not gonna think about it.

She turned away from the mirror. Yes, it wasn't exactly the most mature way to handle her fear, but she didn't care. She could barely put one foot in front of the other. And at this point, she needed to focus on that.

Quinn knocked on the front door again. Annoyance had his shoulders pinching tight, and he glanced down at his watch. Where the hell was she?

Tired of waiting, he left Joe's porch and went around the side of the house. Noticing the door to the backyard shed was open, he headed toward it instead of the back door.

Peering inside the shed, he saw Alex. Clad in enormous sweatpants and an equally oversized, hideous sweatshirt, she was on her knees, her head under a shelf as she reached for something, her backside high in the air.

Not wanting to startle her, he knocked lightly on the shed's doorframe.

She jerked and bolted upright, slamming the back of her head on the shelf with a loud crack.

Fuck. He rushed to her. "Holy shit. Sorry, Alex. Are you okay?"

She scrambled to a seated position, cradling the back of her head with one hand, and holding the other out in front of her.

He recognized her defensive posture and froze. Lifting both arms up, he ever so slowly retreated, giving her as much space as the small shed allowed, then kneeled to join her on the ground.

"Hey, Alex. I'm not going to hurt you." He kept his voice soft and calm. "I'm so sorry I snuck up on you like that. I didn't mean to. Really."

The muted light in the shed was enough to highlight the scatter of healing bruises across Alex's face and neck. The sleeves of her sweatshirt were pushed to her elbows, and one glance at her forearms made his stomach clench. An uncountable number of stitches and butterfly bandages held her slashed skin together.

Defensive wounds.

Her whiskey-brown eyes were wide and frantic, locked onto his. She had the look of a wild, cornered animal. One that was desperate to escape.

"I'm so sorry. I didn't mean to scare you," he repeated,

slowly rising. When she recoiled from him, he knew he shouldn't take it personally. But he did, anyway.

He backed out of the shed, careful to keep his movements gradual and calm. When his feet hit the grass, he turned away, staying in her line of sight so she could track his whereabouts, and closed his eyes, dropping his head. He took a deep breath in, then exhaled.

His eyes snapped open, and he bit back a growl. Yeah. That had done jack shit to calm him. He stormed out of Joe's backyard and toward his own home next door, his anger heating from a simmer to a boil.

Holy. Mother. Fucking. Shit.

He wanted to hit something. Wanted to hurt something. No, he wanted to hurt some*one*. That specific someone being whoever had thought it was a good idea to use Alex as a punching bag and carving board.

A fucking *carving board.*

A helpless rage blurred his vision. He knew violence wasn't the answer—he was the *sheriff*, for fuck's sake—but dammit, that asshole had cut her. *Cut* her. Sliced up her arms like she was a fucking Thanksgiving turkey.

He wanted to find that person. No, he *would* find that person. And somehow, he'd make him pay.

***

She was paralyzed. Only her heaving chest moved; only her ragged gasps filled the silence.

Quinn had left the shed at least five minutes earlier, but her pulse still raced. One hand still cradled the back of her throbbing head. The other remained held out in front of her, protecting her from nothing. But she couldn't move.

Quinn, she thought, fighting to clear her mind. *Not Preston.*

She glanced around the shed, and after a few more moments, came fully back to the present.

Her face flushed as mortification coursed through her. With stark clarity, she recalled the look in Quinn's gray eyes when he'd apologized. When he'd told her he wouldn't hurt her. His gaze had pleaded with her to believe him.

To her surprise, she had. But instead of telling him that, she'd sat there.

Frozen with terror.

Countless months of intense therapy had flown out the window, and she'd waited for him to prove her limited faith had been misplaced. Because that's what strong men did: they hurt her. That's what she'd been taught—no, *conditioned* to believe. For years, that had been her reality.

But it wasn't anymore. Now she knew better. In theory, anyway.

Damn.

Ashamed. *That* was a better word for how she felt right now.

Rising to her feet, she rubbed the lump that was forming on the back of her head. She needed to find Quinn.

She stepped out of the shed and flinched at the bright sunshine. Rolling her neck, she squinted across the backyard to the house next door. While she understood her reaction had been instinctual, she wanted to apologize. Everything was still so raw—*she* was still so raw—but she knew that he wasn't Preston.

Crossing into the neighboring backyard, she saw Quinn through his kitchen window. Catching his gaze, she gave an awkward wave and headed toward the back door. Starting up the steps, her vision briefly cut out. She reached to grab the railing, but her arm was sluggish. She swayed, and her legs gave way beneath her.

Everything went black.

CHAPTER FIVE

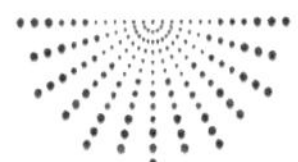

Quinn paced in his kitchen. Frustration clawed at his insides. As he passed the window over the sink again, he looked out toward the shed.

Alex.

She was walking his way. Her hand rose in a hesitant wave as she crossed into his backyard. Even from this distance, he could see the flush stealing over her face. A feeling he didn't recognize settled over him.

He frowned.

The little slip of a thing made him nervous, he realized. Like he was a dumb junior high kid with a crush. Damn, when was the last time his stomach had been this jittery?

He went to the back door, opening it just as Alex crumpled, landing face down and sprawled out on the steps.

Holy shit.

Rushing to her side, he ran his hands over her limbs and spine, checking for anything broken or displaced. Once he was sure he could move her safely, he gathered her in his arms and hurried into the house.

He made his way to his first-floor bedroom and laid her

on the bed. After retrieving a washcloth from the en suite and running it under cold water, he kneeled on the floor beside her. He ran the cool cloth over her forehead, pushing back the black hair that had escaped its tie. Watching the slow rise and fall of her chest, he desperately wished she'd open her eyes.

His gaze trailed over her delicate features. They were marred with fading bruises, the left side more swollen than the right. Clearly, the asshole who'd hit her had been right-handed. Across her high cheekbones, he spied a slight dusting of freckles on her tan skin. Without the bruises, he had no doubt she was stunning.

He ran the back of his fingers along the side of her face. Her skin was so damn soft.

What kind of person would do anything but cherish and protect this woman? If Alex were his, he'd—

He froze, and his eyes widened with surprise. He snatched his hand back as if he'd been burned, rocking onto his heels. What the fuck was he thinking?

Alex *wasn't* his, and he was *not* looking for any sort of relationship. Particularly not with someone who came with a boatload of baggage.

Still . . . there was something about her.

Fuck.

He shook his head in an attempt to clear it. It didn't work. "Get a fucking grip, O'Conner," he muttered as he rose. With a final glance at Alex—just to make sure she was okay—he left the room to call the doctor.

CHAPTER SIX

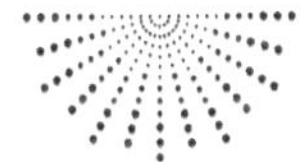

Alex relaxed into the comfort and quiet of the hazy gray fog. She heard voices somewhere in the background, heard her name being spoken, but everything was too muffled to make out what they were saying. She tried to nestle back into the fog, but the voices grew louder.

"She should be fine, but it's hard to say," a male voice said. "I'll stick around until she comes to. I want to check her injuries more thoroughly and—"

"But she'll be fine?" another deep voice interrupted.

She heard footsteps, and then the sound of a door closing. The voices became muffled again.

Prying open her eyelids, Alex scanned the room. The walls were navy blue with off-white trim. The furniture—a dresser, two nightstands, a plush chair, and a bed frame—were rich mahogany. The room had little in the way of decorations, but everything it did have was streamlined and masculine. In the corner, a pair of jeans and a T-shirt were tossed over the arm of the plush chair.

Quinn's room.

She wasn't sure what to make of it. Of what had

happened in the shed, or on the back steps. Of being in his bed . . . Of any of it.

Drawing the soft gray blanket closer to her chin, she curled onto her side. Her eyes caught on a framed picture on the nightstand. Quinn, Roxie, and Joe. Wearing suits and giant smiles, the men made stunning bookends as they flanked Roxie. With her arms linked through theirs, Roxie stood laughing in jeans, a T-shirt, and a paper cone birthday hat.

Reaching for the picture, she ran the tip of her finger over the frame. A wistful longing tugged at her heart. What would it be like to have lifelong friends? She wished she knew. She'd given up so much for Preston.

Loneliness settled over her. But cozied up right next to it was the realization that, more than anything, she wanted to live again. To not let this opportunity pass her by. To make a life that she could be proud of.

"Roxie's thirtieth birthday."

She jumped at the quiet voice. Turning her attention toward the door, she found Quinn leaning against the frame, arms casually crossed over his broad chest. His gaze was on the photograph in her hands, and a soft smile played on his lips.

Her breath came to an abrupt halt. *Whoa.*

She knew from meeting him earlier that Quinn fit the tall-dark-and-handsome cliché to a T. She wasn't blind. But yesterday, she'd been running on fumes and overwhelmed by . . . well, everything. Then, in the shed, he'd scared the living crap out of her. She was sure it had been unintentional, but regardless, the resulting adrenaline had left no room for thoughts beyond *fight* or *flight*.

But now? Seeing him in the quiet? In the calm? Watching that slow smile soften his rugged face? Yeah. The man was more than a little jarring.

At over six feet tall, there wasn't an ounce of fat on him. Wavy, dark, chocolate-brown hair framed his tanned face, and gray eyes the color of the sky before a powerful storm were set above full lips and a strong, angular jaw covered in stubble. He probably would have been considered pretty if it weren't for his once-patrician nose, which looked as though it might have been put back into place a few times. In faded jeans and a casual, long-sleeve button-down, he exuded confidence, but not in a vain, cocky way.

That wasn't Quinn.

And yes, she knew how stupid that sounded. She had just met the man. He was a stranger to her. But she was familiar with arrogant and entitled men. She'd lived with the slyest and most charismatic of them, a devil so pompous he flaunted everything at his disposal to let those around him know he was the biggest man in the room.

And again, that wasn't Quinn.

There was something about him that was different. Safe. He was comfortable in his own skin. He didn't need to play games or show off.

Stepping up to the bed, he took the frame from her hands and kneeled beside her, studying the photo with a faraway smile.

"Joe and I were both living out of state," he said. "We flew in to surprise Roxie for her birthday. We were both with the FBI at the time, and Roxie constantly made fun of us because we always wore suits." He tapped the glass with his knuckle. "Hence why we're decked out in our Sunday best for a back-yard barbeque.

"Killed two birds with one stone, though. When we were teenagers, our version of 'Sunday best' made most people cringe. Our folks were lucky if they managed to drag us to church in clothes that weren't ripped or stained. We figured it'd make Roxie happy to make fun of us, and we also got to show the folks that it was possible for us to clean up."

For Christ's sake, O'Conner. Shut. The fuck. Up.

If Quinn could slap himself upside the head, he would. Reminiscing about his teenage years was not something he did. Ever. And he was sure it was the last thing Alex wanted to hear about.

When he'd come in and found her curled up staring at that photo, something had stirred in him. Exactly what, he had no clue. All he knew was she'd looked so damn tiny in his bed. So alone. So sad. And he'd wanted to comfort her. He'd meant to say something soothing, perhaps ask how she was feeling, but instead, random shit had flown out of his mouth. Fuck if this woman didn't have him all out of sorts.

Trying to reset his mind, he placed the frame back in its spot on the nightstand. Still kneeling, he rested his elbows on the bed next to her.

"How're you feeling?" he asked, proud he'd gotten the question out this time.

"Good." She cleared her throat. "Well, embarrassed, too. I'm not really sure where to begin."

"Nothing to be embarrassed about. I hope you don't mind, but I called the doctor over to make sure you didn't have a concussion or anything."

She smiled and carefully sat up, resting her back against the headboard. "Thanks, but I'm sure I'm fine."

He fought the urge to help her; he didn't want to invade her personal space.

"Quinn, I want to apologize about what happened in the shed. I'm sorry. I had no right to act like you were—"

"Alex, no." He rested his hand on her blanket-covered

ankle, then quickly pulled it away. "I'm sorry. I didn't mean to touch you." He blew out a breath and met her eyes. "There's nothing for you to apologize for. *I'm* the one at fault. Not you. I shouldn't have snuck up on you like that."

"It's okay," she said, nodding to her ankle. "But I still want to apologize, though. I freaked out on you and . . . that wasn't cool." A flush spread over her cheeks. Even bruised and swollen, the woman was adorable.

"We're just going to have to agree to disagree on that one." He placed his hand on the bed between them, palm up. "But I'll accept your apology, even though you have nothing to apologize for. Can you accept mine for scaring you? I really am sorry about that."

She glanced between his face and his offered hand, and he stayed still, hoping she'd accept his gesture. After a few long heartbeats, she did, putting her hand in his. Warmth flooded through him. He wanted to wrap his arms around this woman and protect her from . . . everything.

Keep it light, O'Conner.

"If you don't mind me asking," he said, absently running his thumb over her knuckles, "what were you looking for under that shelf?"

Her flush deepened, and he stifled a smile. Damn, he could sit here with her all day.

"I went into the shed to look for . . . Well, it doesn't matter." She shook her head. "My earring fell off and bounced under the shelf. Like all the way to the very back."

Sure enough, a small gold hoop pierced her left earlobe, and the other was bare. "I'll go snag that for you. In the meantime, you ready to see Doc?"

"Yes. Thank you," she whispered, holding his gaze.

He gave her a slight smile. Then, for a few quiet moments, he simply held her hand.

He wasn't one to over-analyze his feelings. In fact, he'd

been accused of being an emotionless asshole on more than one occasion. And yet, he couldn't help but wonder why *this* woman left him so unsettled. Because she unequivocally did.

He told himself that the reason why he wanted to protect her, to gather her up and hold on tight, was because it was his civic duty to protect the citizens of this town.

But while he knew that was partially true, he also knew it was mostly a load of crap.

A potentially dangerous load of crap. What he needed to concern himself with was Alex's past, and the possible threats that could be following her to Hudson Island. And he would. But right now, if he were being honest, he was more concerned with how soft her skin was. Okay, maybe not *concerned*. More like he was absolutely fascinated by it.

This woman fucking mesmerized him.

And because of that, he needed to get out of here, needed to get his head on straight. Her safety was his top priority. Everything else was noise.

Giving her hand another gentle squeeze, he resisted the urge to press a kiss to her knuckles. Damn, he was a mess.

"You're going to be okay, Alex." He'd make sure of it. Rising, he said, "I'll send in Doc."

CHAPTER SEVEN

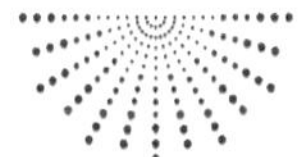

When the door shut behind him, Alex sighed.

Wow. Just wow.

Her insides quaked. She wasn't sure if the cause was her fall or Quinn's recent proximity. Her head told her it was the former, but her gut? Definitely the latter. The way he'd looked at her while holding her hand had been unnerving. In a good way.

But what did she know? She didn't know the man. Even though he made her feel safe—which made *zero* sense—it was no reason to get fanciful.

A frown pulled her lips down. When was the last time she'd allowed herself that luxury?

Still. Dreamed up or not, it had been . . . nice.

Aside from her therapist, it had been ages since anyone had looked at her. *Really* looked at her. Granted, that was partially her own doing. With Preston, she'd made it a point to not get too close to anyone, lest they saw through her precisely crafted facade. However, she'd quickly realized it wouldn't have mattered. People saw what they wanted to see.

She'd been Preston's trophy wife: a much-younger

woman short on brains, high on looks, and easily replaceable. That's all everyone saw. What they'd whispered. After a while, she'd begun to believe it as well. At least the first two points. Preston had made it clear she *wasn't* replaceable. She was his. Forever. No matter what.

"Alex, this is Doc."

She looked up, breaking out of her musings. An older man stood next to Quinn. Judging by the amount of gray liberally sprinkled throughout his blond hair, she guessed he was somewhere in his sixties. Lean and fit, he stood nearly as tall as Quinn. There was nothing out of the ordinary with the man, but goosebumps rose on her arms, nonetheless.

He looked familiar, yet she couldn't quite place him. Her pulse quickened. There was no way the man was from Summerside. But how else would she know him?

"Doc's a—"

"I'm sorry," she said, interrupting Quinn. She met the doctor's bright-blue eyes, and dread turned her stomach. She'd seen those eyes before. She was positive. "You look really familiar. Have we met?" Her voice trembled, and she hoped no one noticed. She clutched the blanket over her lap in a death grip.

"Sean Buchanan. I probably look familiar because I'm Joe's dad."

Absolute relief washed over her. She let out the breath she'd been holding, and the tension in her body eased. Thank. Freaking. God.

"Doc's great," Quinn said, concern evident on his face. "He's been fixing me up since Little League." He playfully elbowed the older man and rubbed the bridge of his nose.

"Son," Dr. Buchanan said with a roll of his eyes, "you've got quite the selective memory." He faced Alex. "It wasn't Little League that broke his nose, my dear. Rather, it was the fist of another little slugger. Get it?" He chuckled at his pun.

Quinn grimaced.

Dr. Buchanan continued, "Even though Roxie was a couple years younger and a lot smaller than all the boys, she had a mean right hook and used it at every opportunity she could. One time—"

"All lies, old man! Don't listen to him, Alex. He's getting senile in his old age." He winked at Dr. Buchanan, but when he glanced at her, his expression sobered. He reached down and squeezed her hand. "Doc will take good care of you. I promise. If you need anything, I'll be right outside."

"Thank you," she said, returning the hand squeeze.

After Quinn shut the door behind him, Dr. Buchanan gestured toward the bed. "May I?"

She hesitated for a split second. Then wanted to kick herself. *Get it together.* "Of course."

Once seated at the edge of the bed, his eyes traveled over her face, no doubt taking in every bruise and cut. Despite what he saw, the doctor smiled pleasantly. "So, you're a friend of Joseph's?"

"Oh, um, yes," she stammered. "He and I . . . uh, well . . ."

Dr. Buchanan patted her leg. "It's okay, dear. I don't need the details." He chuckled and turned to his medical bag. "Could you roll up your sleeve? I'd like to take your blood pressure."

She stared at him, incapable of moving.

"It's all right." He looped his stethoscope around his neck. "I've already seen your arms. We'll talk about that in a minute. First, I just want to check your blood pressure."

She pulled up her sleeve. As Dr. Buchanan fit the cuff around her upper arm and began the process, she closed her eyes. It was humiliating that this kind man had seen what Preston had done to her. What she'd allowed him to do to her.

No! You fought back. And if he comes after you, you're going to fight back again. You're never going back to him.

"One thirty-four over seventy." He removed the blood pressure cuff. "A little on the high side. Nervous?"

Alex nodded. "You could say that." She attempted to give him a small smile. And failed. Her hands shook, and she clutched them together.

"Did they find the person that did this to you?"

She nodded again, her gaze fixing on her hands. Her knuckles had turned white. "Joe told me that he . . . uh, my, um, husband was arrested after all this."

"Good. Look at me, dear." His voice was soft, and he waited until she raised her head. "Did you want anything for the pain? I can prescribe some hydrocodone if you're uncomfortable. Or, if you'd prefer—"

"Oh, no. I can't take med—" She slammed her mouth shut. Crap.

His eyes narrowed, and his head tilted ever so slightly to the side. If she hadn't been watching him closely, she would have missed it.

"Does your husband know about the baby?"

Her jaw dropped, then she cringed. "Was I that obvious?"

"A little bit, my dear." He flashed her a grin that was so much like Joe's she was surprised she hadn't recognized the resemblance right away. "The pregnancy could also explain the fainting, but I'm sure the stress of your situation isn't helping matters. So, does your husband know?"

"Well, he did," Alex whispered. "Joe said he . . . that Preston was told I'd miscarried."

"And if Preston found out that you were still pregnant?"

"I don't know." Worry soured her stomach. "I don't know what he'd do."

"Alex," he said gently. "You'll be safe here. Quinn will make sure of that. So will my Joseph." He reached into his bag again and pulled out a bottle. "Now, let's treat those arms."

As she began to roll her other sleeve up, Dr. Buchanan laid a hand on her shoulder. "If you could take off the sweatshirt and pull up the arms on your T-shirt, that would be better. There look to be some longer cuts on the back of your arm that I'd like to see." He removed his hand. "You'll be okay, dear. You'll be just fine."

She shrugged out of her sweatshirt, and the T-shirt beneath lifted. At Dr. Buchanan's sharp inhale, she stilled, knowing what he saw. Old bruises shadowed the new ones making it impossible to differentiate where one ended and another began. She remembered to breathe when he gripped one of her sleeves and helped her finish maneuvering out of the sweatshirt.

"May I check your back as well?" he asked.

After she replied with a brief nod, he leaned her forward, then lifted the back of her T-shirt, lightly poking and prodding at the various bruises and cuts on her back. Once he completed his examination, he lowered her shirt and helped her settle against the pillows. He got to work on her arms, disinfecting each wound with the application of an ointment.

"Apply a thin layer of this once a day on all lacerations and incisions until the stitches come out. It'll also help with the scarring. Wear loose tops. You want as much air on your wounds as you can get. Also, not too much movement, okay? You don't want any of the stitches popping."

"Okay," she murmured. "I can do that."

"Good. Now, the wounds on your back are considerably deeper than the ones on your arms, so you'll especially want to keep an eye on those to make sure there's no infection. You probably won't be able to reach them, so you'll need to have someone help you with the ointment. You can swing into the clinic every day, or I can talk to Quinn and have him help. Does that work?"

It took all her power to not let her mouth fall open. He had to be kidding.

Trek around in public, every day, with her battered face?

She was familiar with how small-town gossip worked. Hard pass.

Would you rather have Quinn see all the damage Preston inflicted?

Bile rose in her throat. The wounds on her back were the worst. When she'd tried to crawl away from him . . .

She pinched the bridge of her nose and winced. It sounded like a lose-lose situation to her. But she knew which option would make her feel the safest.

She straightened her shoulders and met Dr. Buchanan's gaze. She could do this, dammit. "Quinn."

"I'll get him." Dr. Buchanan stood. "Be right back."

When he returned with Quinn, her earlier embarrassment seemed like nothing. Now? She wanted to die. Yes, she knew what Preston had done wasn't her fault, but it didn't change the fact that she was ashamed.

Ashamed that it hadn't been the first time Preston had hurt her. Ashamed that she had let herself get so complacent. Ashamed that it had taken her so long to leave. So many damn things . . .

She had to give Dr. Buchanan credit, though. He kept it clinical as he pointed out which wounds on her back Quinn needed to prioritize keeping an eye on. Clinical or not, it hadn't made it any less mortifying. When he was done, she adjusted her shirt and leaned back.

Quinn wouldn't meet her eyes. She wanted to know what he was thinking. She didn't know why it mattered, but it did. Was he disgusted by her bruises? Angry? Did he pity her?

"Alex, I'd like to see you at my office in the next couple of days."

She nodded her acknowledgment, and the good doctor let himself out. She continued to stare at Quinn, willing him to look at her. But his gaze stayed glued to the floor.

Silence engulfed the room.

"Quinn, please say something."

He raised his head, and the anger swirling in his eyes was palpable. "What do you want me to say, Alex?"

She inched backward on the bed, pulling her knees close to her chest.

"Don't do that," he said.

She flinched, then held still, observing him.

He fisted his hands in his hair and blew out a breath. "Yes," he said, his voice rough. "I'm pissed, all right? I am fucking livid. But not at you, Alex. Never at *you*. Please believe me when I swear I'm not going to hurt you."

Slamming his eyes shut, he scrubbed his hands over his face. After a second, he let out a weary sigh and dropped his arms to his sides. "But why would you believe me?" he murmured, as if all the anger was seeping out of him. "You don't know me, and I'm acting like a fucking crazy person."

She remained frozen as Quinn came to the side of the bed and perched on the edge, his movements deliberate and slow. He reached for her arm, but stopped before touching her, and pulled his hand back.

"May I?"

Her heart threatened to beat out of her chest. Part of it was pure, instinctive fear. The other part was anger at herself for being afraid in the first place. She detested the quivering mess she'd become.

Determined to be strong, she forced herself to meet Quinn's gaze. His steel-gray eyes still held traces of anger, but they also pleaded with her.

When she nodded, he took hold of her wrist in a tender grasp and turned it so the bruises and stitches on her inner forearm were exposed. Her chest squeezed, and she knew he could feel her trembling.

"Deep breath, sweetheart," he murmured, demonstrating.

As they inhaled and exhaled together, he traced a feather-light knuckle around her stitches. Tears welled in her eyes. She blinked them away.

"When I see these cuts on your arm, the cop in me shouts, 'Standard defensive wounds.' But then I realize it's *your* arm. Not the arm of some faceless, nameless person. It's *you*. And then I look at all the cuts and bruises . . . and I see your back . . . and I want to destroy him." Barely above a whisper, his voice was fierce. "I know you just met me and have zero reasons to trust me, but I need you to understand that I'm *never* going to hurt you. Not only will I swear that to you, Alex, but on my parents' graves, I'll prove it to you."

She could only stare at him as he caressed her arm, a gentle gesture that stood in sharp contrast to the passion in his voice. The weight on her chest eased, and the tension holding her body in a tight coil dissolved.

He was a good man. She'd forgotten they existed.

A soft smile touched the corners of her lips. "I know."

And to her surprise, she did. Even though her head questioned her gut, she still believed him. Believed he'd hurt himself before he would ever hurt her.

Quinn shot her a playful grin that immediately lifted the heaviness between them. "Good, because even though we don't know each other that well yet, I have this crazy need to protect you. I'm the sheriff, you know, so it's my job." Her smile faded, and he tilted his head in question. "Not a fan of law enforcement?"

"Bad experience, that's all." Her gaze dropped to her hands.

He tipped her chin up with his finger. "Tell me what happened. Please. I want to help you, and I can't unless you tell me what's going on."

"I know, and I will. I promise. But not right now. I need some food. I'm actually starving." Her face heated as her stomach let out a loud growl.

He chuckled. "No kidding."

After helping her off the bed, he placed his hand on the uninjured small of her back and led her to the kitchen. The contact quickened her pulse.

Seated at his kitchen island, she watched him put together sandwiches. He kept the mood light by entertaining her with stories of his Little League days. He really was a sweet man. And when he smiled . . . wow.

Whoa—slow it down.

It was *way* too soon to be swooning over anyone's smile.

But she could look, couldn't she? There was no harm in that.

CHAPTER EIGHT

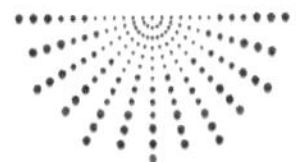

Hours later, they were still in Quinn's kitchen. They'd talked about their favorite movies over sandwiches—action for him, thrillers for her, and superhero movies for both of them. Then, they'd fallen into a comfortable conversation over safe topics, including TV shows, dogs vs. cats, sports, ice cream flavors, and his childhood antics. Now they were at his breakfast table with one of Roxie's blueberry pies between them.

Just as Alex began pondering whether they needed ice cream, Roxie launched through the kitchen door like a rocket.

"I thought I heard voices in here," she said, opening a cabinet. "The least you animals can do is give my pies the respect they deserve." She thunked two plates onto the table and gave them her best mom look.

"Yes, ma'am," Quinn mumbled around a mouthful of pie, grabbing a plate.

Alex wisely swallowed her laugh and followed suit.

Once they'd properly cut and served themselves slices,

Roxie joined them at the table with a triumphant smile. "So, what's all the laughing about?"

"Quinn." Alex chuckled. Her abdomen was starting to cramp from laughing so much. "We were talking about what a wimp he is."

"Of course," Roxie said. She made a circular motion with her hand. "And?"

"And how you broke his nose." She shot him a wide grin.

"Twice, actually," Roxie clarified.

Quinn groaned, and Alex erupted with laughter.

"Seriously, Alex, you should have seen him the second time I smashed his nose. The idiot broke into Ray's Diner when he was about thirteen or fourteen—hey!" Roxie whipped her head around to glare at Quinn.

"What?" His expression was innocent. The guy was so full of crap.

"No kicking under the table, jerk!" Roxie turned back to Alex. "As I was saying—ouch!" She turned and hissed at Quinn. "I swear to god, Quinn O'Conner, if you kick me one more time, I'm gonna shove that fork so far up your ass you're gonna—"

"Roxie," he interrupted with a guileless grin, "I heard you're catering the mayor's big party."

Roxie's face lit up like a light bulb, and Alex bit back a laugh. These two had each other's numbers, that was for sure.

"I know! Isn't that great? The missus stopped by today and put a huge order in. And I mean a *huge* order. It's going to be fabulous! This will really give a lot of exposure to the catering end of the business and—" She scowled. "You're a jackass, Quinn."

"Yeah, yeah," Quinn said. Then, smiling at Alex, he nodded his head toward Roxie. "Attention span of a gnat."

"You know, I'm beginning to hate you," Roxie said, her death glare fixed on Quinn.

He rose and smacked a loud and sticky blueberry pie kiss on Roxie's forehead. "I know."

The two continued to bicker, and she watched their antics with amusement.

Rounding the table, Quinn took her empty plate and shot her a grin that made her mind go blank. "Dinner, sweetheart?"

She blinked at him. "Sure," she said, cringing inside. That one word had come out like a croak instead of the calm, casual reply she'd intended. Good god, this man was starting to fry her brain.

Roxie started chattering again, a steady stream of commentary flying past her lips. Listening with half an ear, Alex grew increasingly distracted as she watched Quinn prepare dinner. Not because she was interested in him or anything.

Nope. No, definitely not.

She simply had a pair of functioning eyes. After all, it was hard not to notice an attractive man moving around the kitchen. Especially when he moved very, *very* well.

Holy crap, woman. Slow. It. Down!

Quinn caught her stare and smiled.

She averted her gaze but couldn't stop the flush that stole over her skin. Good god, she'd been gawking. Like a freaking high schooler. She wished there was a rock she could crawl under.

When the food finished cooking, Quinn dished up their dinners. They sat at the table, and Roxie treated them to the latest town gossip while they ate.

"Between the mayor's upcoming party, the Rotary dinner, and Ray and Martha's anniversary party, it's going to be a busy next couple of months. Oh! That reminds me—" Roxie shot up from her chair and ran out of the room.

With her fork halted midair, Alex shot Quinn a questioning look.

He shrugged. "Who knows? It's Roxie. Just, I don't know, sort of smile and nod at whatever she comes back with." His grin turned mischievous. "That usually works for me."

Chuckling, she shook her head as Roxie burst back into the room.

"Here, I almost forgot," Roxie said, handing her a bag.

Opening it, she removed a navy-blue apron with *Comfort Food* embroidered along the top. As far as aprons went, it was nice and all. If you liked aprons. "Um, thanks. This is for . . ."

"Work. In a couple weeks? At my café? Remember our conversation last night?"

"Oh." She hesitated, her mind drawing a big, fat blank. Was that what she'd agreed to last night? "That's right. Of course. How could I forget?" Apparently, very easily. The giant smile on her face was beginning to hurt. "I can't wait, Roxie. We may have to run through the details again, but—"

"Excellent! I was thinking—" A cell phone rang from the living room, and Roxie held up a finger, rising from her chair. "Hold that thought. I need to get that."

Alex could only blink as the other woman hurried away. She turned and found Quinn staring at her, amusement dancing in his eyes. She cleared her throat. "What?"

"Nothing." The devilish grin on his lips implied otherwise.

"Then why are you smiling at me like that?"

"Because you fascinate me, Alex." He leaned in, and she held her breath. "You are . . . by far . . . the worst liar I have ever met."

She released her breath and grimaced.

Scoffing, he said, "Really, Alex. That was quite impressive in its sheer horror."

Her forehead scrunched. "Was it that bad? Do you think she noticed?"

"Absolutely. But, hey, I wouldn't worry about it. I'm sure it's all part of Roxie's grand master plan." He dropped his voice to a conspiratorial hush. "You know, she probably asked you to work for her when she knew you were distracted. That way you couldn't say no. She's tricky, that one. I'd keep an eye on her." At that, he stood from the table with a wink. "So, when do you start?"

Mouth gaping like a fish, she shook her head. "I have no idea. It's a café, right?"

Quinn broke into a full, belly-rolling laugh. "Wow, you really weren't listening to her at all. And here I thought that was a talent only I possessed. Alex, I am *most* impressed."

He filled her in on all the details she'd missed. As it turned out, Roxie's Comfort Food wasn't a café. Not entirely. It was part bakery, part café, and, as of a few months ago, part catering company. It was open seven days a week, from six in the morning to two in the afternoon, except for Sundays, when they closed at eleven.

Located in the center of the island's downtown district, or as Quinn sarcastically put it, its bustling three-street hub, Roxie's place sold a variety of delectable treats ranging from pies, muffins, cobblers, and cheesecakes to lasagnas, potpies, and casseroles. The fare was traditional and gourmet and everything in between. For anyone who was the slightest bit weight-conscious, Comfort Food sold every possible guilty pleasure imaginable. However, according to Quinn, the food was worth the extra gym time.

. . .

When Alex returned to Joe's house later that night with the navy-blue apron tucked securely under her arm, her thoughts were a chaotic tangle in her head. Everything was happening so fast. But she wasn't quite sure if it was *too* fast.

What she did know was that everything felt surreal.

She'd been on Hudson Island for only two days—two!—and she'd had more fun in those forty-eight hours than she had in years. With people she'd just met and already genuinely liked. It boggled her mind.

Glancing down at the apron, she shook her head. She'd agreed to start in two weeks, giving her injuries more time to heal. She still didn't know what she'd be doing at Roxie's, but one thing she knew for certain was that she was a disaster in the kitchen. Always had been, and likely always would be.

Well, if anything, the work would be interesting.

A job. An actual job. Holy crap.

It had been five years since she'd last had one. How was this her life?

Excitement and nervous anticipation fluttered in her belly.

"It's now or never," she murmured, blowing out a breath.

After triple-checking the locks on both the front and back doors, she climbed the stairs toward her bedroom. As she neared the landing, she slowed, losing momentum.

"A job," she groaned. She lowered herself onto the top step. With her elbows resting on her knees, she put her head in her hands. Uncertainty and doubt took over, vanquishing the earlier excitement in a puff of smoke. "What the hell was I thinking?"

CHAPTER NINE

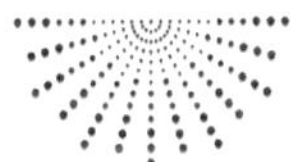

After another restless night of ominous and chaotic nightmares, Alex donned her oversized sunglasses to hide the healing bruises and dark circles under her eyes. She walked to Hudson Island's quaint downtown and wandered about, people watching and checking out the local stores. It was a charming town, roughly the same size as the one she'd fled on the other side of the country.

According to the *Welcome to Hudson Island* informational kiosk she stopped by, the island, which was shaped like a number seven that was tilted at a forty-five-degree angle, was situated in the Puget Sound between the Quimper Peninsula and the center of Whidbey Island. Its sole downtown and main residential area were at the southern part of the island, along with the ferry terminal. In the center, organic farms and two state parks with extensive hiking trails stretched from shoreline to shoreline. Farther north, two award-winning wineries and a multitude of luxury vacation homes dotted the landscape. At the northwestern tip, a five-star wellness resort, along with a world-renowned golf course, attracted tourists from all over.

Joe had mentioned there was a lot of money on the island, but as she observed the fleece-vested people milling about, she couldn't tell a millionaire from a farmer. Hudson Island was the textbook definition of the fabled Pacific Northwest attitude. Laid-back and cheerful, it reminded her nothing of Summerside, the snooty, second-home playground for the Boston elite. On paper, they were comparable: small boating communities with strong fishing industries and upscale resorts. In person, not so much. And that made her smile.

But her favorite part about Hudson Island? No one knew her.

For that alone, she was grateful.

Walking past a number of antique stores, she noted which ones she wanted to stop in and take a better look at later. In her pre-Preston life, she'd loved antique shopping. It had been a treat to find just the right piece for her apartment. Granted, she hadn't had a whole lot of money at the time, so finding something she could afford had been rare. But on those occasions, she'd been thrilled. Preston, on the other hand, was all about interior designers and the most extravagant and ostentatious pieces. He'd put an end to her collection. Nevertheless, now she was free and could do whatever she wanted.

She continued to meander along the town's three main roads and was surprised by the variety of shops she encountered. There was a yarn and fabric store, a bookstore, and several clothing and art boutiques. Along the city park and beachfront was an ice cream parlor, a candy store, and a coffee shop.

The slow pace and mix of tourists and locals charmed her. It seemed everyone she passed gave her a smile or a nod of acknowledgment. Alex welcomed the friendly anonymity with open arms.

In Summerside, if someone hadn't personally known her

or Preston, then they'd at least known *of* her. She'd participated in committees for the Art Council, the Rotary Club, the Humane Society, the Chamber of Commerce, and half a dozen more organizations. It had been endless.

What had frustrated her the most was that even though she'd been in those positions, no one had taken her seriously. She'd just been the pretty wife of one of the town's most influential men. Everyone had been perfectly accommodating to her only because they'd recognized she'd be running the town's social show someday.

Whatever she'd wanted, they'd given. No questions asked. And that had been the problem. All those people and not one of them had been someone she could trust. Someone she could confide in. And none of them had been brave enough to rock the boat by daring to ask if she was okay.

She let out an unsteady breath. This was her chance. Perhaps the only chance she had left. And she'd better make it count.

No.

She *would* make it count.

Coming to a stop, she stared up at the narrow two-story brick building in front of her. Bronze lettering declared it the Hudson Island Sheriff's Department.

She'd tossed and turned all night, knowing she needed to come clean with Quinn today. She owed him the truth. If she worked for Roxie, her past could put the woman in danger. That wasn't an option.

Anxiety constricted her throat as she crossed the street. She knew Quinn would help her. But what if he thought less of her after she told him about her past? What if he thought she was weak? Or worse, that she'd deserved it?

Logically, she knew none of it had been her fault, that she hadn't deserved any of Preston's abuse. After a year of intense counseling, she *knew* that. Still . . . those tiny little doubts kept creeping back, kept getting louder. For the sake of her sanity, she needed to ignore them. But "easier said than done" was a cliché for a reason.

She took a deep, cleansing breath and let it out slowly. Shoulders back, chin up, and one freaking step at a time, she climbed the stairs. In her mind, she ran through the list of bullet points she'd created the sleepless night before. Details Quinn needed to know.

I can do this.

With each step, her confidence grew.

This was it. She was taking back control of her life, dammit.

Striding through the front door and toward the reception desk, she paused when she heard Quinn's deep voice. She turned to search for him and froze.

Holy. Crap. What was he doing here?

A large, blond-haired, blue-eyed Adonis stood next to Quinn. When she met the man's gaze, the blood drained from her face, and the carefully crafted bullet point list in her head evaporated.

CHAPTER TEN

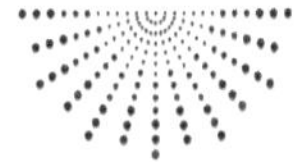

"Joe?" Alex croaked. "What are you doing here?"

"Long time no see, doll." Joe smiled and ran the back of his hand along the side of her face. "You're looking better."

Quinn frowned, and his stomach clenched like he'd been sucker punched in the gut. He might as well have been because Alex hadn't flinched away from Joe's touch. At all.

Fuck, he was an idiot. An idiot who'd read it all—every damn thing—wrong.

When Joe enveloped Alex in a protective hug, whispering something into her ear, it took everything he had to not howl. To not shove his friend away, toss her over his shoulder caveman style, and scream, *Mine!*

Yeah. He was a fucking idiot. And a completely irrational fucking idiot at that.

"Let's take this cozy reunion somewhere private," he growled, turning away from the reunited couple.

Stalking into his office, he focused on keeping his anger in check. But he was pissed. At Joe. At the entire situation.

But mostly, at himself. He fell—no, *almost* fell—for the damsel in distress. Again.

Fucking. Idiot.

He settled behind his desk. Joe and Alex occupied the chairs opposite him. An uncomfortable silence hung in the air. He glared at Joe, and his friend glared right back.

His irritation grew. So did his disappointment, but that was something he didn't want to acknowledge. Nope. He would not go there. Not right now, at least. He had a job to do. But dammit, this whole situation sucked. "So, which one of you two lovebirds is going to sing first?"

Alex's brow furrowed, and her head tilted to the side. "What?"

"You're about to cross that proverbial line, old friend," Joe said, his tone lethal. "You know nothing. And you'll remain in the dark if you don't keep your petty, jealous comments to yourself. So, unless you want to get Alex and her unborn child killed, I suggest you shut the fuck up."

Holy. Shit.

His eyes narrowed to slits as he glared at Joe. His friend had gotten Alex pregnant?

"I could kill you for thinking what you're thinking." Joe shook his head, and the laugh that escaped his lips held no trace of humor. "Really, Connie? She's married, for fuck's sake. Granted, her husband's an asshole, but do you really think that little of me? That little of Alex?"

Married.

Fan-fucking-tastic. Of course she had to be married on top of it all. His chest ached.

"I wouldn't put anything past you, Buchanan." He shoved all his emotions—for Alex, for his best friend, for everything—into a tiny box in his mind and set it aside. "You're an asshole. We know Roxie would vouch for that."

Joe flipped him off, then turned to Alex, dismissing him. The fucker.

"Alex, I wanted to let you know in person that Woodsworth struck a deal. They're going with six months in jail, plus a year of bullshit community service." Joe raked his hand through his hair, his frustration obvious. "I'm really sorry. We were all hoping for a lot longer."

Alex's jaw dropped. She couldn't have heard that right.

"Six months? That's it? Preston almost *killed* me, and he gets *six* months? He also attacked *you*. Isn't there some law about attacking an FBI agent?" Her pulse raced. Disbelief and horror turned her stomach. Her gaze shifted from Joe to Quinn, with a desperate hope that Quinn would tell her differently.

He didn't.

Holy crap. Six months.

The erratic thumping of her heart signaled the beginning of a panic attack. She fisted her hands in her lap, trying to hold it at bay.

"The county prosecutor's office made some clerical errors when they filed the paperwork for his case. There were some other . . . issues . . . on our end that fucked things up, too." Joe pressed his lips into a thin, angry line. "Long story short, they were only able to get one minor assault charge to stick. Everything else was thrown out. I'm really sorry, Alex."

Her chin dropped to her chest. She was pretty sure she already knew the answer to her next question, but she asked it, anyway. "He's not going to serve the full six months, is he?"

"Well . . ." Joe hesitated.

"Don't placate me, Joe." She was tired. Down-to-the-bone weary. "Please. Just tell me how long."

His bright-blue eyes met hers. "If you're lucky, five months. Tops. If he's lucky, then one month. *Possibly* ninety days. My bet is on him."

Rubbing her pounding temple, she sat back and let a frustrated sigh escape. "Mine is, too." She rose from her chair, suddenly antsy, and paced the small room. "Let's say he gets out in a month. Then what, Joe? Does he know where I am?"

"No. And I don't think he knows about the baby."

She spun to face him. "Back in Boston, you said that Preston was told I'd miscarried. Now you don't *think* he knows?" Chills skated down her spine. "Either he knows or he doesn't. Which one is it?"

"I don't know. We aren't sure who he has in his pocket. There's a chance someone could have leaked the truth." Joe pinched the bridge of his nose, then gave her a look she couldn't interpret. Her unease grew and in her gut she knew that she wasn't going to like what he was going to say next.

A loud knock at the door caused her to jump.

"Come in," Quinn called out, his deep voice echoing in the quiet room.

A baby-faced deputy poked his head through the door. "I'm sorry to interrupt, Sheriff. There's an urgent phone call for Agent Buchanan."

Without a word, Joe rose and followed the young deputy out.

When the door shut behind them, she sat down. Hands fisted on her lap, she dug her nails into her palms, leaving little crescent-shaped marks. Her mind raced with everything that had transpired. But there was something in particular that nagged at her. Something that made anger and disappointment battle inside her for attention.

Quinn.

He leaned back in his chair, arms crossed over his chest, eyes locked on his desk.

She stared at him. When he finally met her gaze, the anger won out, and she embraced it. "Do you honestly think I was cheating on my pious and faithful husband by having an affair with Joe? That I'm having Joe's baby and all these bruises and stitches are some wronged husband's justified idea of getting payback on his whore of a wife?"

"Yes. I mean, no! Dammit, no." Quinn sighed, scrubbing his hands over his face. He stood, rounded his desk, and sat in the chair Joe had vacated, elbows on his knees, hands clasped.

She crossed one leg over the other and put her fisted hands on the armrests.

"Alex, I don't know what's going on, but regardless of what happened or what didn't happen between you and Joe, nothing justifies *anyone* raising a hand to you. *Ever.*"

The intensity in his gray eyes had her breath catching, had her recalling how safe she'd felt when they'd spent time together. "No, it doesn't. But you're right. You don't know what's going on."

"Then *please*, explain it to me." Reaching for her hands, he paused midair and lifted a brow in question.

Her heart squeezed, and a tiny bit of the tension in her shoulders eased. She nodded.

He took her clenched fists in his hands. "Alex, I admit that I'm an asshole. I know that. The more time you spend with me, the more you'll come to realize it yourself." His thumb traced the racing pulse along her wrist. "I'm sorry about what I said. What I thought. I want to help you. To protect you—and your baby—in any way I can from this guy. But you've got me in blinders. I have *no* idea what's going on, and I can't do you any good like this."

Her eyes fell to their joined hands.

His claims of being an asshole were all talk. Yes, the man was a little rough around the edges, but she knew men who were real assholes.

Quinn most definitely was not one of them.

She had gotten a peek behind his walls yesterday, and she'd liked what she'd seen.

She wanted to trust him. Hell, a part of her wanted to rely on him completely, to have him make everything bad go away. Because he *would* protect her, most likely by putting his own safety before hers. That's the kind of guy he was. Whether he called himself an asshole or not didn't matter.

But she couldn't hide behind Quinn. No, she *wouldn't* hide behind him. She was done giving all control over to the men in her life.

Realistically, though, she knew she needed help. She was no match for Preston. The countless stitches and Steri-Strips covering her body were proof enough. She'd fought back with every ounce of strength she'd had but if Joe hadn't intervened, she would have left that house in a body-bag. She'd either had to trust Joe or die. This situation was no different. Not really. So, maybe she *should* give over some control to Quinn. Just a little. Just enough to keep her alive.

"I'd go ahead and trust him if I were you," Joe said from behind her. Before she could turn, he walked in and took a knee next to them. "He's a good man, Alex. Annoying as hell, but Connie's a good man. He *will* keep you safe. Despite his lack of social graces."

Quinn scoffed. "Fu—"

"See," Joe interrupted, smiling at her. "That's exactly my point."

Glancing between the men, her brow scrunched in confusion. She pulled her hands from Quinn's warm grip and crossed her arms over her chest. "Weren't you two ready to clobber each other a few minutes ago?"

Joe stood, and the two men nodded at each other, a silent exchange she couldn't decipher passed between them.

Joe rounded Quinn's desk. "Yeah, well, we're always ready to clobber each other." He flopped down into the chair, leaned back, and propped his feet, ankles crossed, on the edge of the desk. "That's one of the many reasons why we don't work together anymore."

Quinn shrugged. "All true."

"So, Alex," Joe began, "I have some official paperwork that should be arriving here to Quinn's attention tomorrow. In the meantime, I have a copy ready for you to review right now. When the originals get here, I need you to fill them out and—"

"What are they?"

"They're your papers, doll." He flashed her a ridiculously sexy grin. She was certain he knew the effect it had on people. Just like she was certain he could pull it out on cue.

She rolled her eyes. Apparently, she was immune to the grin. "What kind of papers would that be, *doll?*"

Quinn chuckled. "Ouch."

"They're the papers that'll make you legal." He looked at Quinn. "You're still in the dark, aren't you?"

Quinn nodded.

Joe gestured between her and Quinn. "Sheriff Quinn O'Conner, officially meet Natalie Woodsworth, soon-to-be ex-wife of Preston Fitzgerald Woodsworth *the third*, deputy mayor of Summerside, Massachusetts. And yes, the pompous asshole made sure everyone used *the third* when addressing him."

Quinn's brow furrowed. "How did the FBI get involved in a domestic abuse case?"

"It wasn't intentional." Joe shook his head. "Off the record, I was undercover as their neighbor with another agent, but that's a whole shit show in itself." Disgust flashed over his face. "We had both Woodsworth and Summerside's mayor on our radar for money laundering and extortion and had built a solid case against them. We were getting set to make a move, but before we could,"—he waved a hand toward her—"Woodsworth went ballistic and put Alex in the hospital. Tried his best to put me in there with her, too. Then, right when we thought we had him, his damn lawyers swooped in. He's one slick bastard."

Alex shifted in her seat. None of what Joe had said was new info. But it was still jarring to hear. Knowing she'd been so blind to it all—the money laundering and extortion, not the abuse—stung.

It also reminded her how lucky she was to have gotten away from him. Bruises and all.

"Afterward, Natalie Woodsworth became Alexandra Garcia. But," Joe said, pulling a manila folder out of his brief-case, "in name only. Alex, I assume you'll need employment one of these fine days. Well, you can't get employment if there's no history of an Alexandra Garcia existing, correct?"

She nodded, and Quinn squeezed her hand, startling her. She wasn't sure if she'd reached for him, or if it had been the other way around. It didn't matter. She took comfort in his touch, in his support.

"As far as the government's concerned, which I am but a humble servant of," Joe continued, sarcasm dripping from every word, "the last known sighting of Mrs. Natalie Wood-worth was at Massachusetts General Hospital in Boston. During this same time period, there's now a record of Miss Alexandra Garcia working in Virginia. In fact"—he flipped through the manila folder—"your verifiable employment record has you as an administrative assistant for the last three and a half years in Quantico, Virginia."

She stared at Joe, and her jaw dropped. She had a work

history now? "You can do that?" She turned to Quinn in disbelief. "He can do that?"

Quinn glared at Joe. "Quantico? Real cute, asshole." Squeezing her hand again, he said, "Alex, you'd *really* be surprised at what can be done as a humble servant of the government."

"What's the big deal about using Quantico?" she asked, leaving her hand in his grip. How the simple contact could be so soothing, she hadn't a clue. But she gratefully took the tiny bit of comfort he provided.

"The FBI Academy is located there," Quinn answered, his glare still fixed on Joe. "Could you be a little more obvious? Fucking feds."

"Hey, the academy isn't the only thing there," Joe countered. "It's a legit place of employment." He looked at Alex. "You've got one of the largest Marine Corps bases in the world in Quantico, which the FBI Academy *just so happens* to sit on. The NCIS Headquarters and DEA training facility are also there. The last time I checked, Connie, all those are notable *and* believable places of employment for an administrative assistant."

Her head spun. "Why can't I just legally change my name to Alexandra Garcia? Why do I have to switch to a whole new identity?"

"Because if you just legally change your name, then there will be a record of it. Name changes are public documents. Anyone looking for Natalie Woodsworth could do a little snooping and find the new Alexandra Garcia. Any decent PI could locate you in two days. But if Natalie Woodsworth *disappears* it'll be much harder to find you, particularly if 'Alexandra Garcia' already exists."

Technically, Joe's explanation made sense. Still . . . unease turned her stomach. "So what about the divorce papers I had filed when I was in the hospital? What happens with that? What happens to my old identity?"

"All that still stands. As for your old identity." Joe shrugged. "Nothing happens with that. It just is. Like I said, the last known sighting of Mrs. Natalie Woodsworth was at Mass Gen. As far as everyone is concerned, you—as Natalie —were released from the hospital and disappeared. No one has seen you since. You went off the grid."

Alex pursed her lips, shutting her eyes. Just like that, her entire past—gone.

"Do you want to start completely fresh or not?" Joe said, no trace of empathy in his voice.

Her eyes snapped open, and she studied him. He was leaving something out. Something big. "What's the catch?"

"Ah, a girl after my own heart." He chuckled, dropping his feet to the ground, then propping his elbows on Quinn's desk. "Let's worry about this supposed 'catch' at a later date. How about you just take a peek at the paperwork? You don't have to commit to anything right now. It's not WITSEC or anything."

"What's WITSEC?" she asked, frowning. When Joe grimaced, as if he'd regretted his words, her frown deepened.

"Witness Protection." Her eyes widened, and he rushed on. "That's not what this is, Alex. This is simply . . . protection. Just look it over. Okay?"

There was something sketchy about this, but she took the folder he slid across the desk. Scanning the contents, the legal jargon made her eyes cross. But she was taking control of her life, dammit. If that meant taking hours to figure out what the legalese said, so be it.

She'd see what the feds were offering, and she'd probably take it. At this point, she'd do just about anything to get Preston out of her life for good. And besides, as far as she was concerned, Natalie Woodsworth had died a long time ago.

Quinn rose, placing a hand on her shoulder. "Don't feel pressured to sign anything you don't want to. We'll let you read those over in private." He nodded toward the door. "I'm gonna have a brief chat with Buchanan outside."

Once the door was securely closed behind them, Quinn spun. Grabbing Joe's shirt with both hands, he slammed his friend against the wall.

"Are you fucking kidding me?" he hissed. "After all she's been through? After all the crap that asshole put her through, you guys are going to use her as fucking *bait*?"

A look of resignation crossed Joe's face. "Look, I understand why you're pissed. I do. But you know how it is. They want Woodsworth. I have no say in this. You know that."

"Fuck," Quinn grumbled as he released his friend. Yeah, he knew. That was one of the reasons why he'd left the FBI. He'd gotten tired of asking, "How high, sir?" every time they'd said, "Jump." And he was now a sheriff, so that said a lot.

"What am I supposed to do, O'Conner? Huh?" Joe raked his hands through his blond hair and began to pace, then jerked to a stop in front of him. "I've got my orders. I'm relying on you to protect her."

"What else do you know?"

"Not much. I thought we fucking had him. Felony assault with a deadly weapon not only against her, but also against *me*, a fucking fed. Case closed. He was going to do serious time for that, and then we were going to stack the white collar shit on top."

Quinn held up a hand. "Wait. You said they want Woodsworth, but they *have* him. He's sitting in a cell."

Joe shook his head. "I wasn't lying about that clerical error. Not only did most of the evidence for our assaults get tossed, but now almost all the evidence we've been gathering for the last eighteen months has gone out the window. These last few days? The shit literally hit the fucking fan."

His brows came together. "How's that possible?"

"Remember that whole shit show I mentioned?"

Quinn nodded, and the hairs on the back of his neck rose at the abject revulsion on Joe's face.

"My partner and I went under as a husband-wife power couple playing the married-for-the-money roles. She played the role too well. My partner is now a *former* Special Agent and being detained herself."

Of all the things he'd expected to hear from Joe, that hadn't been it. "The fuck . . ."

"She was fucking Woodsworth, leaking information, and destroying evidence. A complete clusterfuck. The powers that be still want Woodsworth. No, I take that back. They want the higher-ups on the food chain. We know Woodsworth will give them up because he's a pussy. Any man who beats on a woman, let alone a woman who's half his size, is a man who'll rat his friends out to save his own sorry ass."

"Agreed." Damn. He didn't envy his friend's predicament. At all.

"We need a little more time to build our case back up and then a way to get Woodsworth back into custody. There's no way in hell he's serving the full six months. Alex can give him to us on a damn platter with a fucking apple in his mouth."

Things still didn't quite add up. Not that they ever fucking did with the feds. "Why didn't Alex go straight into WITSEC? Why is she at *your* place?"

"When she was in the hospital, we thought we still had Woodsworth, so she wasn't approved for it. It truly wasn't even an issue then. I sent her here because I knew she wanted a fresh start. I just wanted to help her get away from all that bullshit."

Quinn crossed his arms over his chest. "And now?"

"Fuck, Connie. The powers that be. They want what they want, but only when they fucking want it. *Now* they deem her important, but still not vital enough for WITSEC." Joe let out a weary sigh. "I wasn't lying earlier. They did approve a modified protective custody." He shrugged. "And here we fucking are."

Quinn pictured the bruises on her face, and his molars ground together. They were going to risk Alex's life by dangling her in front of that piece of shit? After everything she'd already been through?

"You know they're going to do this with or without me, Connie. I'd rather be in the know. I'm sure you'd agree."

Fuck. His friend wasn't wrong. Joe was in the shittiest of positions. But Alex was in the crosshairs. And that was unacceptable.

He scrubbed his hands over his face before planting them on his hips. "'I am but a humble servant of the government,'" he parroted with equal sarcasm. "Fucking hell, man. What do you need me to do?"

Joe stared at him for a moment, the seriousness of his expression setting off warning bells in his gut. "Keep her safe. She's going to need it. And if she starts working for Rox like you said she plans to, promise me you'll keep them both safe."

"Of course."

"I'll tell you what I can, but you know how it is. It's all need-to-know, and most of the time, I don't even make the damn cut." His eyes narrowed as if he were debating something in his mind. "Off the record?"

Quinn nodded.

"Call in Gavin's crew if you need to."

The warning bells were now blaring. When an FBI agent suggested enlisting the help of a private security company, shit was beyond fucked. He nodded again.

"Above all, O'Conner, make sure you get her to talk to you, to trust you. Woodsworth is going to come after her, and you need to be by her side when he does. Because I can guarantee you it's not going to be pretty. He's a sick son of a bitch. And worse? When he gets out, he's going to be a *desperate* son of a bitch."

Quinn crossed his arms over his chest. That fucker was *not* going to get near Alex. Not on his watch.

"I need to get back," Joe said, pulling his phone from his pocket. "I'll be back and forth between the Boston and Seattle offices until this is resolved. I'm going to run in and say goodbye to Alex now, but I'll be in touch." He stepped toward Quinn's office, then paused. "Can you tell Roxanne that—" His mouth slammed shut. "Never mind," he muttered before vanishing through the door.

CHAPTER ELEVEN

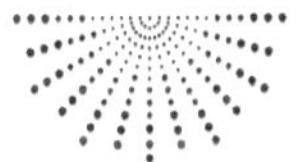

"**D**amn, dude. What the hell did that heavy bag do to you?"

On an exhale, Quinn swiped at the sweat dripping into his eyes with his forearm. His muscles shook from exhaustion.

He lifted his chin at his friend Cade, the co-owner of De La Rosa Gym. "Long fucking day, man."

Quinn usually came to the gym in the morning, but after seeing Joe this afternoon and hearing the bomb his friend dropped, he'd needed to hit something. Preferably not Joe's face. Though that thought still held appeal. A tiny part of him was also avoiding going home. He didn't want to run into Alex.

After Joe had left, he and Alex had shared a few moments of awkward small talk. She'd mentioned she had swung by Doc's clinic and gotten the nurse to help her with the wounds on her back, so she wouldn't need his help there. Then she'd grabbed the manila folder Joe had left her and hightailed it out of the building. All the ease they'd built the day before, all the friendly comfort, had been obliterated.

"Long day?" Cade glanced at the bag with one brow arched. "I'll bet. But if you break it, you buy it, fucker." He nodded toward an MMA cage where a lone man was shadowboxing. "Want to spar?"

"With Alvarez?" he asked, surprised by the suggestion.

Matt Alvarez was an old friend of Cade's who'd come to Hudson Island to wait out his medical leave from the Seattle PD. Quinn had never sparred with the other man, but he knew the guy was a beast.

"Nah, not with Alvarez. He hasn't gotten the okay yet," Cade said as they made their way to an empty boxing ring. "Besides, when he does get cleared, you're not gonna want to be the first man up. Dude's got so much pent-up shit, he'll rip your head clear off."

"Like you're not gonna," he grumbled.

"True." Cade laughed. "But lucky for you, I don't have months of rage built up." He smacked his gloves together. "Let's go, Sheriff."

Thirty minutes later, Quinn's gloved hands were on his knees, and he was bent over, gasping for air, praying he didn't puke.

"Good job, brother," Cade said, smacking him on the back. "See, once you let loose and stop thinking, your form gets a shit ton better."

"Thanks." He wheezed. "Holy shit. Why do I feel like I'm gonna die?"

"Because you've never full-out sparred that long. Congratulations."

"You're not even short of breath. I think I fucking hate you."

"I'm a professional. What can I say?" Cade shrugged, a shit-eating grin on his face. "Can I assume your 'long day' has something to do with the mysterious guest at the Buchanan house?"

Quinn straightened, then yanked open the Velcro closure on one of his gloves with his teeth. "How do you know about that?"

Cade scoffed. "Small town, dude. Small town."

"What have you heard?"

"Beat-up midsize sedan. Tiny female in ill-fitting clothes with long black hair. Name is Alex. Wears giant sunglasses that do a shit job hiding the bruises on her face."

He shook his head. "Jesus."

"If it's any consolation, Roxie was scolding everyone about gossiping."

He snorted. "Roxie? That girl's café is gossip central."

Cade grinned. "I know, right? But in the twenty minutes I was there, it was clear she's very protective of Alex."

"Good." He tugged off his other glove.

"I take it this"—Cade indicated the ring they'd vacated—"is also because of the other nugget of gossip flying around town?"

"And that would be?"

Cade grinned. "Joe's back."

He withheld an eye roll. Barely. "Yeah. That fucker swooped in for an hour, stirred up shit, then swooped on out."

"Last time I checked, that's what he does." Cade nodded to a couple guys at the heavy bags. "Me and Alvarez are going to grab a bite at Monty's Tavern. Come have a beer with us and you can set us straight on all the Hudson gossip."

A beer and shooting the shit sounded a lot better than going home and wondering about Alex. If she was settling in okay. If she needed anything. If it would be weird if he stopped by.

Fuck.

"Count me in, man."

CHAPTER TWELVE

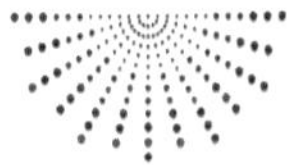

Alex sat on one of the rocking chairs on Joe's front porch. A glance next door revealed a dark, still house. Her plan had been to wait for Quinn to come home from work so she could apologize for bolting out of his office like a madwoman. Seeing Joe had taken her by surprise and sent her mind reeling. But that was no excuse for being rude to someone she hoped was becoming a friend.

The sun had set almost an hour prior, and it was closing in on nine. Still, no Quinn. Her apology would have to be added to the top of her to-do list tomorrow. Not that she had a bustling list. Swinging by the clinic for her back and grocery shopping were the only other two items.

She melted into the cushion she'd placed behind her back and closed her eyes. The quiet night enveloped her. Focusing on the gentle, rhythmic sway of the rocker, she fought to slow her breathing and willed her mind to calm.

Just over a year ago, by a stroke of luck, god, fate—whatever you wanted to call it—she'd stumbled upon a pair of women who had righted her sinking ship. Those two strangers had given her the tools she'd needed to not only survive, but more importantly, the tools she'd needed to *overcome*. The ongoing counseling and therapy they'd provided had helped her realize that she needed to leave her husband.

She'd known she couldn't just divorce Preston. He wouldn't allow it. So, she'd designed her escape. Meticulously. Unfortunately, the age-old adage about best laid plans going awry was so, so true.

Looking back, there had been some glaring holes in her scheme. Probably thanks to watching *Sleeping with the Enemy* one too many times.

Now, Alex had a month. Just one short month before she might have to fight for her freedom all over again. She wanted to believe Preston wouldn't come after her, that he had bigger things to worry about. But she knew better.

Once he was released from jail, the clock would start ticking. Within hours of ascertaining her location, he'd be knocking down Joe's door. Even faster if he knew the miscarriage had been a lie.

For the millionth time, she wondered how Preston had learned about the pregnancy in the first place. She certainly hadn't told him. But somehow, he'd found out. During that final attack, he'd screamed something about the baby not being his. The accusation of infidelity had been less surprising than his knowledge of the baby. *Whore, cunt,* and *cheating slut* were his go-to insults any time he beat her.

She wasn't sure why Preston had attacked her that final night—then again, he'd never really needed a reason—but regardless of the cause, regardless of whether he was aware of the baby or not, she knew without a shadow of a doubt that he blamed her *completely* for everything that had happened. His arrest. His jail time. She was at fault. Always.

When he found her, he would take none of the responsibility. Instead, he'd lay the blame solely at her feet. Reprimand her for airing their "personal issues" in public and ruining his precious image. He would claim it was her, and her alone, who'd destroyed his political career—and hence, his entire life—by ending up in the hospital.

And that made her nervous.

No. It petrified her.

Because his professional aspirations were everything to him. Preston Woodsworth *III* had been groomed since birth to become a member of the political elite.

Now it was over.

And he'd want his revenge.

She opened her eyes, and an icy chill ran through her body. Her trembling hands reached for the pack of cigarettes sitting on the little table next to her. She'd come across the open pack in one of the kitchen drawers and had been staring at them ever since.

She used to smoke. A horrible habit, for sure, but it had been her crutch. However, a year ago, Preston had . . . convinced her . . . to quit.

But right now, she was craving a cigarette. Desperately.

She shouldn't smoke, especially since she was pregnant, but she pulled one out of the box, anyway. Putting it to her lips, she struck the match and inhaled.

Her chest seized.

Holy shit.

It wasn't like riding a bike. At all.

She coughed. The smoke was so much thicker than she'd remembered, the taste more bitter. A wave of nausea consumed her. With watering eyes, she bolted out of the rocking chair. Gripping the porch railing with one hand— the other still held the cigarette—she leaned over and emptied her stomach onto the shrubs below.

Once her insides settled, she sank back into the chair. With the rocker in motion, she eyed the offending cigarette in her hand. "There goes that."

She put the cigarette out on the bottom of her shoe. Its burning ember slowly went out with a soft, sizzling hiss, and the sound took her back in time.

Preston strode up behind her. Without giving her time to turn, he grabbed the cigarette from between her fingertips and slapped the side of her face. She teetered on unsteady feet, but his hand fisted in her hair, steadying her. Fire exploded along her scalp as he dragged her through the French doors and into the house. She'd rather have fallen.

"Natalie, really. You shouldn't smoke," he said, his own cigarette dangling from his lips. "What would the neighbors think?"

Yanking her toward their rectangular breakfast table, he shoved her into a chair and laid her still-lit cigarette in the glass ashtray in front of her. He set his own half-smoked cigarette next to hers.

She didn't dare take her eyes off him. With her heart pounding, she sat still, completely mute, as he lit up one cigarette after another, lining them all along the edges of the ashtray. When the pack was empty, he sat down to her right at the head of the table.

Preston caressed the side of her face, pushing her hair off her neck, and she forced herself not to recoil. Her breath caught when he leaned forward and kissed her chin, repeating the soft kisses along her jaw. When his lips reached her ear, his voice was soft, seductive. "You need to be taught a lesson." Pulling away, his tropical-blue gaze met hers. "Don't you agree?"

Her heart knocked hard in her chest, but she remained silent.

He ran tender fingers through her hair and settled his hand against her nape. "Darling," he murmured a fraction louder, "I asked you if you agree."

Goosebumps erupted over her skin. But still, she remained silent.

The fingers along her nape crept to the front of her neck. They tightened. Black spots danced in her vision, but she didn't care. She'd rather suffocate than agree with him. She'd rather die than give him permission.

His eyes narrowed, and rage contorted his features. "I'll take your silence as a yes, darling."

He released her. Before she could gasp for breath, his hand swung out, and his fist landed square on her chest. Her lungs compacted, and her shoulders rolled in. She clutched her torso. For a desperate moment, there was no air. The black spots grew larger. As she fought to breathe, he grabbed her arm and pinned it to the table.

"A lesson, you stupid little cunt," he spat.

Picking up one of the lit cigarettes, he brought it to her forearm. He slowly waved it back and forth, hovering it just a hair over her soft skin. She wanted to escape the heat of the ember, but terror froze her limbs.

"Lesson number one. When I ask you a question, you answer. Simple enough. Right, love?"

He crushed the burning cigarette into her arm.

A scream tore through her as it scorched her skin. The pain was sharp and icy hot. She struggled to free herself, but he held her outstretched arm in place.

Letting go, he punched her in the stomach. She wheezed and fell limply against the chair, cradling her arm. The small circular burn had already gone numb.

"Some things are meant to be . . ." serenaded her softly in the background.

"Lesson number two," Preston continued, his voice mellow. "Do not fight me. The more you struggle, the worse it's going to be. Look at me, my darling wife."

He selected another lit cigarette and took a pull as he waited for her to meet his gaze. She tried to blink back the tears, but it was no use. She met his eyes, disgusted by the twinkle of smug satisfaction she saw in them. He pushed the cigarette slowly into her arm.

Her nerves sizzled down to her fingertips. Agony screamed from every pore. And more tears fell from her eyes.

But she didn't move. She didn't dare. An anguished whimper snuck past her lips. Preston didn't seem to mind.

"Good girl," he said. "See, that wasn't so bad, now was it? Just a few more."

"Alex? Are you okay?"

Somehow, she stifled her frightened yelp. Looking up, she saw Roxie standing at the base of the steps, concern apparent on her face. Blinking rapidly, she placed the crushed cigarette onto the small table and wiped her clammy palms on her pants.

"Sorry." She cleared her throat. "I, um, didn't hear you."

Roxie nodded toward the discarded cigarette butt. "You smoke?"

The now-faint scars on her forearms tingled. She cleared her throat again and shook her head. "Not anymore. I just tried to, but it made me sick." She gestured toward the railing. "Literally."

Roxie grimaced. "Mind if I take them?"

"Not at all," she said, tossing the pack over.

"Thanks. Don't tell Quinn, though, he'd kill me." Climbing the steps, Roxie settled into the rocking chair opposite her. "We both used to smoke. I think he did it because it was the perfect accessory for that stupid tough-guy image he liked to project. Naturally, I started because I wanted to do everything that Quinn and Joe did." She dug out a cigarette. "Do you mind?"

"Go for it," she said, nudging the matches toward the other woman.

She desperately needed a distraction. Thankfully, Roxie could provide one.

Roxie lit up, lazily inhaled, smiled, and exhaled. "I guess you could say I idolized the guys. I'm three years younger than them and, as you know, we all grew up on this street. There weren't any other kids our age on the block, so it's safe to say that I've been running around after them all my life. I was that annoying kid who wouldn't leave them alone and pestered them until they just resigned themselves to hanging out with me. We're all singletons and just took to each other."

Roxie pulled her knees up to her chest, setting her rocker in motion. "A few years ago, Quinn and I made one of those pacts you make when you're completely hungover. Sort of like the I'm-never-gonna-drink-again thing, but not as drastic, of course." She took another drag of the cigarette. "Well, a *different* kind of drastic. We both quit smoking cold turkey. Over the years, I've snuck in more than my fair share, but Quinn's been so good. No cheating or anything. So please don't tell him. I'd never be able to live it down."

Alex smiled as her nerves calmed. She sent a mental thank you to the universe for sending Roxie over tonight. "I'm sure Quinn's not as perfect as you make him out to be."

"Oh, you'd be surprised. I mean, sure, the guy can be the biggest jackass you've ever met, but overall, he's pretty close to perfect."

She frowned. If Roxie thought the man was so wonderful . . . why weren't they together? Rather than ask, she said, "You're serious, aren't you?"

"One thousand percent." All of a sudden, Roxie's eyebrows nearly hit her hairline. "Oh, shit. I see what's going on. You think that since *I* think he's so perfect, then why aren't we involved? Right?"

Wow. Her poker face must really be crap. She tried for a casual shrug. And was pretty sure she failed. "It crossed my mind."

"Well, honestly, it's crossed my mind, too. I think I was eight or nine at the time." Roxie smiled and put out her cigarette, placing the butt on the table. "Seriously, though, Quinn and I don't go there. We never have. I think it would be too weird. Incestuous, really. He's always been a big brother to me, and I always try to have his back. But nothing remotely beyond that. Behind his bluster, he really is a wonderful guy. More than that, he's a protector, and I always worry someone will try to take advantage of him."

Roxie's face scrunched, as if she'd smelled something foul. "There was this one girl, a real piece of work. I never met her, it was when he was working down in San Francisco, but man, she did a real number on him and—"

Silence.

Alex waited, more curious than she'd ever admit out loud. "And . . ."

"Sorry. Not my story to tell." Roxie shook her head. "But I hate the bitch. Juvenile, I know. But I do. Quinn's my pseudo-big brother, and no one messes with him without messing with me, too."

Alex admired that kind of loyalty. She knew firsthand what a rare thing it was. "And Joe? Is he your other pseudo-big brother?"

"Good freaking god, no. Joe's definitely more in the pain-in-the-ass category." Roxie rolled her eyes. "So tell me, Alex —and yes, I am *blatantly* changing the subject now—what were you thinking about when I walked up? You looked really intense, and, if you don't mind me saying so, not in a good way. You okay?"

Roxie didn't need to know all her baggage—no one did, really—but Alex had been in counseling long enough to know that she needed to be honest. With herself. With others. No more lies. No more hiding.

Her therapist's advice, once again, echoed in her head.

It's time to let go of the guilt and allow yourself to move on.

But damn, this opening-yourself-up thing was scary. Necessary, but so. Damn. Scary.

She took a deep breath and slowly let it out. Baby steps. She opened her mouth to explain what had happened with Preston and the cigarettes, but instead, she blurted, "I'm pregnant."

Roxie's jaw dropped, but no words came out. She was pretty sure that was an unusual occurrence. It would have been amusing, except the woman was now deathly pale, and Alex had no idea why.

"Joe's?"

Annnd that was why. A world of emotion and turmoil hid behind that one name, but she was nowhere near close enough to Roxie to begin unpacking any of it.

"No. It's not Joe's," she said, borderline insulted by the assumption. "It's my husband's—well, soon-to-be *ex-*husband's." Irritation festered beneath her skin, and she began to regret bringing up the baby. "You know, Quinn thought the same thing. I don't get it. You two are supposed to be Joe's closest friends, yet you seem to think pretty poorly of him. He didn't lure me out of some perfect marriage to have a hot, steamy affair. Joe is a wonderful man. It confuses me, and honestly annoys me, that his oldest friends jump to the worst conclusions about him."

Roxie said nothing for a moment, then shrugged. "Joe and I have history. Why do you have him on a pedestal?"

She crossed her arms over her chest. "I don't."

Roxie scoffed. "You do. Shit, I just got mom-lectured by you because I thought he knocked you up." She grimaced. "Sorry. That's a horrible expression. The thing is, Joe has never played well with others. Ever. So, the fact that you think so highly of him is fascinating. The question is why?"

She was being overly defensive with Roxie. Snappy. She knew this. And that furthered her irritation. What if this was her new default attitude? God, she hoped not. She really needed to get a grip.

After counting to ten in her head, she said, "Do you want the long story or the short?"

"Either will do." The bright-green eyes staring back at her communicated patience and curiosity. Not judgment.

With a deep inhale and exhale, her hackles lowered.

"I suppose I can give you both because, well, my idea of long stories is probably your version of short ones. No offense, of course."

"None taken." The corner of Roxie's lips tipped up. "Go on."

She blew out a breath. "Joe Buchanan can do no wrong in my eyes because he saved my life. Literally. And not once, but twice." She drew her knees to her chest and wrapped her arms around her legs, mirroring Roxie.

She wished she were still angry. Because anger was better than embarrassment. Would she always feel like an idiot when she talked about—hell, *thought* about—her marriage? She hoped it would get easier, that the shame would one day cease.

Instead of meeting Roxie's gaze, she studied the grain of the porch's wooden planks. At last, she said, "I was in an abusive marriage. For years. It wasn't all bad. At least, not at first."

She liked to think she would have gotten out earlier if the relationship had started out as ugly as it had ended. But who knew? Preston had been so good at manipulating her, at making her believe that everything had been her fault, that she'd deserved it all.

"As the years went on, it got worse. Then, two and a half weeks ago, I came home from running errands, and he attacked me." She hadn't even made it fully out of her car before she'd been mauled. "It's embarrassing to admit, but he'd hurt me before. Pretty badly sometimes. But never like that. This last time was . . . I thought he was going to kill me."

Her heart galloped as memories flashed across her vision like a fucked-up horror film. She rubbed her arms, but her body continued to tremble.

"I guess I should backtrack. Prior to that day, Joe was an acquaintance at best. He and a female agent were posing as our super-rich, society-type neighbors, though I obviously had no clue they were undercover FBI agents until"—she indicated her bruised face—"all this. They'd lived next door for about a year and a half, and Joe and I had talked maybe a handful of times."

Handful was an exaggeration. She and Joe had spoken just twice in the eighteen-odd months they'd been neighbors. Their first meeting had taken place in Joe's front yard the week he and his pretend wife had moved in.

She remembered the exact timing not because of their captivating conversation, but rather the aftermath. When she'd returned home, it had been the first time Preston had given her a "real beating," as he'd called it. Sure, he'd struck her before, but only a punch or just a slap. Nothing major.

Shame turned her stomach. *Just* a slap. *Only* a punch. *Nothing major.* How could she have accepted that? Why had she stayed with him for so damn long? And why did she still downplay her abuse in her mind?

Stop. You have nothing to be ashamed of. Nothing. It's time to let go of the guilt and allow yourself to move on.

Her second encounter with Joe had occurred at a charity auction a few months ago. She'd tried to avoid him, but when he'd asked her to dance, she'd accepted. That had been the polite thing to do, and she was always polite. She'd naïvely thought Preston wouldn't mind. After all, she'd danced with many men that night, including Preston's boss, Mayor Downing.

When Preston had chatted with Joe after their dance, setting up a tee time for the following week, she'd thought everything was okay. But the moment they'd arrived home, she'd found out otherwise.

She cleared her throat and ignored the hammering of her heart. "When he attacked me that last time . . ." She fumbled for the words to describe the confusion, the chaos, the utter horror, but came up blank. "I don't know how to explain it. One minute I was in the garage, then the next, I was in the house, and Preston was beating the living shit out of me."

Alex remembered the devastating disappointment that the hours upon hours she'd spent planning her escape had all been for naught. Because her husband was going to kill her. In her own damn kitchen.

"Then, out of nowhere, Joe was there. Somehow, he pulled Preston off me and stopped him." Everything after had been a blur. Police, doctors, FBI agents, nurses. "I woke up in the hospital the next day. I was still alive. So, yeah. You can say Joe's on a pedestal."

Roxie chewed her lip, processing Alex's words. "You said Joe saved your life twice. If you don't mind me asking, when was the second time?"

"After. When he sent me here." She sighed. "I don't recall being admitted to the hospital, but when I woke up, Joe was there. I don't know what I would've done without him. I don't have any close friends, and my family . . ." Her chest tightened painfully, and her eyes dropped. "I haven't spoken to them in years. I didn't have anyone to call."

Her face heated, but she continued, swallowing past the lump lodged in her throat. Everything was so damn embarrassing, so damn shameful. "Joe helped me get out. No questions asked. He found me a car, dyed my hair back to black, and gave me money and a single piece of paper with driving directions to this house. He told me I'd be safe. And here we are."

Too scared to look at Roxie, too scared to see if there was judgment and disgust on the other woman's face, Alex lowered her chin to her knees and stared at her hands, which were still locked around her shins.

"Jeez, Alex," Roxie whispered with a loud sniff, rising from her chair.

She glanced up just as Roxie hugged her. When she tensed, Roxie hugged her harder.

For the first time since she'd started telling her story, a smile touched her lips, and the heavy weight on her heart eased.

Roxie let go and sat back down, wiping away her tears with another sniff. "Sorry, I'm a hugger. And obviously a crier, too. But damn." Roxie looked at her thoughtfully. Alex tried not to squirm. "With all you've been through . . . you're still standing. Don't forget that."

A tiny seed of hope took root in her chest. Her eyes welled, and she blinked back the rush of tears. Apparently, Roxie wasn't the only crier. "Thank you for that."

"I'm sorry I talked badly about Joe. I didn't mean to upset you. It's just that Joe and I have a . . . strained relationship. Part of it is we've known each other for forever, and the other part is . . . well, strained. He knows how to push my buttons, so he does. A lot. And we tend to yell at each other. Again, a lot."

Roxie shrugged. "In any case, I promise I'll try to be better about criticizing him. I don't want you to feel uncomfortable. But enough about me." She clapped her hands, and a brilliant smile lit her face. "You're pregnant!

Congratulations!" Her eyes widened, flickering with panic. "Or, um . . ."

Alex winced and chuckled. Two things she didn't know she could do at the same time. But there it was. "'Congratulations' is fine. You know, the pregnancy thing is still a bit of a shock." Terror, elation, excitement, and dread all swirled within her. "But thank you. I think I'm okay with it." Mostly? Maybe?

"That's completely understandable, Alex. Holy hell. You've been through a lot." Roxie gave her the once-over. "From your teeny-tiny body, you're pretty early on?"

She nodded. "Barely a month."

"If there's anything I can do to help, anything at all, just let me know, okay? I mean it. If you want company at your doctor appointments or need anyone to set them up or someone to go baby clothes shopping with? I'm your girl."

The hope in her chest began to bloom.

Friends.

A real life.

She wanted to pinch herself.

"Um, I have an appointment to see Dr. Buchanan in a couple days. If you really wouldn't mind, I mean, I don't want to impose—"

"Done," Roxie said without hesitation. Standing, she bent over and gave Alex another hug. "No, don't get up. Let me know what time you're seeing Doc, and I'll pick you up. Are you going to be okay tonight? If you don't want to be alone, I can crash in one of Joe's guest rooms or you can slumber party at my place."

She wanted to accept Roxie's offer, but she bit her tongue. She needed to practice independence. No more hiding behind other people. "Thanks, but I'll be fine."

"Thank you for trusting me with your story. I know it couldn't have been easy."

"Thank you for listening. Really."

"Any time. And Joe's right, you know. You'll be safe here."

Roxie waved goodbye and headed down the steps. Halfway across the lawn that separated the two houses, she turned back. "Oh, Alex? Come over tomorrow for dinner. I've got a new recipe to try out, and I need the opinion of someone who *isn't* my bottomless pit of a landlord. Night!"

CHAPTER THIRTEEN

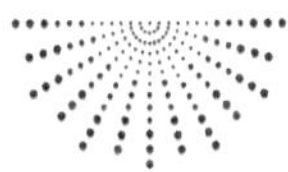

Two weeks into her time on Hudson Island, Alex had fallen into a routine. She started her days hovering over the toilet, heaving as the room spun around her. An hour later, like clockwork, her stomach would settle, and the nausea would pass. She'd then head over to Roxie's Comfort Food to get acquainted with how the operation ran. She came away from all her visits a little more excited about her upcoming job. She enjoyed the company at the café. The community.

It didn't hurt that Roxie's smoked ham and Gruyère quiche was one of the few things she'd been able to keep down lately. It also didn't hurt that Quinn joined her each morning. Sitting across from the man when he was freshly shaven and dressed in his perfectly pressed sheriff's uniform was no hardship at all.

After Comfort Food, she would then go sightseeing for a few hours. It wasn't a large island by any stretch of the imagination, but there was plenty to do. She wanted to explore Whidbey Island, Hudson's northeast neighbor, too, just . . . not quite yet. For now, she was content with her little routine, which ended each day with dinner at Quinn's house. Roxie had been joyfully testing out delicious new recipes on them.

As she prepared for bed, she studied her face in the bathroom mirror. The swelling was finally gone, and most of the discoloration had vanished, except for a couple of marks along her jaw. But that wouldn't be a problem at work. She was an expert at concealing bruises with makeup.

She frowned. How sad was that?

A wave of shame surged over her as she scanned the rest of her naked body. Most of the bruises on her torso and abdomen had faded, though, like on her jaw, there were a couple of lingering marks. As for her stitches, Dr. Buchanan had removed the last of them earlier that afternoon. The slashes across her arms and back were now dull-red scars. Scars that mocked her. That made her want to hate herself.

It would be so easy to give in. To let her self-disgust drown her.

But she didn't.

Her therapist's soothing words had become her new mantra: *You have nothing to be ashamed of. Nothing. It's time to let go of the guilt and allow yourself to move on.*

She took a deep breath in and shoved her negative thoughts away.

"No more, Alex," she murmured. "No more. Never again."

She refused to let Preston win.

The sharp ring of the telephone made her jump. With a hand over her racing heart, she slipped on her robe and walked into the bedroom.

"Hello?" She answered the old-fashioned rotary dial phone that sat on her nightstand.

Silence.

"Hello?"

She waited another second. "Hel—"

The caller hung up.

Huh. She placed the receiver back onto its cradle and absently played with the dial. The click, click, click as it spun made her smile. She couldn't remember the last time she'd encountered a landline, let alone a *rotary* phone.

Simple things. She wanted to appreciate the simple things. With this new life of hers, she vowed to do just that.

Heading back into the bathroom, she disrobed and stepped on the scale. Ninety-three. Damn. Same as it had been at Doc's earlier that afternoon.

"You need to put on weight, Alex," Doc had kindly scolded. "Being under a hundred pounds is underweight for someone of your height. Let's see." He'd swiped to a different screen on his tablet. A grin, so much like Joe's, had spread across his face. "Ah, yes. You measured in at five feet, one inch."

"And a half," she'd added. "That's important."

"Right. Five feet, one and *a half* inches. Either way, you'll admit that you're below your normal weight, correct?"

"Yes, sir." She'd bitten back a smile. Apparently, Joe had come by his interrogation skills naturally. "Usually, I'm at a hundred pounds. One-oh-five at the most."

"And before your ex-husband?"

Though she hadn't wanted to, she'd held his gaze. "One-fifteen. One-twenty."

"Good." He'd nodded and patted her hand. "Aim for that. I understand that you're queasy and are having a hard time keeping things down—all normal for your first trimester—but keep eating. I want you to try to get back to the one-fifteen, one-twenty range in the next couple of months. Once you're there, your goal should be about a twenty-pound additional weight gain for your pregnancy. For now, take your prenatal vitamins, keep hydrated, find what foods you can tolerate, and eat up. You start work tomorrow with Roxie?"

She'd nodded, a nervous smile touching her lips.

"Good. Eat, eat, eat, my dear. Tell Roxie that it's the doctor's orders."

Looking at the bathroom scale, she shook her head. *Gain weight.* She'd never thought anyone would tell her to do that. With Preston, it had always been the opposite.

Throughout their marriage, there had been months when he'd weighed her daily, noting every fraction of a pound she had gained or lost. Yet another giant red flag she'd ignored.

If she had ever gone over 105, even by the *slightest* margin, he had berated her.

The one time her weight had hit 110, she'd discovered his affinity for kidney punches. They were devastating, and the bruises remained hidden. When he'd finished teaching her a "lesson" about willpower and moderation, he had put her on a strict diet of celery, laxatives, and water for a week.

She'd never gone over 105 pounds after that.

Dressing in her cozy pajamas, she tried to shake off her mood. She knew she deserved to be happy, that it was okay to allow herself to move on. But there were moments, like this one, when it was just so damn hard. Harder than she'd ever thought it would be.

Her therapist had told her it would take time to heal emotionally, that it would often be one step forward and nine steps back. That the doubts and self-loathing would be some of the biggest hurdles. Now, Alex was finding out how true that wisdom was.

One moment, she would be embracing her fresh start, enjoying her new friends and town, and the next—bam!— something would trigger her, reminding her of Preston. Then, just like that, a devastating, drop-you-to-your-knees shame would engulf her, making her want to crawl into a dark cave and disappear.

She swiped away a few renegade tears as she climbed into bed.

Please let this get easier. Please.

One day at a time. That was all she could do.

But it *had* to get easier. It had to . . .

CHAPTER FOURTEEN

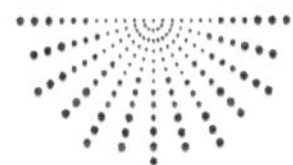

Wearing her Comfort Food apron, Alex stood next to Roxie, notepad in hand, pen racing over a fresh page.

"It's a standard point-of-sale system: touchscreen, cash drawer, receipt printer. We'll go through how to work it in a little bit, but it's fairly straightforward."

Holy crap. Her hand was cramping, but she didn't have time to shake it out. She was pretty sure Roxie hadn't taken a breath since she'd arrived.

"One of the things you'll do is make sure this baby"— Roxie patted the top of the refrigerated display case that stood next to the register—"is fully stocked."

"But you don't want it full at all times, do you?" she asked. Roxie looked at her in confusion, so she hurried on. "Say someone orders a slice of pie and there's only two slices left. You don't want me to put out a new pie, right? I mean, if we don't, then the other customers will think, 'Ooh, there's only a couple slices left. I'd better get one before it's all gone.' Right?"

She gave Roxie a smile, but it was weak. They both knew it.

Good lord, what had she been thinking when she'd taken this job?

Roxie tilted her head to the side. With a brisk nod, she said, "That can work. But don't overthink this, Alex. Seriously. Read the customers and do what you feel is right. Believe me, if I don't like something you're doing, I'll be the first person to let you know." She winced. "But for the love of god, if I do, *please* don't take it personally. It's not. It's just business."

Nodding again, Roxie turned and gestured past the refrigerated display case. "Espresso machine. Some people love it; some people fear it. Do you know how to make coffee?"

Holy crap. Work Roxie was a whole lot more intense than Friend Roxie. And Friend Roxie was pretty damn intense.

"Yes," she said. "I can do basic lattes, mochas, and Americanos." Using her old machine at home. Not this gleaming silver beast that took up the entire side counter. "I'll, um, need a refresher, though."

"Not a problem. Nina can run you through it," Roxie said, referring to the woman currently baking up a storm in the kitchen.

Nina Castillo was roughly Alex's age, of Filipino heritage, and Roxie's only full-time employee. Comfort Food had two part-time employees, June and Ella, a mother and daughter who were dead ringers for Goldie Hawn and Kate Hudson, respectively. Like Alex, June worked Wednesdays through Sundays. She was on the early shift—five to nine in the morning—while Alex worked from nine to two, eleven on Sundays. Ella, who was in her first year of online college classes, worked the same nine-to-close shift, but only Fridays through Sundays.

"Now," Roxie continued, "when it's quiet up here, I'll need you in the back . . ."

The next couple of hours were a blur as Roxie led her through a thorough description of what her new job entailed. Which was way more than she'd anticipated. Not that she minded. She wanted to pull her weight. Needed to be useful. Not only for Roxie, but for herself as well.

Gnawing on her bottom lip, she listened to Roxie explain the minute-by-minute schedule of what went into which ovens when. She had thought she was simply going to be dishing out food and coffee, wiping down counters, smiling, and making change, but apparently, she was going to be cooking, too.

"Um, Roxie," she interrupted. "I'm really not much of a cook, and I'm an appalling baker. No exaggerations." The other woman's brow arched, and she couldn't tell if it was in question or annoyance. "Are you really sure you want me doing this? I mean, I'd hate to mess things up." Or burn the place down.

A memory played in Alex's mind.

She'd ruined dinner. Again. Not only had she over-cooked the steak—Preston preferred his blue-in-the-middle rare, and she'd broiled it to medium—but she'd also burned the pie, which she'd attempted to make from scratch, crust and all. Preston had been furious. The "lesson" that night had been about following simple directions. He'd decided to beat her with what he had deemed an "appropriate apparatus."

The rolling pin.

The welts on the backs of her thighs had been so painful she hadn't been able to sit for nearly a week.

"Oh, don't worry about it," Roxie said, bringing her back to the present. "I've burned my fair share of food. Everyone does it. It's a learning process. Besides, I have a small staff.

With their staggered schedules, I need everyone cross-trained."

Judging by Roxie's tone, she knew it wasn't open for discussion.

When Roxie dismissed her to lunch, her head was spinning, and her little notepad was crammed full of customer favorites, cooking times, and oven temperatures. Sitting at the corner table by the window, she inhaled the aroma of freshly baked chocolate chip cookies. The morning had been so overwhelming, but underneath her nerves, she tingled with excitement.

A job. Friends. Financial independence.

Freedom.

She was getting her life back. Even though she knew she still had a long way to go, she couldn't stop the smile that spread across her face.

Two women, both in their late sixties or early seventies, approached her table. She recognized them as Mrs. Yoshida and Mrs. Abbot, the Comfort Food regulars she had met last week.

"You'll get the hang of it, honey," said Mrs. Abbot.

"Make sure Roxie doesn't work you too hard," chimed in Mrs. Yoshida. "She's a steamroller, that one. Make sure she doesn't go and run you off like she did the last girl." She turned to Mrs. Abbot. "That one made it what? Three days?"

"Hmm. I think it was only two. Didn't stand a chance, poor thing." Mrs. Abbot smiled at her. "But don't mind a word we're saying, honey. I'm sure you'll do just fine. You have a smart and patient look about you."

"Thanks." She returned their smiles. "That's very kind of you. I do hope I get into the swing of things before Roxie boots me out of here."

"Oh pa-tosh! That's nonsense," Mrs. Abbot said. "You seem like a nice—"

"Well, if it isn't the two most beautiful women in the world."

She swung her gaze toward the familiar baritone, and her breath caught in her chest. Quinn. In uniform. With a wide smile and mischief twinkling in his gray eyes. Wow.

"Mrs. Abbot, Mrs. Yoshida, it's always a pleasure." He raised each of their hands to his lips as they giggled. He shot a wink at Alex. "You're not too shabby, either."

Heat zinged through her body, and she felt a flush creep over her face. She was pretty sure her mouth had fallen open. She prayed she wasn't drooling.

Friendly, neighborly Quinn? She was familiar with that.

Playful and flirty Quinn?

Holy. Crap.

Next level.

Words failed her, and she could only watch as Quinn led Mrs. Abbot and Mrs. Yoshida to a nearby table, where they proceeded to fall over each other to get his attention. And Quinn, sending the occasional smile her way, kept them entertained.

She straightened in her chair and tried to refocus on her notes. Every few seconds, she was distracted by the women bursting into laughter with a "Oh, Quinn, you devil!" or a "Aren't you just the cutest, Quinn?"

The distraction was real.

So the man was charming. So what? Lots of people were charming. Just like lots of people looked that tempting in a sheriff's uniform.

Wait, what? Tempting? Good grief, woman!

He didn't tempt her. Definitely not. She was only watching him out of the corner of her eye to make sure the customers were comfortable.

Yeaaah. She didn't buy it either.

Quinn rose, excusing himself from Mrs. Abbot and Mrs. Yoshida, and walked to her table.

All Alex's thoughts came to a halt. She held her breath.

Holding your breath? Not a good sign.

He sank into the chair next to her. "How's your first day going?"

"Busy," she said, willing her racing pulse to slow. "I mean, I knew there would be stuff to learn, but . . ." She held up her notepad, fanning out the pages for him to see.

"It's surprising, isn't it?" Leaning forward, he tucked a stray lock of hair behind her ear.

His touch sent an electric current of awareness through her veins. Her heart tripped.

When they'd first met, he'd waited for permission before touching her. He'd always been respectful, always given her the opportunity to pull away. As they'd gotten to know each other better over the last couple of weeks, she'd become more comfortable with him, allowing more of his casual touches.

Quinn smiled at her, a look of longing seemed to flicker across his face.

Wait.

Longing?

No way. She was losing her damn mind.

She swallowed against her suddenly dry throat. "What's surprising?"

He traced the side of her jaw with the back of his finger, his gaze tracking the movement, before lowering his hand and relaxing against his chair. "Roxie. She seems pretty scattered in her regular world. Flighty, some would say. But here . . . I don't know . . . she's more like a . . ."

"Drill sergeant?" She adored Roxie, she really did, but Work Roxie was truly someone to be reckoned with.

He laughed, and the deep rumble warmed her. "Yeah, that sounds about right."

His amusement made her smile.

"You know what, Alex?"

Her heart skipped. Having him so focused on her did something to her insides. It was impossible to form a coherent thought.

"What?" she managed to say.

"You have the sweetest smile I've ever seen."

Heat tore through her cheeks. "Um, thanks," she stammered. Clearly, coherent thoughts were still not her friend.

"I promise that's not a line. It's just a very pleasant fact of life." He slowly stood from his seat. "I have a great idea. In honor of your first day at work, I think you should have dinner with me tonight. No Roxie this time, just you and me. Besides, after today, I'm sure the last person you're going to want to spend extra time with is Sergeant Jameson. What do you say?"

Coherent thoughts moved from *not her friend* to *mortal enemy*. She feared her mouth was gaping open. Again.

"Great," he said. "It's a date, then."

Wait. What?

That flirty grin graced Quinn's lips, and she melted.

She now understood why Mrs. Abbot and Mrs. Yoshida had dissolved into a fit of giggles upon having it directed at them.

"Your place, sweetheart. Six thirty. I'll cook and bring over everything I need." He bent down and brushed his lips across her forehead. "See you then."

He was out the door before she'd recovered. Her jaw remained hanging open.

Holy shit. What had just happened?

Peeking at Mrs. Abbot and Mrs. Yoshida's table, she saw them watching her with curious, twinkling eyes.

"Looks like our little Roxie isn't the only steamroller in town," Mrs. Yoshida said with a chuckle. "Aside from when he was a tiny thing, I don't think I've ever seen that boy move that fast before." She nodded to Mrs. Abbot. "You?"

"No." Mrs. Abbot winked at Alex. "No, I can't say that I have."

CHAPTER FIFTEEN

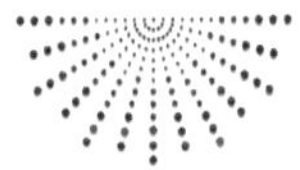

Alex ran through the front door and tossed her keys and purse onto the small entryway table. Six fifteen. How had it gotten so late? She dashed up the stairs to her bedroom, a trail of scattered clothing marking her path.

Flinging open the closet door, she frowned.

"Well, what's it gonna be?" she asked herself, standing in her underwear. "The gray Unabomber sweatshirt or the equally blah T-shirt?"

The other clothing in her closet was more or less the same, only in different colors.

We're not in Kansas anymore.

Her old wardrobe had been a whole lot nicer than the one in front of her now. While the practical part of her was fine with it, the vain part shuddered.

She pulled on a fresh pair of jeans and turned toward the vanity, searching for a brush.

"Don't be so nervous," she muttered. "Quinn's just being a good neighbor. It's not like a *date* date or anything—"

Hadn't there been that little flicker of interest in his eyes earlier? She could have sworn she'd seen something . . .

She shook her head. Nope. "Don't be an idiot, Alex. This is *not* a date. He's not interested in you like that."

Technically, she was still married. And overall, she was a flaming-hot dumpster fire. A *pregnant* flaming-hot dumpster fire.

Yeah. She scoffed. What sane man would want to get involved with her?

Catching her reflection in the vanity mirror, she scowled. "Get over it, Alex. That man is *not* for you."

She abandoned her search for a brush and returned to the closet. After pulling on a black T-shirt and the gray, zippered sweatshirt, a glance at the clock showed she had five minutes.

Giving herself a final once-over, she winced. To say she looked like a frumpy mess would be generous. Her makeup-free face was flushed from the mad dash, and her long black hair had fallen out of its makeshift bun and settled around her in a wavy mess. To top it all off, her ill-fitting clothes dwarfed her petite frame.

She pursed her lips. It would have to do.

Besides, there was no need to dress up tonight. Because it *wasn't* a date. It was just dinner between two friends. That's it.

Turning away from the mirror, she twisted her hair into a knot, clipped it up, and then rushed through the house, picking up her scattered clothes.

Freaking relax already, Alex!

If only the stupid butterflies in her stomach would get the memo . . .

At six thirty sharp, Quinn strode across Alex's front porch.

Armed with a bag of groceries and two bottles of wine, he pressed the doorbell.

Shoulders tense, he shifted on his feet.

Christ, O'Conner, calm the fuck down.

He was just doing his job. That's it. Just being a damn good neighbor.

Alex peeked out the side window, then the door swung open.

"Hi. Come on in." A shy smile graced her face. She had a pile of clothes balled up under her arm. "Sorry, I was just picking up. Let me put these away." She gestured toward the kitchen as she turned to the staircase. "I assume you know where everything is?"

"Yep. All good," he said, watching her disappear up the steps, her sweet, hesitant smile permanently etching itself in his brain.

Who the fuck was he kidding?

There was nothing neighborly about what he felt for her. Unless wanting to toss her onto the nearest flat surface and devour every damn inch of her was neighborly. If that were the case, then yes, he thought of her in a neighborly way.

His dick twitched. And that made him want to clobber himself in the head. Both heads.

He was acting like a goddamn randy teenager, and it was completely inappropriate. Now was not the time or the place. Thankfully, he was pretty sure she had no idea what was going on in his head. His thoughts would probably scare the hell out of her. And even if they didn't, she deserved so much better than him. Especially after everything she'd been through.

An image of her battered face flashed in his mind, and a chill raced down his spine. *Fuck.*

With a shake of his head, he unloaded the groceries onto

the island and made himself at home in Joe's kitchen. As he started their simple dinner, conflicting emotions made a muddled mess of his mind.

When Alex had arrived on Hudson Island, given the circumstances, he'd quickly filed her away as a damsel in distress. And if there was anything he avoided at all fucking costs, it was DIDs. He'd been burned by one before, and he wouldn't let it happen again.

Isabel.

He shuddered.

A few years back, when he'd still been with the FBI, he'd met Isabel at a friend-of-a-friend's party. The moment he'd seen her, he'd been stunned by her beauty. Then, when some guy had started being aggressive toward her, he'd stepped in. From that moment on, she'd treated him like her white knight. She'd fawned over him and, though he hated to admit it, stroked his ego. She'd made him feel fucking invincible.

That feeling of invincibility had transformed him into a complete idiot as far as she'd been concerned. Hence why he'd turned a blind eye to her faults, of which there had been many.

Isabel had lied, manipulated, and schemed. Always the victim, nothing had ever been her fault. Ever.

But Quinn had eaten all that shit up because he'd believed he, and he alone, could do what no one else had been able to do: save her from her shitty past.

Being with Isabel had been emotionally exhausting. She'd been unstable. Narcissistic. Sociopathic. He'd recognized all that. And had ignored it. What he'd missed? She'd also been an addict.

If it had been anyone other than Joe who'd found Isabel's gigantic stash of cocaine in Quinn's bedside table, his career would've been over. He would have been booted from the

FBI, and he sure as shit wouldn't have become the sheriff of his hometown.

It had taken that threat to his career to lift the fog over his vision. He'd cut her loose without a second thought.

But it still pissed him off that it had taken him so long to see what had been clear to everyone else. So many people had told him that she was trouble, that she was playing him like a fucking fiddle, but he had been so content in the damn white knight role that he'd ignored them all.

For his own sanity, he needed to treat Alex like she was just as dangerous as Isabel. He *had* to.

But he couldn't.

The more time he spent with her, the deeper she got under his skin. His gut said she was *nothing* like Isabel, but his head reminded him that he'd been tricked before. It was a fucked-up internal tug-of-war. But his gut was winning out.

These last two weeks, he'd stopped by Comfort Food every morning to sit and have coffee with her. Every evening, they'd had dinner together with Roxie. Day after day, as her bruises had slowly faded, she'd gradually begun to open up.

He wouldn't fool himself. He knew Alex's increasing comfort was all thanks to Roxie. His friend had the uncanny ability to make people feel at ease. He was just happy to be along for the ride. The glimpses he'd caught of Alex's strength, determination, and feistiness, combined with her lingering vulnerability, tugged at his heart. Hell, at every part of his being.

Then there was the physical attraction he had for her. It was borderline ridiculous. He could stare at her for hours— and he'd done just that during their nightly dinners. Her whiskey-brown eyes held tiny flecks of gold, and he could have sworn they sparkled when she laughed. Sappy as fuck, for sure. But he was okay with a little sappiness when it came to her.

He loved how petite she was—her head barely came up to the middle of his chest. He'd had more than one fantasy about pulling her small frame to him and removing the claw-looking contraption from her hair. He wanted to tangle his fingers in those soft black waves. And her lips . . .

With a groan and a quick glance around to make sure he was still alone, he adjusted himself. *Shit.* He had to stop thinking about her like that.

Dinner, dammit. He needed to focus on dinner.

Tonight was about getting to know each other. *Without* Roxie. He was reluctant to get involved with anyone again—

No. He wasn't going to lie to himself. There was no point.

He *wanted* to get involved with Alex. And he *really* wanted to be Alex's white knight, to slay every one of her fucking dragons, even knowing how that had turned out for him last time.

That should worry him. White knight syndrome led to disaster.

But strangely enough, when his relationship with Isabel had imploded, his heart had been fine. Only his pride had been wounded.

With Alex, something told him it would be much more complicated. But that same something told him it would be worth it.

Returning to the kitchen, Alex paused in the archway. A smile spread across her face as the savory aroma of sautéing garlic and onions engulfed her senses. Her mouth watered.

"Jeez, I leave you alone for a few minutes and you have

the place smelling divine." She joined Quinn at the stove. "What are you cooking?"

"It's a surprise." He grinned. "You like garlic?"

"Who doesn't?" She reached for the covered pan to sneak a peek and chuckled when he playfully swatted her hand away.

"Go make yourself useful," he said, gesturing toward the kitchen island. "There are a couple bottles of wine in the bag. Can you bring them over?"

At the island, she paused. And stared.

She watched as he added more spices to the mystery concoction, and a sigh escaped her lips. The man was ridiculously attractive. And cooking. For her. How could that not make her sigh?

Dressed in a button-down flannel and worn jeans, his simple outfit accentuated his broad shoulders and powerful chest. The sleeves were rolled to his elbows, and the muscles of his forearms popped and flexed as he cooked. She wasn't quite sure how forearms could be sexy, but they were. Ridiculously so.

She had no doubt that beneath the flannel were hard, chiseled abs that tapered to his strong hips and long, muscular legs.

"Yes?"

She blinked. Her gaze shot up Quinn's body to his face. A sly smirk played on his lips.

Heat flooded her cheeks. He knew where her mind had been. She busied herself with unloading the wine.

"Um." She cleared her throat, her gaze locked on the grocery tote in front of her. "Which wine did you want again?"

She jumped when gentle hands settled on her shoulders. Despite the layers of clothes, her skin tingled.

He slowly turned her, putting her back against the kitchen island. She held her breath.

His hands cruised down her shoulders, then her arms, until they settled on the counter on either side of her, loosely caging her in. He hovered over her, but she didn't feel threatened, not in the least bit. Instead, an electric current zinged through her body, and for the life of her, she couldn't look away.

"Sweetheart, if you want to sneak a peek, I don't mind at all. But if you want a better look . . ." He paused to stroke his finger over the racing pulse at her neck. "All you have to do is say so."

Her blood burned. And it had nothing to do with fear.

The corners of his lips tipped up in a sexy smile, and his smoky-gray eyes heated.

No, she hadn't been wrong before. There was no mistaking the cloud of desire in his gaze now.

She wanted him closer, wanted something more. Exactly what, she didn't know. But she needed it. Him.

He leaned down, and her stomach fluttered with anticipation.

The sizzling hiss of water boiling over jerked them apart.

"Damn," he murmured, stepping away to take care of the overflowing pot.

Her breath left her in an unsteady whoosh.

Wow.

She willed her erratic heartbeat to return to normal. To no avail. Like a video on repeat, the moment replayed in her mind: the smoldering fire in his gaze, the scents—leather and forest—that were uniquely him, the warmth of his nearness . . .

Quinn cleared his throat.

She startled. Great, he'd been talking to her while her scattered thoughts had swirled around in the gutter. Nice.

"I'm sorry. What?"

He chuckled as he uncorked a bottle of red and poured some into another pan, that sexy, satisfied smirk dancing on his face. "I said, don't worry about the wine. The alcohol will cook off, so you don't have to worry about it."

"Worry about what?" Her mind was mush.

His chuckle turned into a full-on laugh. "About the alcohol hurting the baby."

"Oh, right. Of course." Heat crept up her neck, and she fought a cringe. She'd forgotten she was pregnant. What the hell did that say about her?

Focus, Alex!

On anything *other than Quinn!*

Scanning the kitchen in desperation, she spotted the second bottle of wine. "Do you want me to open the other bottle for you?"

She started searching for the wine opener but stopped short when she saw it on the counter. Next to Quinn. She glanced up at him, and the heat crawling over her face intensified. The grin splitting his lips was knowing.

"No, that's okay," he said. "That one's a replacement for one I swiped a while back." After lowering the stove dials, he gestured to the refrigerator. "There's grape juice in the fridge. I figured we could pretend it was wine . . . or something."

Uncertainty crossed his expression, and he turned back to the stove. Her insides, as if they'd needed extra prodding, melted a little more. Was this guy for real? Gorgeous and thoughtful?

She moved to stand next to him and laid her hand on his forearm. "That's really sweet of you, Quinn. Thank you."

He mumbled something she couldn't decipher.

Her eyes widened. Was he *blushing*?

"Really, it's no big deal. I happen to be a big fan of grape juice." After giving a spoonful of sauce a quick blow, he lifted it to her lips, cutting off any reply. "Does it taste all right?"

She closed her lips around the spoon and her tastebuds exploded with flavor. Ripe tomatoes, garlic, and oregano with a hint of sweetness and a kick of spice. "Oh my god, Quinn," she said, licking her lips. "That's delicious."

He blinked, his eyes locked on her mouth. "Sorry, what?"

She smothered a grin. "I said it's absolutely fantastic."

Good to know she wasn't the only one affected by whatever this was between them.

CHAPTER SIXTEEN

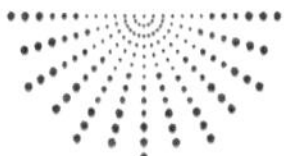

Dinner ended up being chicken rigatoni in a creamy red wine tomato sauce with a side of thick, crusty Italian bread slathered in a homemade roasted garlic and parmesan butter. If Alex hadn't witnessed Quinn making it all, she would've sworn he'd picked it up from a restaurant. It was *that* delicious.

There was something about a man who was at home in a kitchen. There was especially something about *this* man.

As they finished their meals, he regaled her with light-hearted tales of small-town crime. When he spoke of one of his deputies foiling the local high school's senior prank, she found herself laughing, completely at ease. For the hundredth time that night, she wondered how that was possible.

The whole situation should've made her nervous. A one-on-one dinner with a man? Whom she'd only known for a couple of weeks? Who not only dwarfed her physically, but was also the town's sheriff?

The fact that none of it triggered her anxiety, the fact that it all felt so normal and so right, was astonishing.

Even more astonishing? As she sat across the kitchen table from Quinn, listening to him talk, a calm unlike any she'd ever known enveloped her.

"Alex, you okay?"

She pushed her musings away. "Sorry about that. I really was paying attention to you. Promise. And we've established my poker face is nonexistent, so you know I'm not lying."

"That's very true." Setting their now-empty plates to the side, he relaxed in his chair. "What's on your mind?"

"Oh, it's silly, really." She hesitated, unsure how to continue. "I just . . . I don't know . . . I feel comfortable around you, and I guess it makes me nervous because I'm *not* nervous." She grimaced. "Does that even make sense?"

He leaned forward, elbows on the table. "What you're saying is you feel like you *should* be nervous around me, but you're not. And because you're not, *that's* making you nervous. Right?"

Her lips pressed into a tight, embarrassed line. "That about sums it up." She shrugged. "Stupid, huh?"

"Not at all." Reaching across the table, he held out his hands, palms up.

She knew what he was waiting for. He was leaving it up to her.

She took a deep breath, exhaled, and placed her hands in his.

He gave them a delicate squeeze, tracing little circles on the insides of her wrists. If he was trying to distract her with his touch, well . . . it was working.

"If you feel comfortable around me, then I, for one, am glad." He shot her a lopsided smile.

She couldn't help but return it.

One of his hands left hers, rising to toy with a strand of her hair that had fallen free. "This piece does not like that claw thing you've got going on. And frankly"—he paused and unclipped her hair—"neither do I."

Her hair tumbled down around her shoulders and arms, and her jaw dropped. "Now, why did—"

She fell silent as he ran his fingers through her waves.

She swallowed; her throat was suddenly dry.

"You have such pretty hair," he murmured. His eyes smoldered.

He caressed the side of her face with the backs of his fingers, sending her pulse into overdrive.

"So beautiful." His voice was barely above a whisper. Then he met her gaze. "Tell me about yourself, Alex. I want to know you. All there is to know."

He traced her bottom lip with his thumb, and she leaned closer. "Quinn, I—"

The sharp ring of the telephone broke them apart.

She leaned back in her chair. Her pulse was still pounding, her stomach still fluttering. She missed his soft touch.

Whoa. Easy there, Alex.

"Sorry, let me . . ." She pointed to the living room and stood, hustling toward it.

Confusion, uncertainty, and excitement clouded her thoughts. Part of her wanted to explore this simmering thing between them, but the other part still doubted her instincts.

Desperate for a distraction, she picked up the ringing telephone. "Hello?"

Silence.

"Hello?"

With a sigh, she hung up. Interrupted for nothing. Or maybe not. Maybe it had been a sign. A big ole slow-it-waaay-down sign from the universe. She pursed her lips.

Quinn strode into the room and crouched in front of the fireplace. "Want a fire?"

"Uh, sure," Alex mumbled, distracted by how his jeans

tightened around his firm backside and thick thighs when he crouched. She could watch him arrange logs in a fireplace all freaking night.

After a few moments of silence passed, she realized he'd said something else, and she'd missed it. *Holy crap.* She really needed to stop gawking at the man. "I'm sorry, what?"

He glanced over his shoulder, an eyebrow raised in question. "Who was on the phone?"

"No one. Wrong number, I guess." Leaning against the sofa's arm, she shrugged. She was aiming for casual, but by the way the corners of his lips twitched, she was pretty sure she was failing.

The fire roared to life, and Quinn rose. He took a seat on the sofa, playfully patting the spot next to him. How he could be so gruff and adorable at the same time was beyond her.

Unable to hold back a smile, she settled cross-legged onto the cushion opposite him, her back to the armrest. "I assume this is the getting-to-know-you portion of the evening?"

He laughed, and the sound warmed her chest. Not that she was getting gushy over him or anything.

"First question goes to me, then. When you were little"— his voice dropped to match the inflection of a game show host—"what did you want to be when you grew up?"

She didn't think it was possible, but her insides melted even more. Not once in their entire marriage had Preston asked that question. Now that she thought about it, he'd never expressed any interest in her life prior to him.

Yet another giant, waving red flag she'd ignored.

But that was the past, dammit.

She was done with Preston. She would overcome how he still made her feel. She would. She had to.

Taking in the man across from her, she wondered if it was delusional to entertain the teeny-tiny possibility of moving forward with him. Was it too soon?

Probably.

But if she'd learned anything over the last month, it was that life was short. So, she planned to enjoy every moment.

A weight lifted from her shoulders.

Pretending she was a contestant on his game show, she leaned forward and spoke into an imaginary microphone. "A ballerina."

His face lit up with a grin, and she almost swooned.

"Why a ballerina?" he asked, switching back to his normal baritone.

She shrugged. "I loved the sparkle and costumes and how they were just so graceful."

The fire, plus the flush of shyness from talking about her long-forgotten dream, had her overheating. She pulled off the gray sweatshirt and tossed it to the floor, then shifted to hug her knees.

"I always loved the beauty of it all. How ballerinas could take beautiful music and make it even more beautiful." A smile grew on her lips. "I must admit, though, the ballerina I wanted to be was not your average, ordinary ballerina. Oh no. She was also—secretly, of course—a superhero."

"Really?" He drawled out the word, amusement on his face. "Please, do go on."

"Well, growing up, my family had season tickets to the ballet. My sister, Kayla, and I were fans. We took classes, dressed up. The whole bit. We were complete girly girls."

Kayla.

Her heart ached. Despite Kayla being three years older, they had always been best friends. Until Preston.

God, she missed her sister.

She pushed down the sadness and tried to focus on the happier times. "For my seventh birthday, my parents arranged for me to go backstage after one of the performances. It was *Sleeping Beauty*, which was my favorite, of course."

"Of course."

She chuckled. "After the show, we went backstage and met all the ballerinas. I distinctly remember how tired they were. They were all still gorgeous, mind you, but exhausted. They'd unwrapped their feet, and their poor toes were just mangled. Blistered and bloodied. Being so young, I got scared and immediately burst into tears."

"You were sweet even as a kid," he said.

"I guess." She gave him an embarrassed smile. "Anyway, the lady giving us the tour was the director. She sat me down and told me not to worry. She said, 'Ballerinas are tough. They aren't scared by a little blood and pain. Ballerinas are *superhero* tough.' Being the wise age of seven, I took what she said literally and believed that all professional ballerinas fought crime when they weren't onstage."

She stretched out on the sofa, enjoying the memories. "From then on, I always wanted to be a ballerina-super-hero. You know, fighting crime and preserving justice, but doing so in pretty, sparkly tutus with nice background music."

Quinn pulled her ankles onto his lap and began massaging one of her feet. "You know, that explains a lot about you."

She scrunched her face. "I'm not sure if that's a good thing or a bad thing."

As he pressed his thumbs into her arch with the perfect amount of pressure, she relaxed into the couch.

Heaven. His hands were heaven.

"What about you? Did you always want to be in law enforcement?"

"Not at all." He shook his head. "I was more of a trouble-maker than anything. There was definitely no crime fighting

—in sparkly outfits or otherwise—on my agenda. I guess you could say I was more of a practical kid."

"Well?" She waved her hand in a circular get-on-with-it motion. "What did you want to be?"

His mouth opened, then shut. The corners of his eyes crinkled. "You have to promise you won't laugh."

She scoffed. "Are you kidding me? There's no way I'm promising you that, mister. Well?"

"Tough crowd." He chuckled. "Okay, when I was little, I wanted to be an ice cream truck driver."

She burst into laughter. Of all the things he could have said, that was the very last thing she would have guessed. "Seriously?"

He grinned back at her. "Come on, Alex, it's not *that* funny. But think about it. What could be a cooler job than that? Really. All the ice cream you could eat, sitting right there at your disposal? Check. Driving an awesome truck that played awesome music? Double check. Being the most popular person in town? The guy who causes kids to literally lose their freakin' minds when you drive down their street? Triple check."

She tried to control her laughter. She really did. But he was too much. Too cute. Too everything.

He sighed. "Hey, it sounded like a win-win situation to me at the time."

"Ah, you crack me up." She wiped a tear from her eye. "You're right, though. When you put it that way, being an ice cream truck driver would be the best job ever. It definitely makes a lot of sense to a kid. But instead, you joined the FBI with your best friend, and then became sheriff of the town you grew up in."

He stared at her for a second. The air around them grew heavier. "Yeah. It's funny where you end up, isn't it?"

"I'll say," she murmured.

Her heart hurt for that little girl who'd wanted to be a ballerina-superhero. She had been so happy and secure. She'd had a wonderful childhood. Parents who'd not only loved and supported her, but also each other. There had been no violence in her home. At all. And she could count on one hand how many times her parents had raised their voices at each other.

She was an example of how domestic abuse could happen to *anyone*—not just those who had grown up in the abuse cycle.

Her eyes met Quinn's, and resolve filled her.

She wanted him to understand, wanted him to know she truly was trying to move forward with her life. Especially since that life could possibly include him.

Yeah, she was probably jumping the gun big-time, but she no longer cared. And while her situation was beyond complicated, she wanted to trust him. If anything, they were friends. Beyond that . . . who knew?

As he sat there quietly, waiting for her to choose where the conversation went next, she called on the tenuous thread of hope inside her. She met his gaze, deep gray eyes that held no judgment, and took that step.

"It's strange, Quinn," she said at last. "It really is."

"How so, sweetheart?"

"It's like . . ." She hesitated, searching for words. "Like the last five years of my life happened to someone else. I grew up with loving, regular, middle-class parents. I was a regular, middle-class kid who idolized her big sister and dreamed of becoming a ballerina-superhero. I played soccer on the weekends. Took ballet and swimming lessons. Sold wrapping paper, candy bars, and Girl Scout cookies to all my neighbors every year. I was taught to respect myself and to respect others."

She shook her head, mystified. "When I look back at my

life with Preston . . . at how I was and how I allowed myself to be treated—and how I'm *still* afraid of him—I just can't explain it."

"How did you two meet?" Quinn's voice was low and soothing. He continued massaging her feet.

"I was twenty-five and on my way to a job interview with his boss, the mayor," she said. "I literally ran into him and spilled my coffee all over him. He was really nice about it, and I'm embarrassed to say that he completely dazzled me. He was a handsome guy. I suppose, technically, he still is. Physically, anyway. He has these beautiful blue eyes that just make you want to trust him."

Rolling a strand of hair through her fingers, she continued, "At the time, he was everything I was striving to be. I wanted to be involved in politics. Not necessarily as a politician, mind you, but I wanted to be surrounded by them. The whole circus of government fascinated me. Preston was the city's deputy mayor and an up-and-coming political figure, so when he took an interest in *me*—little old me—it seemed too good to be true."

She looked down at her hands in her lap. She knew hindsight made everything clear, but she still felt like an idiot. A naïve, stars-in-her-eyes idiot.

"When I got the position with the mayor, suddenly I had this exciting job and life was great. Then Preston and I started dating, and he swept me off my feet. Yeah, I thought it was a little strange at first, considering our age difference. I mean, what did a twenty-five-year-old from the suburbs have in common with someone who was forty-one and a member of one of Boston's oldest political families? But hey, I trusted him. Believed in him completely. If he said everything was fine, then things were fine. I was a sucker and drank the Kool-Aid. Hell, I *made* extra batches of the Kool-Aid."

She'd been such a wide-eyed, gullible fool.

"I think, deep down, I truly believed he was better than me. And that was the opening he needed. Within months, we got married. I stopped working, and before I knew it, I'd lost contact with my family and friends. And myself, I suppose. Then all hell broke loose."

Quinn's grip on her feet tightened ever so slightly.

She sighed in dismay. "I don't think you can understand how strange it is to hear myself say these things. To know that all that"—she waved her hand around— "actually happened to me. *Me*. That I *allowed* it all to happen. It's so surreal. And honestly, if it weren't for this baby, I would believe it was all a horrendous nightmare. I can't even begin to explain it."

"Alex, sweetheart, you don't have to explain anything."

"I feel like I do." Her lips pursed in frustration. "I *need* to. Because it doesn't make sense."

"Well, maybe you'll learn more about how it happened if you look at how it ended." His gray eyes were intense, challenging her to tell him more. "Was there something that made you say, 'Enough'?"

She nodded. "I met a pair of angels."

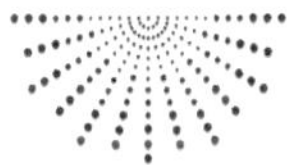

CHAPTER SEVENTEEN

"Pardon?"

"Angels." Alex grinned at the stunned expression on Quinn's face. "Not the halo-and-wings type. Lina Grable and Melissa Suarez. Two strangers who became *my* angels."

His brow furrowed. With her talking in circles, it was no surprise he wasn't following.

"My main job as Preston's wife was to look good," she said. "No one cared what I did or said as long as I presented a pretty package."

At first, she hadn't minded. She'd wanted to make Preston happy. But the constant disregard from everyone—particularly her husband—had eaten away at her spirit to the point where she'd stopped caring. Until her angels had forced her to see what was happening.

"For years, me and a couple other trophy wives would take the ferry into Boston for a spa day. Massages, facials, mani-pedis. The whole deal. At least once a week, sometimes twice. Our favorite was the Silver Angel Spa."

"Hence, the angels," Quinn murmured, a contemplative look on his face.

She nodded. "Lina was my regular masseuse. About a year and a half ago, while she was massaging me, she said, 'Just because you're in an abusive relationship, doesn't mean your life is over. You can still have a happy, full life, but the only person who can move you toward that is you.'"

The fine hairs on Alex's arms rose as the memory echoed in her mind. Her throat grew tight.

That day had changed her life.

"I wasn't sure I'd heard her right. I was ready to bolt, but she kept talking quietly and massaging. She told me about her ex-husband. How he'd beaten her. How he'd convinced her that it had been all her fault. How, after he beat her, he'd get the ice pack and gently hold it to her face and tell her how much he loved her. She told me about how she'd cut off ties to her family and friends because she'd believed her ex-husband when he said that they were just jealous of her."

Quinn's hands stilled. Two heartbeats passed before she glanced up, catching his gaze.

He held out his arms. "Come here, sweetheart."

The gentleness in those three little words had her leaning toward him. He pulled her close and positioned her back against his chest. With his arms wrapped around her in a comforting embrace, she relaxed. She hadn't realized how tense she'd been.

After a moment of silence, she said, "Hearing Lina's words . . . Her former life was such a reflection of mine. It was devastating. I couldn't hide from the truth of what my life had become anymore. This woman who I'd seen weekly for years but didn't know anything about . . . she saw my life for what it really was. All I could do was lay there and cry. She didn't judge me. She didn't censure me or lecture me or tell me I was an idiot. She just shared her story with me."

"She let you know that you weren't alone," he said, holding her tight as tears welled in her eyes.

She nodded. "It was the most amazing gift. I'm *so* grateful for that day."

He pressed his lips to the top of her head, and her tears began to fall.

"I went back later that week and we talked more," she continued. "Lina convinced me to meet her good friend, Melissa, who was also the spa owner's sister. Turned out, Melissa was a psychologist who worked at a domestic violence shelter. From that moment on, I met with them under the guise of massages, facials, and pampering. Twice, sometimes three times a week.

"Talking with Melissa and learning from Lina healed a part of my soul that I hadn't realized had been pummeled. After a few months, I started to put together an escape plan. Because of who Preston was, I knew it had to be well thought-out. In the meantime, whenever he beat me, they documented the abuse and helped me recover as best as they could. The police were never an option because he'd made it clear that they were *his* friends. He said they'd never believe 'a dumb piece of pussy.'"

Quinn tensed behind her, but he stayed quiet, letting her get it all out.

"It took almost a full year to finish my escape plan and squirrel away enough money. But everything flew out the window when I found out I was pregnant. It was a shock on so many levels."

Hell, it was *still* a shock.

"We hadn't . . . he and I didn't . . ." They'd only had sex a handful of times, at most, in the last year. He'd berated her, constantly telling her how awful in bed she was. "I knew he'd been cheating on me for a while, but I was fine with it." His taunts and comparisons to the other women had stung, but the less he'd touched her the better. "The last time we'd—" Her words caught, and bile surged up her throat. "After he hit me, he'd usually leave me alone. But that time . . ."

He had been so angry. She'd thought she would suffocate from his punishing grip on her throat when he'd bent her over the dining table and shoved her bruised and bloody face into the unforgiving wood. But she hadn't. She'd been fully alert, praying he would just kill her already, when he'd slammed into her, tearing her flesh. The memories threatened to drown her.

Goosebumps tore across her skin, and a shiver racked her body.

Strong hands ran over her arms, soothing her, pulling her back to the present. She let out a shaky breath and pushed the memories away. When she inhaled, her senses flooded with a spicy, woodsy scent.

Quinn.

She leaned into the solid chest behind her and focused on the arms holding her steady.

Quinn.

"I'm so damn sorry, Alex," he murmured, his voice rough. "I'm so sorry that happened to you, sweetheart."

She nestled into him. It took another moment before she could continue. "Early on in our marriage, we tried to have a baby with no luck. After countless tests, our doctor told us that my chances of getting pregnant were almost zero. Preston didn't believe in IVF or surrogacy. Said it was 'unnatural.' Adoption was out of the question because he 'didn't want to raise someone else's bastards.'"

"Damn," he muttered. "I didn't think it was possible to hate the fucker more, but there you go."

The corners of her lips twitched. "I'd resigned myself to knowing I'd never have kids. So, I was beyond shocked when the doctor said I was pregnant. Looking back on it, I should have realized my doctor would call Preston the second I left his office. At least, that's what I'm assuming happened. As you heard from Joe, the mayor and Preston had a lot of people in their pocket. They owned our town. Judges, lawyers, police, doctors. Everyone. But at the time, I was so stunned. Preston's reaction to the pregnancy was the last thing on my mind. And I sure as hell wasn't prepared for when I got home."

Images tumbled in her mind.

Preston's face contorted in rage.

The blur of his fist flying toward her eye.

The unforgiving cement of the garage floor.

"It was chaos. One second, everything was moving in slow motion. The next second, it was all a crazy, mad blur. I'd barely stepped out of the car when he came at me and punched me right in the face. I fell, and he dragged me inside by my hair. It's sad, but I remember my first thought was, 'He's hitting my face. I must have screwed up something *really* big.'"

"None of it was your fault, sweetheart," Quinn whispered. "None of it."

"I know that now. Or at least, I try to." She sighed. "But that night, he was *screaming*. And that scared the shit out of me. He was usually eerily quiet when he beat me. I couldn't think straight. I remember not being able to focus on one thing. There was just too much going on."

Quinn rubbed his hands over her arms, chasing away the goosebumps.

"My whole body was on fire. Everything hurt at once. Then, all of a sudden, there's this sharp pain in my shoulder, and it burned like nothing I'd ever felt before. When I turned to see what happened, there he was. My husband. The man I'd vowed to love, honor, and cherish. The man who'd pledged to do the same for me." She let out a bitter chuckle. "He'd stabbed me with a kitchen knife. Everything after that was a blur of noise and sensations and images. And pain. The most awful, all-consuming pain."

She tilted her head to look back at him. "I'm so sorry, Quinn. That was probably waaay more information than you were looking for."

"No, sweetheart." He dropped a kiss to her forehead. "Like I said earlier, I want to know everything. Even if hearing what happened to you makes me want to gut the bastard." Anger swirled in his gray eyes, but she knew it wasn't directed at her. "I want to know about this, about you. And you need to get it out. It's good to talk about it."

He moved her so they were sitting face to face, then cradled her hands in his. "Alex, it means the world to me that you shared your story with me. I promise I'll do everything in my power to keep earning your trust. And if he comes after you, I will do everything I can to protect you. Everything."

He squeezed her hands, and her heartbeat quickened.

"Can you trust me to protect you?" he whispered.

Reaching up, she framed his face with both hands, smoothing her fingers along the stubble of his jaw.

This man. This sweet, fierce, gentle man . . .

She nodded. "I do trust you, Quinn."

His gaze flicked to her lips. Her breath caught, and she pulled him close. A split second before their lips touched, her chest kicked, and her courage fled.

Holy shit. What the hell was she doing?

She turned her head, and his lips landed on her cheek.

<hr>

Quinn couldn't help the smile that tipped his lips. He had no problem with her last-second evasion. He'd been shocked as shit when she'd pulled him close. Things were moving too fast.

He placed another kiss on her forehead before pulling away.

Then his heart nearly stopped.

Her whiskey-brown eyes were tinged with panic, and her lips were pressed in a firm line. Before he could react, she scrambled off the couch.

"I'm so sorry, Quinn. I shouldn't have done that."

He tracked her anxious pacing with his gaze, holding completely still. The last thing he wanted was to make her uncomfortable. Well, *more* uncomfortable.

"I can't. I'm sorry. It's not because I don't want to. Because I do," she said, her words stumbling over one another. "It's just . . . It's not . . . The timing is shit, and I'm not being fair to you."

He knew she had to work out what was going on in her head for herself. And he'd be a patient friend—because, first and foremost, that's what he was. Right now, she needed someone who would listen and *not* wrap her in his arms. Even if it killed him.

She stopped and faced him, wringing her hands. Tears slipped down her cheeks. "I'm a mess. And I don't want to make your life a mess, too. It's not fair to you."

He ached to hold her.

She hurried on, her eyes ping-ponging around the room. "I know I'm not making sense right now. But you don't really want to get involved with someone like me. And don't get me wrong, I like you, Quinn. I really do . . . Probably more than I should. Well, for sure more than I should."

His lips curved up. Thank god for small miracles.

"Don't grin," she huffed. "That's not the point, Quinn."

The point—to him—was that the panic in her eyes had eased. It sure as fuck was still there, but it was a lot less.

"I'm not going to lie and say that I'm not attracted to you. I am. You're a really great guy. But I don't want to mess things up for you, and that's what will happen if you get involved with me. My god, Quinn, I'm still married—"

"Technically." He shrugged. As far as he was concerned, her sack-of-shit spouse had been revoked of all his husband privileges the second he had hurt her. "And you filed your divorce papers before you left Boston."

"—and I'm pregnant on top of it all," she continued as if he hadn't spoken. "My life is a soap opera, and I don't want to lead you on. I'm just not good for you and . . ."

She fell silent, looking everywhere but at him as he rose to his feet. He closed the distance between them, and she rushed on with more excuses.

"Really, Quinn, I'll ruin your life. I don't know—"

"Let me ask you a question," he interrupted, standing before her, though not so close as to crowd her. He wasn't sure the nudge he was about to give her was the wisest decision, but he didn't have the willpower to change course.

He waited for her slight nod before continuing. "Back there?" He gestured to the couch with his head. "Did you want to kiss me?"

Her eyes widened, and her lips parted with a nearly inaudible gasp. But after a few beats of silence, she gave another slight nod.

He held out his palms, and when she placed her tiny hands in his, the tightness in his chest dissolved. The amount of trust in that one act wasn't lost on him.

Knowing he needed to keep things light, he led them back to the couch. They assumed their previous seats at opposite ends, facing each other.

"Well." He held his arms out wide and shot her what he hoped was a playful grin. "Have at it."

Her eyes narrowed in disbelief, and a flush reddened her

cheeks. But he didn't miss how the edges of her lips ticked up. "What? Just lay one on you? Just like that?"

"We've become friends, right?"

She nodded. There was no hesitation and that made him want to grin like a fool. He ignored the urge.

"We're attracted to each other," he said. "But what happens next is up to you. You're in the driver's seat, Alex. We move as fast or as slow as you want. I'm not going anywhere."

Doubt flickered over her face. She shook her head. "That's not fair to you. What if I'm all gung-ho, like earlier, and then . . . can't? What if—"

"Like I said, you're in the driver's seat, sweetheart. I'm happy with whatever you're willing and comfortable to give. You want to just hold hands for a year? I'm good with that."

Her brow arched, calling bullshit, and he grinned.

"Seriously, Alex, I'm not a teenager who can't control things. What matters is *you*. And you being comfortable with me. However long it takes. I want to get to know you. See where this"—he waved a hand between them—"goes."

She studied him, absorbing his words. His heart raced, and he was sure she could hear the thudding.

Had he just fucked it all up?

Yes, he wanted to see where their attraction went. He hadn't lied about that. But he also valued their newfound friendship and didn't want to jeopardize it.

He tried not to squirm under her stare. She was looking at him like he was a puzzle, and he didn't know how he felt about that.

Abruptly, she scooted to his end of the couch, settling next to him. He reminded himself to breathe.

"I don't want to make things complicated for you," she whispered.

Their gazes locked.

She reached for his face, hesitating midair.

He held absolutely still.

Whatever she saw in his eyes must have been enough to reassure her, because a moment later, her hands gently framed his jaw. "But I really want to kiss you."

He broke out into a wide smile. Damn, this brave woman was stunning.

Closing the distance between them, he reveled in the soft touch of her lips. One arm went around the small of her back, drawing her closer, while the other cupped her jaw, tilting her face up. She tensed for a brief second, but then her arms wrapped around him and she melted.

He traced the seam of her lips with his tongue, wordlessly begging for entrance.

Her lips parted and her tongue met his, tentative at first, then growing bolder. He groaned. Needing her closer, he changed the angle of his head, deepening their kiss. Her hands moved to his chest, grabbing onto his shirt.

The press of her body against his had all his blood rushing south. He gently nipped at her bottom lip, and she let out a quiet moan that had his cock weeping. When her fingers ran through his hair and fisted, he prayed she would never stop.

But he knew *he* should. As much as he didn't want to.

He pulled away, breathless and dazed. Then, unable to help himself, he dropped another kiss to her perfect, kiss-swollen lips, this one quick.

"While I appreciate your concern," he said. "Don't worry about complicating things for me, sweetheart. I'm a grown man."

She shifted against him, and he didn't miss how his hard length pressed against her.

"No kidding," she murmured as a blush stole over her cheeks.

"I can make my own decisions, Alex, and I know what I want." Her brow scrunched in question, and he chuckled. "You. Just as you are. Whenever you're ready."

His heart stuttered as she leaned into him and gently pressed her lips to his. The kiss heated, and their tongues danced. Attraction was definitely not their problem. But he wouldn't rush her. He'd pushed enough.

With a pained smile, he pulled away again. "I'm going to go, sweetheart." He untangled himself from their embrace. They stood, and he tucked her to his side as they headed to the front door. "Tomorrow, then."

"Tomorrow?" she asked. The caveman in him took great satisfaction in how her voice trembled on that one word. "What about it?"

The hazy, lust-filled look in her eyes made him grin. He'd done that, put that dazed look on her face. And confirmed that slowing things down was the right decision.

He held her face in his hands. He couldn't help it; she had the softest skin. "I want to see you again tomorrow. We're not done with the getting-to-know-you part."

She looked up at him with those beautiful whiskey-colored eyes, and he felt an unfamiliar tug in his chest. He kissed her, making sure not to linger too long, then turned to leave.

"Thank you for spending tonight with me. I'll see you tomorrow," he said. Closing the door behind him, he added, "Don't forget to lock up."

CHAPTER EIGHTEEN

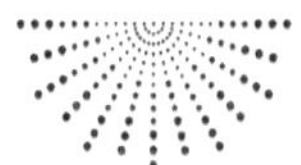

*S*he giggled as Preston carried her through the front door, over their proverbial threshold. Married! Glancing up at her new husband, she let out a blissful sigh. She couldn't believe she was officially this wonderful man's wife.

Setting her down, he went to his home office to check his messages.

She scanned their crowded living room in delight.

"Preston," she called out, adjusting the spaghetti strap of her summer dress. "Do you want to go through this stuff now or later?"

Countless gift boxes, delivered while they'd been away on their two-week honeymoon, were mixed with moving boxes from her studio apartment. Everything was stacked neatly, labeled, and organized by size.

"Wow, your assistant definitely needs a raise because—"

The words died on her lips as Preston stalked back into the living room. His face was red with fury, his eyes blazing. What was going on?

Run, a voice in the back of her head whispered.

But that was ridiculous. He was her husband. "Preston, what's wrong?"

His expression turned glacial. Dread curdled her stomach, and her heart began to pound.

The living room spun, and when her vision refocused, it was nighttime. She was in the entryway. And Preston was prowling toward her. She stepped backward and tripped on the hem of her evening gown.

Preston, clad in his perfectly tailored tuxedo, remained unnervingly calm. "Who is Joe?" he demanded. "Did you fuck him?"

The back of his hand cracked against her cheek, stunning her. She turned to run but was too slow. Her scalp stung as he grabbed her by the hair and hauled her to him. His knee connected with her ribs, and she crumpled to the ground.

The room spun again. Now she was in the kitchen. Curled into a little ball on the floor. The sweater she wore was tangled around her torso. Numbness threatened to envelop her. And she welcomed it. Who was this man?

Preston's fist connected with her nose, and she saw stars. Warm blood oozed across her face. She tried to fight back, but her limbs wouldn't move. She tried to cry for help, but her voice was gone. She tried everything she could, but it was all useless.

He loomed over her. His eyes, once gentle and calm, were now those of a monster. His fist rose, a kitchen knife clutched within it.

Everything slowed.

Her mouth opened, but before she could scream, the knife came crashing down, stabbing into her stomach. Again and again and again . . .

Alex shot up in bed, gasping for breath. Heart racing, her gaze darted around the dark room, frantic and disoriented. Her hands flew to her stomach.

Blood!

Her heart stopped.

Pulling her damp fingers away from her body, she held her shaking hands in front of her face.

Seconds passed before her brain caught up with her eyes.

No blood.

She patted herself down, confusion muddling her thoughts.

Sweat. It was only sweat that had her nightshirt sticking to her. Not blood.

Gripping her blanket to her chest, she continued to quake.

A dream. It was just a dream.

She flinched when the phone next to her rang.

Holy crap. Had it been ringing the entire time? She snatched up the receiver.

"Hello?" she answered, her voice wobbling.

Silence.

A glance at the clock told her it was nearly three thirty in the morning. Out of sorts and anger building, she opened her mouth to give the caller a piece of her mind. But the words caught in her throat.

A noise.

A quiet murmur at the other end of the line.

Chills inched down her spine.

The voice in her mind screamed for her to hang up the phone. But she ignored it.

Instead, she sat frozen, the phone clasped in a death grip against her ear. As if the harder she pressed the phone to her head, the more she'd be able to discern what she heard.

Her eyes stayed locked on the clock as she focused on the low hum. It was so distant, but strangely familiar, and not at all comforting.

Recognition hit.

A violent shiver racked her body, and the tiny hairs on the back of her neck stood at attention.

She slammed the receiver down onto its cradle and scrambled away from the phone.

No. It couldn't be. It couldn't.

As the hours passed to sunrise, she sat in the center of her bed, trembling, knees tightly clutched to her chest. She tried to breathe through the panic, tried to remember her therapist's words.

But it wasn't working.

Nothing was working.

Maybe she'd dreamed the phone call, just as she'd dreamed of Preston.

No. She knew better.

The quiet tune she'd strained to hear over the phone was now playing on repeat in her mind.

"Like a river flows surely to the sea, darling, so it goes. Some things are meant to be . . ."

She was in trouble. Big, big trouble.

He was coming for her.

CHAPTER NINETEEN

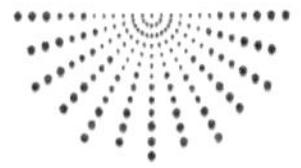

"Alex!"

She whipped around. "What?"

Roxie stared at her, one eyebrow raised in question, both of her perfectly manicured hands resting impatiently on her slim hips. With an over-obvious gesture, Roxie nodded toward the women who were standing at the counter behind Alex.

She spun to face Mrs. Abbot and Mrs. Yoshida, who were patiently waiting for her to take their orders. She cringed. How long had they been standing there?

"Oh, right. Sorry," she said, her face heating. "Good morning. What can I get you, ladies?"

"There's no rush, dear," Mrs. Abbot said. "We'll take our usuals when you get a chance."

"No rush at all, dear," parroted Mrs. Yoshida as she nodded to an empty corner table. "We'll just settle in over there."

"Sure thing. Your usuals, coming right up." She knew her reply held too much enthusiasm—hell, it was grating to her own ears—but she pasted a smile on her face and turned to the espresso machine. She tried to recall what their usuals were, but her sleep-deprived brain was mush.

"You okay?"

"Jeez!" She jerked, hand to her chest, and looked at Roxie.

"A little jumpy today?"

She fumbled with the espresso machine. "Um, yeah . . . sorry. Mrs. Abbot and Mrs. Yoshida want their usuals and I . . ." She sighed, exhausted, and her shoulders slumped. "I have no idea what that is."

"Didn't you write it down in your little book?" Roxie asked, sarcasm dripping from each word.

She stiffened at Roxie's tone. Peeking up, she winced. There was zero humor on the other woman's face. Great. Piss off the boss. Excellent way to start the freaking day.

"Uh, yeah, I did actually. But I, uh, left my notebook at home. Kind of a rough night."

More like a terrifying night.

"Yeah, sure." Roxie scoffed, folding her arms across her chest. Irritation radiated from her in waves. "Since the day these doors opened, Mrs. Abbot has ordered a blueberry scone and a nonfat vanilla latte. Mrs. Yoshida has a cranberry muffin and a two percent peppermint mocha."

"Thanks. And sorry, Roxie." Head down, she bent to grab plates from under the counter. When Roxie caught her arm, she froze.

"Look. I get this is all new and that it's only day two for you," Roxie said, hushed yet authoritative. "But as my employee, I expect you to not only show up on time, which you didn't, but when you're here, to be focused and attentive. Which you're not. That includes greeting customers when they walk in and actually taking their orders." Roxie glanced pointedly at Mrs. Abbot and Mrs. Yoshida as she released Alex's arm. "If your extracurricular activities happen to leave you sleep-deprived and floating around in la-la land, that is not my problem. I expect you to show up, work, and not waste my time and money by daydreaming. Got it?"

"What the hell do you think you're doing, Roxie?" a low voice interrupted.

Not taking her eyes off Alex, Roxie said, "First off, Quinn, you don't work here. So use the front door like every other paying customer. Second, just like every other customer, you have no right being behind the counter." She turned to glare at him. "Third, this is between me and my employee and, frankly, none of your goddamn business."

"What the hell crawled up your ass, Rox?"

"Go. Away."

As they continued to hiss at each other, Alex shut her eyes.

Breathe. Just breathe.

Her anxiety spiked. She knew she was wasting space today. While Roxie's anger was adding to Alex's distress, it wasn't the cause. The only thing her mind could focus on was the song. That damned, static-filled hint of a song that had teased her from the other end of the line.

"Take my hand. Take my whole life, too. For I can't help falling in love with you."

Her chest tightened.

She couldn't breathe!

Inhale. Exhale. Just breathe, dammit!

"Alex?"

She startled when Quinn touched her arm. Her eyes flew open, and she stifled a scream. She slammed her hands over her mouth.

"Sorry," she whispered. Concern had the skin between his brows crinkling. Tears welled in her eyes. "Sorry, Quinn," she repeated, struggling to regain her composure.

He held her face with gentle hands and tilted her head up so she could meet his gaze. "What's wrong, sweetheart?"

She blinked back her tears and concentrated on the warmth of his hands, the calm gray of his eyes, and his steady breathing. Miraculously, her nerves began to settle.

"Ahem."

Her attention flew to Roxie, and she grimaced. If someone looked up *annoyed-borderline-pissed* in the dictionary, they would find Roxie.

With Quinn's hands still framing her face, she tried to pull away.

"Ignore her, Alex," he said. "Look at me. Tell me what's wrong."

"Okay, that's it," Roxie growled, smacking Quinn hard on the shoulder. "I don't care what you do in your free time or if she happens to be your new flavor of the month, but you need to leave. Right now."

Alex's eyes widened with surprise as Quinn released her and pivoted toward Roxie, disbelief dominating his expression.

"I'm running a business here," Roxie said. "I will *not* have you strolling in here like you own the damn place. Do you seriously think you can just waltz in and distract my employees whenever you feel hard up? Leave. Now." She pointed at the front door. "I mean it, Quinn. Get the hell out."

Roxie stormed into the kitchen.

What. The. Fuck?

Quinn looked back at Alex. Dark circles shadowed her brown eyes, which were a little too frantic. He wanted to scoop her up and figure out what had shaken her.

But first things first.

Giving Alex's slim shoulders a delicate squeeze, he dropped a kiss to the top of her head. "Be right back."

He had to deal with his crazy-ass friend who'd just run off.

Ignoring Nina's confused stare, he followed Roxie into her cramped office. Crossing his arms, he propped himself against the doorframe. And waited. Her back was to him, and tension strained her muscles as she scrubbed her hands through her hair.

Turning, she glared at him in that special way of hers that never failed to annoy the shit out of him. She tilted her head and raised her eyebrow in challenge.

He hated that damn eyebrow raise. God, she could be so damn irritating.

Taking a deep breath, he strived for calm. "What the fuck is going on with you, Roxie?"

"I asked you to leave, Quinn." She huffed, as if shooing away a fly.

She attempted to walk by him, but he shifted to the other side of the doorframe and blocked her.

Pausing in front of him, she eyed him up and down, her chin lifting. Even though she was a few inches shorter than him, she was damn intimidating. She'd perfected the princess-to-peon look by her tenth birthday.

"Really, Quinn. She's married, and she's pregnant. I didn't think that was your style."

Holy. Fuck.

His blood ran cold, and his earlier exasperation morphed into full-blown outrage. Leaning down so they were eye to eye, he got right in her face. "I thought she was your friend, Roxie? Why are you being such a goddamn bitch?"

He had to hand it to her; that damn haughty look remained firmly in place. Didn't even fucking waiver.

"Alex is my friend, jackass. It's currently you I'm beginning to wonder about." She put her hands on her hips. "Now move."

He shook his head in disgust. "I'm disappointed in you, Roxie. I don't know what's going on in that warped mind of yours. But whatever the hell you're, know that you are *completely* wrong."

He pointed toward the front of the café. "That woman out there trusts you. And you're treating her like absolute shit. You know I love you like my goddamn sister but sort your shit out before you go anywhere near Alex. She's not just your employee, Rox. She's supposed to be your goddamn friend. A friend who's been through hell and back. Don't fucking forget that."

He left Roxie alone in her office.

Something had to be wrong if Roxie was acting like such a crazed bitch. He was too livid to stick around and figure out what it was, though. Did ditching her when she was clearly upset make him an asshole? Probably. But at this point, he didn't care. Roxie was stubborn as fuck and would tell him what was wrong only when she was good and damn ready. Which could be never. So, yeah, he was okay being an asshole.

CHAPTER TWENTY

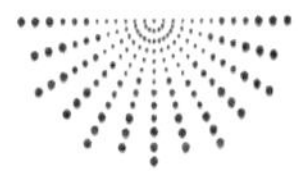

After assuring Quinn she was fine and simply tired, Alex did her best to stay out of Roxie's way. Unfortunately, the tension continued throughout the rest of the morning.

She tried to pull it together, she really did. But she was having the hardest freaking time concentrating. Between last night's call and Roxie, Alex's nerves were shot. She was one giant, frazzled, jittery mess. It didn't help that her veins held more caffeine than blood.

When Roxie suggested she switch with Nina and work in the back office on inventory, she was grateful. However, guilt flooded her when she overheard Roxie apologizing to Mrs. Abbot and Mrs. Yoshida for the earlier blowup, bribing the women with treats to gain their discretion regarding the gossip-worthy incident.

Engulfed in a small mountain of paperwork, Alex lost track of time until a knock interrupted her.

Nina stood in the doorway holding a large white box tied with a giant red bow. "Hey, hun. Delivery for you." She stepped fully into the office and placed the box on top of the stacks of papers.

A tingle of unease slid down Alex's spine.

"Well?" Nina asked, eyeing the box. "Don't you want to open it and see what it is?"

No. Not even a little bit.

She swallowed hard. "Um, sure."

Reaching for the bow, she fought the tremble in her hand. She could do nothing to stop the nervous roiling of her stomach. Or the bile creeping inch by inch up her throat. Bile that had nothing to do with the baby.

It couldn't be. It wasn't possible. There was no way in hell it could be what she thought it was.

Though undoing the bow took only a few seconds, each one felt like a lifetime. With her heart hammering in her chest, she peeked into the box. The blood drained from her face.

It was.

Holy shit.

Beneath the box's lid lay four dozen long-stemmed white roses.

It's just a coincidence. It has to be.

She knew it wasn't.

Her hands shook violently as she tore open the card. Her vision swam with unshed tears when she read the message.

Please forgive me. I love you.

She broke out into a cold sweat. Saliva flooded her mouth, and her stomach lurched. She bolted out of the chair, knocking into Nina as she ran for the bathroom.

Dropping to her knees in front of the toilet, she retched until there was nothing left. Dry heaves had her entire body cramping, and she clutched the porcelain as the room spun.

Oh my god, this can't be happening.

She collapsed onto the bathroom floor and curled into a

shivering ball. Closing her eyes, she prayed for mindless oblivion.

She thought she heard Nina and Roxie calling her name, but they sounded far away, like they were at the end of a long tunnel. Gentle hands touched her back, and she recoiled away from them. She curled herself tighter and blocked everything out. She had to.

Mindless oblivion. That's what she needed.

And when it was finally within her grasp, she welcomed it.

CHAPTER TWENTY-ONE

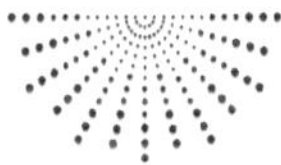

Another damn interruption, Quinn thought, glowering at the ringing phone on his desk. He debated whether to answer it or toss it across the room.

Mercifully, the ringing stopped.

He looked back at the dreaded stack of papers before him, applications and resumes for the department's new deputy position. They were the last thing he wanted to deal with right now.

The shrill sound of the phone broke the silence again.

"Goddammit!"

After the morning's drama with Roxie, to say he was in a piss-poor mood would be a gross understatement.

When Alex had told him she was fine, his frustration had grown. He didn't know shit about women—what man did?— but he knew *fine* wasn't a good thing. Her beautiful whiskey-brown eyes had been filled with fear, and her damn hands hadn't stopped shaking.

So, no. He didn't believe for one damn minute that she was *fine*.

But what the hell was he supposed to do?

He snatched up the phone and barked, "Sheriff O'Conner."

"It's Roxie."

He sighed. She was the last person he wanted to talk to. "Look, Rox, I'm really not in the mood for your bullshit right now—"

"Shut up and come over," she interrupted. Her tone had his Spidey-senses tingling. "Something's wrong with Alex. I'm not sure if I need to call the paramedics, too, but you need to get over here. She got a delivery—"

He didn't hear the rest of her sentence. He was already out of his office and bellowing for one of his deputies to meet him at Roxie's.

Racing the few blocks to Comfort Food on foot, he barged through the front door. Ignoring the stares of the customers, he ran behind the counter to Roxie. Before he could open his mouth to ask about Alex, Roxie placed a finger over her lips.

"Don't let anyone in the back," she whispered to Nina.

Nina nodded, but the concern on her face filled him with trepidation.

"What the hell happened?" he asked Roxie as they hurried to the back.

"I don't know." Her voice trembled, and that trepidation grew. "Alex was in the office doing paperwork and a delivery came in for her. Nina brought it to her. She said when Alex opened it, she started looking queasy. Then, when Alex read the card, she got sick. Literally. She ran into the bathroom and puked."

Shuddering, she continued, "Nina and I tried to help her, but she kept throwing up. When she started dry heaving, I got scared with her being pregnant and all. Then she started shaking. She wouldn't respond to us when we called her name, and she started shaking even harder when I tried to get close. That's when I called you." Roxie gestured to the partially closed bathroom door. Her green eyes shone with worry and guilt. "She's still in there."

Every part of him wanted to rush into that bathroom and see what was wrong. To wrap Alex in his arms and offer her whatever comfort he could. However, considering what Roxie had told him, he needed to exercise caution, needed to gather as many facts as possible first. There was no way in hell he was going to risk scaring Alex any further.

He needed to be logical. He was the sheriff, for fuck's sake. Logic was his job. But damn if his emotions weren't all over the place. Emotions he hadn't even known he was capable of feeling until this morning, when Alex had brought them out in him.

Duty, he reminded himself. *Do your fucking duty. That's how you can help Alex.*

"What was it?" he asked.

"What?" Roxie replied.

"The delivery."

"Oh. A bunch of flowers. White roses. A few dozen of them."

"They still here?"

She nodded. "Yes."

He appreciated Roxie's to-the-point answers. She knew him well enough to understand he had very little patience when he entered what she deemed "cop mode."

"They're still in the office. No one has touched them since she ran out of the room."

He glanced at the archway leading to the front of the café. "Deputy Chase should be here any minute. Tell him what happened and have him find out where those flowers came from."

"Okay. Um, Quinn?" Her cheeks flushed a fiery red. "About what happened earlier—"

"Not right now, Roxie." He pushed a hand through his hair. "We'll deal with all that later."

He approached the bathroom door with caution, nudging it all the way open. The air left his lungs in a rough whoosh, as if someone had slammed him in the ribs with a two-by-four.

Alex was in the fetal position on the bathroom floor, hands clasped and tucked under her chin, knees drawn protectively to her chest. The side of her face rested against the tile floor, and her eyes were wide open. Unfocused. Blank. Her entire body trembled.

Seeing her like that . . .

His heart fucking broke. There was no other way about it.

"Sweetheart," he whispered, crouching before her.

His blood thrummed loudly in his ears. He reached out and touched her shoulder. She flinched away from him, vibrating with terror. A lump formed in his throat. He raked his hands through his hair and blew out a breath, not knowing what to do.

Fuck logic.

Following his gut, he placed his hands firmly on Alex's shoulders. She froze. As gently as he could, he wrapped his arms around her, cradling her against his chest.

"Alex, you're safe," he murmured. "Come back to me, sweetheart. Please. You're safe. I promise . . . Just please come back to me."

Through a thick fog, Alex heard a muffled voice. She strained to listen.

Quinn?

No, that couldn't be right.

She tried to make out what the voice was saying, but it

was too far away. She gave up, focusing on the warmth surrounding her instead. It felt wonderful. Cozy. Soothing.

After a few moments, her fingers and toes tingled, as if she were recovering from frostbite. The numbness protecting her mind began to ease. She still couldn't grasp the voice's words, but they were growing louder. The suffocating fog dwindled away, freeing her senses. She inhaled, and the faint scents of leather and forest surrounded her, enveloped her, calmed her.

Opening her eyes, she winced at the scratchy feel of her lids. A few blinks cleared her sight, bringing the face above hers into focus.

She frowned. What was going on?

"Quinn?"

His embrace tightened around her, and she felt the warm press of his lips on her forehead.

"Sweetheart, you're safe," he murmured, rising from the ground with her still tucked in his arms.

He carried her out of the bathroom, and her pulse picked up when she saw a young man dressed in a law enforcement uniform. Holding the white box of flowers, the man nodded to them as he passed.

"You're safe, Alex," Quinn repeated, entering Roxie's office.

He sat behind the desk, positioning her on his lap. He was a cocoon of warmth, and she snuggled into him, nuzzling her forehead between his neck and shoulder. She remained still, absorbing his strength, his spicy scent, and most importantly, the feeling of security his arms provided.

Eventually, she found her voice. "What happened?"

A strained chuckle rumbled in Quinn's chest. He leaned back so he could look her in the eyes. "I was hoping you could answer that for me. That's twice now, sweetheart." She must have given him a confused look because he clarified,

"That's the second time you've scared a few years off my life."

Her brow furrowed. "Second time?"

"The first was when you passed out after I scared you in Joe's shed." He touched his forehead to hers. "Please let this be the last time. I don't know if my heart can take anymore."

Pulling back, she took in the care, concern, and adoration in his misty gray eyes. She held his face with unsteady hands, and her throat grew thick, tears filling her vision.

This man. This sweet, wonderful man . . .

A feeling she couldn't put into words flooded through her.

"Thank you," she managed to whisper.

"For what?"

With her hands still framing his face, she ran a thumb along his chin. "For being here. For bringing me back from the fog. For making me feel safe." She leaned forward and laid her lips on his. "Thank you."

"You're welcome, sweetheart. I'd pretty much do anything for you, you know."

She smiled, tucking her head back into that perfect spot between his neck and shoulder. Her trembling subsided as they sat in silence.

"Do you need to get checked out by Doc?"

She shook her head, not wanting to move.

"You sure, sweetheart?"

"Positive," she murmured.

"Let's get out of here, then. I'm sure Roxie will let you take off early. Okay?"

"That'd be great."

How could she not want to be with this man? She believed he meant what he had said. He'd do anything for her. All she had to do was trust him.

She knew she could. And should. But *would* she? That was the question.

Taking a deep breath, she sat up, and his arms loosely encircled her waist. "Can we swing by your office first? I think I should file a report. No. I *need* to file a report."

"Of course." He tucked a lock of hair behind her ear. "The flower delivery?"

She nodded, then hesitated, chewing her bottom lip.

Trust him.

"Also . . . well . . . there have been some phone calls."

He tensed beneath her, and that crinkle between his brows popped. "What phone calls?"

CHAPTER TWENTY-TWO

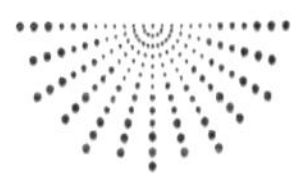

Alex sat on the uncomfortable guest chair in Quinn's office as he tried unsuccessfully to get off the phone. She studied him. Noted how his dark-brown hair was just a little bit too long. How his forehead scrunched when he didn't like what he was hearing. How he absently twirled a pencil in his large, calloused hand as he spoke. Even out of uniform, dressed in jeans and a corduroy button-down, the man had a commanding presence about him.

This was his element. This fit him.

She couldn't imagine him doing—*being*—anything else.

"Sure. Right. Thanks," he muttered, then hung up the phone. "Sorry about that. The mayor's a talker." An enormous exhale left him as he grabbed a notepad from his desk drawer. "Whenever you're ready, Alex. Start from the beginning."

You have nothing to be ashamed of. Nothing. It's time to let go of the guilt and allow yourself to move on.

Squaring her shoulders, she took a deep breath in, then let it out long and slow.

"It started a few days ago," she said, "but I'm not sure

which day. It was just a phone call with no one on the other end. I figured it was simply a wrong number, you know? I hung up and didn't give it much thought. Then another hang-up call happened last night when you were over. Um, when we were about to . . ."

"Kiss."

Heat spread across her face, but she was determined to maintain eye contact. Even when the corners of his lips twitched. She cleared her throat. "Right. Again, I didn't think anything about the call."

Because you distracted me.

She cleared her throat again. She needed to force herself to stick to the facts and not random details like how it had been so hard to think straight with Quinn's undivided attention on her.

Facts. Right.

As she recalled the previous night, all gushy thoughts fled. A shiver coursed through her. "This morning, I had a nightmare that woke me up." She pursed her lips in thought. "Actually, I'm not sure if it was the dream that woke me or the phone. Either way, I woke up, and it was three twenty-two in the morning."

The glowing numbers on her bedside clock were seared in her brain. That was the exact time she had recognized the song.

"It was silent on the other end, and I was about to hang up. But then I heard this soft hum. It sounded familiar, but I couldn't quite place it. And when it got a little louder . . ." Ice crept down the back of her neck, and she wrapped her arms around her middle. "I knew. I got scared. Really, really scared. I remember slamming down the phone. And then I just sort of . . ."

"Sort of what?"

She opened her mouth, but no words came. Her eyes dropped to her clenched hands.

In her peripheral vision, she saw him push his notepad aside. He leaned forward with his elbows on his desk. "Sweetheart, look at me." She did. "Alex, tell me what happened next."

Please don't think I'm a complete nut job.

Her teeth caught her bottom lip, and she waved helplessly. "I sort of, I don't know, checked out . . ."

She tried to gauge his reaction. Unfortunately for her, he had an excellent poker face.

"Sometimes when Preston would hit me, when it got really bad, I would make myself check out." Damn. There was no way around it. She sounded batshit crazy, even to herself. "I guess what I mean is if I concentrated really hard on something, like a painting or a doorknob or whatever, I could make myself mentally leave the situation I was in."

She shifted in her seat, her gaze everywhere but on Quinn.

And now for the extra crazy part . . .

"Toward the end—the last three months, especially—it seemed like everything I did made him snap. My mind would automatically check itself out, so I don't really remember what happened during that time. It's all . . . hazy. But maybe my subconscious does?" She shrugged. "I've had some crazy nightmares. They're always a jumbled mess, but so damn vivid."

Too vivid.

She could still feel the blood trickling from her body, her lungs seizing after being punched in the stomach. Her nightmares were pure chaos, but they felt *so* real. When she was in them, she never knew what was imagined and what was remembered.

"The end of the nightmares is always the same. He always

stabs me. Over and over and over again." She shook her head, hoping to clear it, but the images remained. "Sorry, I'm rambling." She sat taller in the uncomfortable chair. "So yeah, I guess when things get to be too much, my head knows its own limit and shuts down. Does that make any sense?"

"It does." His deep voice was steady, and his expression was relaxed. "And you're not crazy, sweetheart. I can see that's what you're thinking. What your mind does is completely normal. It's self-preservation at the body's most basic and instinctual level."

She released the breath she'd been holding. Though she was certain he didn't know it, his calm, matter-of-fact explanation had helped soothe her frayed nerves.

Glancing down, her eyes caught on Quinn's white knuckles. He was holding his pencil in a death grip. He was keeping his anger in check.

For her.

A grateful smile lifted her lips. The man would never understand how much she appreciated him in that moment.

"So, after the last phone call," he continued, "was it an automatic thing, or did you make yourself check out?"

"Automatic."

"Why, Alex? What did you hear on the other end?"

Fear dried her throat.

"The song," she whispered.

His gray eyes implored her to continue.

"Preston is a big Elvis fan, basically because people call him *the King*. Our wedding song was 'Can't Help Falling in Love.' You know, the 'fools rush in' song? He thought it was apropos to our relationship. He talked about how he thought of me every time he heard it. How he felt it represented our love. How us loving each other was as natural and meant to be as the rivers flowing to the sea."

And she'd fallen for that cheesy bullshit. Hook, line, and sinker.

A bitter laugh escaped her lips. "He even made a special playlist and had the gall to title it 'Preston loves Natalie.' It had all the different versions: Elvis, UB40, and all the countless covers. This last year, he always made sure it was playing in the background when he'd wail on me. It would play over and over again. He said it was so I wouldn't forget how much he loved me, or that the 'lessons' he taught me were for my own good. To make me a better wife."

"Jesus, that's *completely* fucked up." He jerked, seemingly surprised he'd spoken out loud. "Sorry, please go on."

Despite the subject matter, she smiled. Just a little.

"After a minor lesson, where he'd simply slap or punch me or grab me by the hair, he'd usually apologize, maybe cry a little, and I'd forgive him. But after a big lesson, where he'd hit me somewhere he wasn't supposed to—my face, arms, places that I couldn't easily cover up—he would always send me a box of four dozen long-stemmed white roses with a note. It was always the same. 'Please forgive me. I love you.' Then he'd cook me dinner, draw me a bath, and treat me wonderfully."

Deep down, she'd always known that Preston didn't really mean his apologies, that he would only play the good, doting, and caring husband until the bruises faded. But she'd gone along with it all because she'd been desperate for the affection, the attention, the hope that Preston still loved her.

God, what a naïve idiot she'd been.

No.

She had to stop berating herself. She wasn't an idiot. She was a survivor.

Once her angels had opened her eyes, she'd only gone along with Preston's sick manipulation because she'd been biding her time until she could escape.

She'd gotten through five years of his abuse; she'd get through this, too.

Straightening her spine, she asked, "I thought Preston was still in jail?"

The calm, neutral expression on Quinn's face wavered, and he snapped his pencil in two.

"He is." Tossing his destroyed pencil aside, he grabbed his coffee mug and took a long sip. She fought the urge to hug the man. To give him some of the comfort he'd given her. If he could be professional, so could she. "I spoke with Joe yesterday, but I'll call him again when we're finished here."

"It doesn't matter, Quinn. Preston knows where I am. And he's coming." She placed her hands over her abdomen. Knowing she had to face Preston didn't make it any less terrifying. "I don't think there's anything you or Joe or anyone can do about it."

"You're wrong, Alex." The first hint of anger entered his voice. "I am going to get this asshole, I can guarantee—"

"Quinn," she interrupted with a shake of her head. The sleepless night and the morning's drama—hell, the drama of her *life*—were catching up. Her determination waned alongside her energy. "I'm so tired. So damn tired of being afraid of him."

Quinn leaned into his desk, and his eyes filled with fervor. "You don't have to be afraid anymore, Alex. I *will* protect you." She opened her mouth to respond, but he hurried on. "I don't care if you don't think you need protecting. *I* think you do. *Joe* thinks you do. I also don't care if you think that me protecting you won't do any good. Because I *know* it will. If that makes me some sort of caveman, then so be it. If you're tired of being afraid of him, then fine, you'll face him. But Alex, I will be damned if you're going to face that bastard alone."

Was he for real?

His blind support overwhelmed her. She didn't know how to react. How to *trust*.

"Thanks, Sheriff," she said, drawing into herself. She'd tried to keep her tone cool, distant, but there'd been a tinge of panic. She hoped he hadn't heard it.

Quinn slammed the mug onto his desk, and it broke with a loud crack.

"Dammit," he growled. He mopped up the spilled coffee with tissues, making a bigger mess. Frustration emanated from his pores as he pushed the soggy heap to the side.

"Don't do that, Alex. Don't 'Thanks, Sheriff' me. You know damn well that this has nothing to do with me being the sheriff."

"Do I?" The moment the words left her mouth, she regretted them. Why was she suddenly hell-bent on pushing him away?

"Yes. You do." He met her stare. "Regardless of whatever walls you want to build around yourself to keep me out, regardless of whatever crap comes out of Roxie's damn mouth, yes. You do."

She crossed her arms over her chest like a sullen child. Her emotions ricocheted around like out-of-control pinballs.

"Alex, if you want to pick a fight with me because you're mad, that's fine. If you want to pick a fight because you're scared, no problem. But if you're doing it to get a rise out of me—to make me berate you or hit you—then you're out of luck. Because *that* is never going to happen."

She wanted to scream. What was wrong with her? She *did* know he cared about her beyond his civic duties. His actions, his words . . . that kiss . . . They were all proof.

Maybe he was right. Maybe part of her *was* looking for a fight. Simply put, the man was too good to be true. And that was petrifying. If he was going to hit her, she'd rather it happened sooner than later. Then she could run away and say she'd been right.

She knew she wasn't being fair. She knew good men existed. But even if Quinn was one of them—and she believed he was—then she still had to contend with her insecurities. Her doubt that she deserved to be with a man like him.

What a freaking mess she was making of things.

"You're right," she said on an exhale, taking in the man before her. "I am picking a fight with you, and I'm sorry. I'm not being fair to you and—" Wincing, she pointed at his hand. "Uh, Quinn, you cut yourself."

Glancing at the blood dripping from his palm, he muttered a creative obscenity. With a growl, he excused himself.

A few minutes later, he returned with his hand bandaged. A young, uniformed man with bright-red hair and a face full of freckles accompanied him.

"Alex, this is Deputy Chase. He was at Roxie's place earlier today."

She rose and shook the deputy's outstretched hand.

"Chase will be helping out in our investigation. He's looking into the flower delivery and checking with the phone company on all the calls to your landline since you've arrived. Thanks, Chase. That'll be all for now."

"Nice to meet you, ma'am." He flashed her a smile, then gave Quinn a nod before taking his leave.

Once again seated behind his desk, Quinn said, "It's almost noon—"

At the same time, Alex asked, "Why aren't you—"

"Sorry," he said. "What was that?"

"No, go ahead," she urged.

He gestured with his bandaged hand for her to continue.

"Well, it's kind of a stupid question, but why aren't you wearing your uniform? Everyone else is. Day off?"

With that lopsided grin that made her heart ping, he shook his head. And just like that, all their earlier tension evaporated.

"No, it's not my day off. It's pretty simple, really. The way I figure it is that I'm the boss and, as the boss, if I don't want to wear a uniform, then I don't have to. See, simple."

"Don't you mean, 'pretty arrogant'?" She gave him a saccharine smile. No way was she buying what he was saying. Not only was he usually in uniform, but he was the last person to act like he was better than anyone. Boss or not.

"Semantics, darlin'." He shot her a wink and stood from his desk. "I'm totally kidding about the uniform, by the way. I almost always wear mine in. You have to lead by example, have to have pride in what you do. And I do. It's truly an honor to wear the uniform and—"

He stopped abruptly, and she could have sworn she saw a flicker of surprise and embarrassment cross his face. Like he'd said more than he'd intended.

She stared at him. He was a man who obviously took pride in his position but didn't go on and on about it. For some reason, that fascinated her. *He* fascinated her.

"Truth is, I was at the gym this morning and ended up running late. I didn't have time to swing back to my house to grab my uniform. Luckily, I had these in my gym bag"—he indicated his outfit—"or else I'd still be in sweats and a T-shirt."

Nodding toward the door, where a garment bag hung from a hook, he added, "I always have a couple extra uniforms here. I planned on changing, but the morning . . . got away from me."

She grimaced. "Imagine that . . ."

"Yeah, imagine that." He chuckled. "Care to join me for lunch? We can go over what Chase finds when we get back."

"Sure," she said, rising from the chair. She snuck peeks at him as she put her jacket on.

"What?" he asked, noticing her observation.

"I can't figure you out," she said. "One minute, you're the tough Sheriff O'Conner who's all professional and bad-cop mean—"

"Mean?" He laughed. "I'm never mean. I'm *direct*. If you think that's mean, then you need to toughen up, sweetheart."

She rolled her eyes. "And then the next minute, you're back to being easygoing and flirty. I can't figure you out."

He opened the door and placed his hand on the small of her back. "I don't think anyone has ever described me as easygoing before. I'll take it, though. And, for the record, I *don't* flirt."

It was her turn to laugh. "Sure you don't, mister. I bet Mrs. Abbot and Mrs. Yoshida would beg to differ."

As would she. Not that she minded him flirting with her. Not at all.

CHAPTER TWENTY-THREE

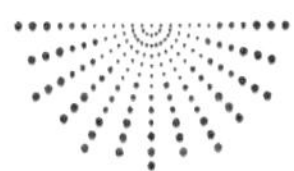

Beating the lunch rush, Quinn and Alex settled into a booth at Ray's Diner. Shouting over his shoulder to a line cook, the diner's owner, Ray, tossed a set of menus on the table. He put two glasses of water down without looking up, muttering something under his breath about the line cook.

"Sheriff. The usual, I assume?" Ray lifted his head and froze when he saw Alex. The man stood taller and fixed his suspenders. "Well now, Sheriff. Who's this lovely little thing you've got here?"

Quinn rolled his eyes, which earned him a scowl from Ray. He wisely smothered a snicker. He knew from much experience that a warning scowl from Ray was usually followed by a smack to the head.

"Alex, this is Ray. Ray's second-in-command here. His much better half, Martha, runs the show. Ray, this is Alex."

"Don't you mind that fool, sugar," Ray drawled, bringing Alex's hand to his lips.

Quinn laughed. "Now *that,* sweetheart, is what you call flirting."

Ray continued as if Quinn hadn't spoken. "This fool's been the laziest of the lot since he was knee-high. Since you're obviously new to town, I ought to warn you that you'd best start keeping better company. This one will get you into nothing but trouble."

Alex's eyes widened, and her expression became innocence personified. "How's that possible, Ray? Quinn's the sheriff."

God, she was adorable.

"Don't let that ugly mug of his fool you, honey. He's nothing but trouble," Ray repeated. "Now, how 'bout I fix you up something special?" He gave Alex the once-over before heading toward the kitchen. As he walked away, he called, "I'll have my Martha put a little extra in it. You look a bit food-deprived."

Alex choked on her water. "'Food-deprived?'" she croaked once Ray was out of earshot.

He shrugged. "Ray likes his women with a bit more meat on their bones. Besides, you are a bit on the scrawny side."

In this case, scrawny equaled petite, delicately curved in all the right places, and smoking hot. But he had to hassle her.

"I am *not* scrawny."

"Sweetheart, you're what? Five feet tall?"

"I'm five foot *one and a half*, thank you very much."

Yup, fucking adorable.

"Oh. Pardon me. And you're what?" He gave her the same once-over Ray had—though he was positive he appreciated her figure much, much more than Ray. Meat on her bones or not, he liked every damn thing about her. "A buck-oh-five soaking wet with combat boots on?"

She crossed her arms over her chest and glared, but not before he saw a flicker of amusement in her eyes.

"Exactly, sweetheart. You have to admit, from up here, you're pretty scrawny."

"'From up here'?" she mimicked playfully. "What's that supposed to mean?"

"I'm six-two and have more than a hundred pounds on you." He looked her over again. But slower this time. Much slower. "Not that I'm complaining. Because—between the two of us, of course—you're absolutely stunning."

Her cheeks turned pink. "You think you're so charming, don't you, Quinn O'Conner?"

"No, not really." He reached across the table and tucked a renegade lock of hair behind her ear. "It's usually too much effort. But there's something about you . . ."

He meant to pull his hand away, but instead, he lingered. He couldn't help it. Her breath caught as he caressed her jawline with the back of his finger. He traced the pulse along the side of her neck, and satisfaction surged through him when it quickened.

What he would give to taste that soft, delicate spot. He traced her pulse again.

Right there. And a little bite, too.

"Ahem."

He leaned back in the booth. Good fucking god. He'd forgotten where the hell he was. All he'd been able to focus on was the sweet, kissable spot that he was dying to—

Holy. Shit.

Focus, O'Conner. You're in the middle of the damn diner.

Glancing up, his eyes locked with Martha's. The ruler of Ray's Diner, clad in her trademark bubblegum-pink 1950s diner uniform, was carrying two plates heaped with food and sporting the biggest shit-eating grin he'd ever seen. The woman loved it when she had a scoop for Hudson Island's gossip mill.

"Now, you must be Alex," Martha said, placing an ungodly amount of food in front of her. "Ray did say you were a wee little thing."

He chuckled as Martha set his plate down in front of him. Then, before he could blink, she smacked him on the back of the head. Hard. "Don't tease the little thing, young man. Last time I checked, you weren't in elementary school."

Alex's eyes went wide, and her mouth fell open. He couldn't tell if she was horrified or amused. Probably a little bit of both. He rubbed the back of his head and bit down a smile. "Sorry, Martha," he mumbled.

"Alex, it's nice to meet you. I'm Martha. If there's anything else you need, you just holler. Or my little Scarlet"—she pointed across the diner to a young waitress whose brown hair was liberally streaked with teal, pink, and purple—"can help you out as well. Don't let the rainbow on her head fool you; the sweet girl has a memory like a steel trap. Also, please don't pay any mind to what my Ray says about Quinn here."

The woman paused to pat him on the head. Like a dog. "Quinn is just the sweetest thing you'll ever meet. Granted, he can be as stubborn as a mule and sometimes he makes me want to box his ears, but that's okay because he truly is a good boy."

He closed his eyes. *Holy shit, kill me now.*

"And as you can plainly see for yourself, our Quinn's not hard on the eyes. Not one bit. Well, I'll let you enjoy your food. And Quinn?"

To his dismay, Martha smoothed the collar of his shirt and patted his cheek. Like a four-year-old. Heat engulfed his face. "Yes, ma'am?"

"You make sure she eats up. We need to get some padding on those little bones of hers. Winter will be here before you know it. We can't have her freezing to death."

He watched as Martha shuffled away, paused, then looked

back at them. She shot him two thumbs-ups before disappearing through the kitchen door.

"Why, Quinn O'Conner, are you blushing?"

Alex's eyes danced with delight. The heat on his face intensified. He cleared his throat and pointed to her plate with his fork. "Eat."

Face glowing with merriment, she took a bite of her perfectly golden hash browns and closed her eyes in blissful appreciation. His thoughts immediately hit the gutter.

Damn, she was gorgeous.

"'Winter will be here before you know it.'" She laughed and forked a bite of her scramble. "Good thing I still have time to add on some extra 'padding.'"

He hadn't seen Alex this relaxed, this carefree . . . at all. Not even once.

Embarrassment be damned. He'd let Martha fawn over him every damn day if it allowed Alex to momentarily forget her troubles.

They finished up at Ray's and walked back to the station. Quinn was well aware of the many local eyebrows that were raised in response to his long lunch and stroll with the town's mysterious stranger, but he paid them no mind.

Stacks of manila folders greeted them when they entered his office.

"Looks like Chase is earning his keep." He pressed a button on his landline and called in Deputy Chase. As Alex seated herself at the worktable at the far end of his office, he shot her a wink. "Sorry, sweetheart, but I guess it's back to bad-cop mean."

Deputy Chase arrived with his laptop, and they turned to the task at hand.

"What did you find, Chase?"

"Over the past three weeks, there have been twenty-seven calls to the Buchanan house's landline," the deputy said, reading from a paper in one of the folders. "Eight of those were either from Doc Buchanan or his clinic. With the exception of three calls, I was able to track the rest to known solicitors and robocall centers. The first unknown call was two days ago on Tuesday at 10:47 p.m. Duration under a minute. The next unknown was yesterday at 8:07 p.m. Again, under a minute. The most recent was this morning at 3:21 a.m. This one was just under three minutes."

After a few clicks on his laptop, Deputy Chase projected a map of the United States onto Quinn's whiteboard and marked three cities. "The first call was from Louisville, Kentucky. The second was near Sioux Falls, South Dakota, and the third was from Sturgis, South Dakota. All calls were placed from different cell numbers—looks like burner phones—but they all pinged near rest stops along the major interstates."

Pausing, Deputy Chase opened another folder. "Petal Pushers on Front Street delivered the flowers today. Jenny—" He turned his attention to Alex—"she's the flower shop's owner. Anyway, she said the order came in this morning via phone. The only thing she could recall was it was a man who placed the order."

"How'd he pay?" Quinn asked.

"Credit card. We're checking with the credit card company now. If the guy's an idiot, then he'll have used his own. Unfortunately, chances are it's a pre-paid deal that's registered to a fake email. Jenny said the phone order came in just after eight this morning, and she sent them out on their 9:30 a.m. delivery route. I checked with the phone company, and they have that call coming in from Sheridan, Wyoming. Another cell that pinged near a rest area on I-90."

Quinn frowned. If you followed I-90 all the way west, it took you right into Seattle. From there, it was one ferry ride —or two, depending on which route you took—to Hudson. *Fuck.*

"Hang on," he said, moving to his desk phone. As soon as the call connected, he said, "It's O'Conner. Call me back and make it private."

Within seconds, his cell phone rang. He pressed the speakerphone button. "O'Conner."

"You summoned?"

"I've got you on speakerphone with Deputy Chase and Alex—"

"Hey, doll, how are you?" Joe crooned.

Quinn continued before Alex could respond. "Alex has been getting phone calls at the house. Chase traced them." He relayed the dates, times, and locations of each call. "The last one included a subtle personal message. Then, around eight this morning, a man near Sheridan, Wyoming placed an order with Petal Pushers to be delivered to *Alex*. Not *Natalie*. The delivery address was Roxie's café. The flower selection and personal note included with them clearly indicated Woodsworth's involvement."

He paused to take a breath. Adrenaline coursed through his veins. The sensation was familiar, but this time, its cause wasn't the thrill of a new investigation; it was pure rage.

Somewhere out there, a bastard had the balls to threaten Alex.

Quinn wouldn't stand for it.

"Someone's on the move, Buchanan, and I want to know who the fuck it is."

"Well, it's not Woodsworth, if that's what you're thinking. I'm in Boston now, and he's still locked up nice and tight here."

"Visitors?"

"Only one. His lawyer. Last visit was two days ago. No one else."

Scenarios and possibilities raced through Quinn's mind. "Does he have internet access?"

"Yeah, Woodsworth has access. But no, that's not it. We've been monitoring that."

"Phone calls?"

"Again, only his lawyer."

"It's the lawyer then." He slapped his desk. That had to be it.

"Strike three, Connie. Sorry. We've got an ear on all the lawyer's conversations, both in person and over the phone."

Alex's eyes narrowed in confusion.

"What is it?" Quinn asked her.

"Isn't wiretapping a person's conversations with their lawyer illegal? Even if you're the FBI?" Alex shook her head. "Not that I care about Preston's rights or anything, but aren't you going to get into trouble for doing that?"

"There are a number of federal provisions and technicalities that give us the okay," Joe answered. "Off the record, of course."

Quinn leaned back in his chair and scrubbed his hands over his face. He was close. He could feel it in his gut. But where was that damn missing piece?

"So, who is it then, Buchanan? It has to be someone connected to Woodsworth. A cellmate? A cellmate's contact, maybe?"

"I don't know. I'll see what I can find out. Hey, Connie, I have to go," Joe said in a rush. "I'll look into things and let you know. Good work, Chase. And Alex?"

"Yes?"

"Hang in there, doll. O'Conner's got your back."

With that, the line went dead.

Quinn growled. All his muscles were coiled tight.

After all that, he was no closer to knowing who was threatening Alex. He just had more questions than ever and not a single answer.

Damn. Wasn't that always the way of things?

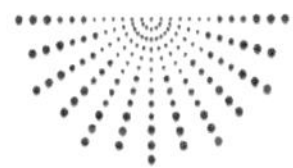

CHAPTER TWENTY-FOUR

Quinn sat on his living room sofa staring at the logs crackling in the fireplace. The Pacific Northwest's weather was temperamental, so even though it was late April, the brisk chill had yet to leave the air.

He heard the water running in his master bathroom and tried not to think about the fact that Alex was currently naked in his tub.

Yeaaah. Who was he kidding? He wasn't trying that hard.

Restless, he tromped to the kitchen and popped open a beer. His thoughts kept returning to Alex. Her heartbreaking words echoed in his head.

I guess when things get to be too much, my head knows its own limit and shuts down.

What he wouldn't give to make everything better for her . . .

Beer in hand, he settled back onto the couch, replaying his last face-to-face conversation with Joe in his mind.

"How involved with Alex are you really?"

"Not in the way you're hinting at, asshole," Joe replied. "When Alex was Mrs. Natalie Woodsworth, my job was to watch her pompous, jackass douche of a husband. I tried to befriend her to get an in, but both times I talked with her, she got her face pummeled. So, I kept my focus on him and off her."

Joe laughed, but the sound was hollow. Humorless. "The reason Alex is here is a goddamn fluke. The powers that be were getting impatient and told me I needed to make contact immediately. So, I went over there that day for a neighborly cup of sugar."

Quinn's stomach clenched as disgust colored Joe's features.

"I was walking up their driveway and saw their garage door was open, so I headed that way. When I peeked in, I saw the interior door was open, too. There was really loud music playing, but I could hear Woodsworth screaming like a fucking lunatic. I crept in closer, and he was kneeling on the floor over something, but I couldn't tell what. My gut was howling that something was wrong, so I moved closer and saw her lying under him. Woodsworth was fucking wailing on her."

Nausea washed over him, and he took his seat behind his desk.

With an aggravated sigh, his friend laced his fingers atop his head. "Damn woman was a trooper, though. She was trying to fight back and defend herself. Then the next thing I know, Woodsworth pulls a knife off the counter. I'm running toward her. She's trying to scramble away. Then, for a split second, I swear our eyes locked. She almost managed to crawl away . . . but she didn't. In the few seconds it took for me to get to them, he just fucking hacked away at her. It was like the goddamn shower scene in Psycho."

Joe's hands dropped from his head, and his shoulders slumped. "When the paramedics arrived, she was unconscious. Barely breathing. I thought she was dead. It was fucking awful."

The haunted misery in his friend's eyes was something he'd never witnessed in all their years together. It had Quinn's simmering anger boiling over to a white-hot rage. He had to take a few deep breaths before he could speak.

"How did you not kill that motherfucker?" he ground out at last.

Not only did he want that asshole destroyed for Alex's sake, but now for Joe's, too.

"It was tempting, believe me." He shook his head. "I was with her in the hospital when she woke up. She barely remembered Woodsworth attacking her or seeing me. Thank fucking god she blacked out most of the details. Sucks for us, witness-wise. But it's probably better for her."

"What are you doing in here by yourself?"

He kept his gaze on the fire and didn't bother to mask his annoyance. "Roxie, can't a man sit by the fire in his own fucking living room and drink a beer in silence?"

"Nope. At least not if I live nearby. And don't swear at me, asshole. Why is your water running?"

He groaned in frustration and twisted to face Roxie. She stood in the living room archway, hands on her hips, poised for a fight.

"Alex is taking a bath. She had a rough fucking day. I figured she could use a nice, *quiet* soak in the tub somewhere safe. You got a problem with that?"

She threw her hands up in surrender. "Jesus, Quinn. I'm sorry, okay! You know I hate apologizing—"

"I really don't care, Roxie." He turned his attention back to the flames dancing in the fireplace. "It's been a long-ass day, and I'm not in the mood for you right now."

"That's fair."

The lack of sarcasm in her voice had his gaze swinging back to her. His brow furrowed. A tiny part of him felt bad for his friend. But the other part was still pissed.

"Look, I know I was a total bitch today. And I'm really sorry. I was super stressed out because I've got my first big catering gig tomorrow night, and Mayor Green's wife has been *hounding* me since five thirty this morning. Then, when Alex showed up to work late and was acting all out of it, it pushed me over the edge. My imagination got away from me because I knew you were over at her place last night and—"

Whoa. He flinched. Hard. Like she'd dumped a bucket of ice water over his head. "What the hell, Roxie?"

"Ewww, Quinn. I wasn't thinking of you like *that.*" She shuddered, and her face scrunched in revulsion. He had never been more thankful. "My point is I wasn't rational. I let my temper stew, and I didn't think. Then you mosey on in, completely ignore the fact that I'm running a friggin' business, and start coddling her like she's some broken little child, and, I don't know, I just snapped, okay?"

"Was there an apology somewhere in there?" A non-apology apology. Classic Roxie.

She frowned. "Now you're just being a jackass. You know I hate it when you're mad at me. I said that I was sor—"

"Rox," he interrupted with a tired sigh, the fight in him gone. "I don't care what you say to me. I never have. You can tell me to fuck off and spit nails at me for all I care." He rose, crossed the room, slung his arm over her shoulder, and yanked her into a hug. "I've heard it all from you before, and sure as shit, I'll hear it all again." He pulled slightly away to look at her. "The apology you owe is to Alex. Not me. And when you go and tell her you're sorry, it'd be appreciated if you—oh, I don't know—painted me as less of a man-whore to her."

"Yeaaah. About that." Her eyes closed, and she grimaced, embarrassment staining her cheeks. "Sorry for the flavor-of-the-month bit. I think I was projecting." His brows lifted at her explanation, but she didn't give him a chance to comment. Her eyes flew open, and she said, "I know! How about I make you guys dinner tonight? I'll make a fabulous meal and leave. I promise. Will that make up for it?"

Classic Roxie. Her mind was like a crazy multi-ball pinball machine.

"That works for me. But stay for dinner."

Worried green eyes met his.

"Talk to her, Roxie. Make it right. She needs all the friends and support she can get right now."

———

Utterly relaxed, Alex sank deeper into the tub. Quinn had been right. A long soak was exactly what she'd needed. It had been a rollercoaster day, but when she thought back on her lunch with Quinn, she couldn't help but smile.

For one brief moment, she'd been a regular woman having lunch with a man who—if she were being completely honest with herself—she was wildly attracted to. It'd been just food, conversation, and perhaps a little bit of flirting, but the simplicity of it all had made her feel so blessedly normal.

Foreign, giddy hope had stirred in her belly while they'd sat in their booth. As if whatever they had between them— the comfort, the electricity—could lead to something more. Something meaningful.

But then lunch had ended, and they'd returned to the stark reality of her life: her pregnancy, her not quite ex-husband . . . the flowers, the mystery calls. Talk about a letdown.

Her heart sank.

How could being reminded of her pregnancy be a letdown?

She was an awful person.

Stepping out of the tub, she picked up a plush towel and began to wipe herself dry. When she got to her abdomen, she paused.

There was a tiny little baby in her womb.

Years earlier, when she'd been told that she couldn't have kids, she'd been devastated. So, now that she was pregnant, she should be thrilled.

And she was. Most days. But when she really thought about the enormity of what was to come . . . she panicked.

She knew women had children by themselves all the time. But still. The idea of raising this child on her own terrified her. Though, it wasn't the logistics of single parenthood that kept her awake at night, that crippled her with waves of anxiety. It was doubt.

What if she couldn't fully love this baby?

The thought alone made her feel like a monster.

Her chest squeezed painfully hard. Shame and fear brought stinging tears to her eyes.

She'd always wanted to be a mother. But what if she was a horrible one? What if, when she looked at her baby, all she could see was the abuse and violence Preston had subjected her to?

A shiver racked her body.

No, dammit. She couldn't think like that.

She had to stay strong. To remember that despite its dark and heartbreaking conception, the baby was *hers*. Not Preston's.

She had to stay strong. She had to.

She finished drying herself off, repeating her mantra.

You have nothing to be ashamed of. Nothing. It's time to let go of the guilt and allow yourself to move on.

When both her mind and spirit had calmed, she wrapped herself in the soft, fluffy towel and glanced at the fresh clothes Quinn had laid out for her. Donning the oversized garments, she caught her reflection and smiled, a miracle considering the darkness of her earlier thoughts.

Simply put, the clothes were ridiculous. The faded, tissue-soft T-shirt—which she imagined fit Quinn quite well—came down past her hips, and the sleeves past her elbows. The jogging shorts, even when rolled at the waist, hit below her knees.

After towel-drying her hair, she pulled on a pair of too-large socks, knotted the shirt at the small of her back, and chuckled at her outfit. It would do.

The aroma of something spicy and Italian tickled her nose as she left Quinn's master suite. Her mouth watered and her stomach growled in appreciation. She entered the kitchen and came to a halt, her jaw dropping at the spread laid out on the dining table. A loaf of steaming garlic bread sat next to what had to be the best looking—and smelling— lasagna she'd ever seen.

"I hope you don't mind."

Shoulders tensing, she turned to find Roxie. A quick scan showed no sign of Quinn.

"I put together the lasagna earlier today as kind of a peace offering." Roxie shoved her hands into the pockets of her jeans and shifted on her feet. "I was hoping to have a chance to talk to you as well." Abruptly, she went to a cabinet, pulled out three wine glasses, and began filling two with wine. "I know I can be a lot at work. I get stupidly territorial over my café. But that's no excuse for the way I acted today. I'm really sorry I got snappy at you this morning."

Alex waited. When someone apologized, there was usually a catch.

"It's not an excuse, but Mrs. Green, the mayor's wife, has me so freaking stressed out. They're having a big party tomorrow night, and I know she took a chance hiring me for their catering instead of their usual people. God knows the woman's told me enough times what a giant risk it is for her."

Roxie pinched the bridge of her nose. "I didn't realize things were off with you. I just thought you were being flaky. But that's *my* thing, not yours. And . . . you really should know I hate doing this . . . but I *am* sorry for being such a bitch to you. I'm also really sorry I made those jabs about you and Quinn. I was being a complete jackass." Roxie shrugged. "There is one thing I can't apologize for, though."

Of course. Here was the catch. "And that would be?"

"Alex, I love Quinn. I love him with all my heart. I really do."

Her breath lodged in her throat.

Holy hell. She *loved* him? She could've sworn Roxie had said there was nothing between them. Damn. Did Quinn know?

Holy shit.

Did he feel the same way?

The possibility that Quinn was just messing around with her, that he didn't care at all, that she really was his flavor of the month, had the blood draining from her face.

"W-wow," Alex stammered. "I thought you said the two of you weren't . . ." Swallowing, she willed her brain to find the words. Any words. "I'm *so* sorry. I truly didn't realize—"

Roxie gasped. "Oh, shit! No, no, no. It's not like *that*," she said in a rush. "Listen, I love Quinn. I do—though I often wonder why—but not in the way you mean. Like I said before, he and I, as a romantic couple, would never work. But I've known him my entire life, and he's my best friend. Don't get me wrong, Alex, I like you. I really do. But I *love* him. There are only a handful of people I truly love with all my heart. And Quinn's one of them."

She crossed her arms over her chest. Where was Roxie going with this?

"Alex, I know you mean a lot to him, and I *suppose* my shitty attitude this morning may have included some petty jealousy. I'm sorry for that. But I'll be honest with you"—a hint of challenge entered her voice—"in my own little way, I'll test you, whether consciously or not, because Quinn deserves the best. I mean no offense at all, but I'm not sure yet if that's you."

Her brows hit her hairline. Well, then.

What had just spewed from Roxie's mouth was a bit insulting, and yet oddly admirable.

"Fair enough," she said. "You're entitled to your opinions, and I can respect that. Honestly, I'm glad he has a loyal friend looking out for him."

"I do truly apologize if I hurt you with my earlier oh-so-mature behavior . . . and my flavor-of-the-month comment. I hope you know that Quinn's really not like that. So, I'm sorry." With a hopeful smile, Roxie extended her arms out to Alex. "We okay?"

As far as apologies went, Roxie's might have been the most rambling one ever. But it *was* an apology. With no apparent catch.

"We're good," she said, giving the other woman a hug.

Beaming, Roxie turned and opened the refrigerator. She retrieved two cartons of grape juice, one red and one white, and held them up for inspection. "Merlot or chardonnay?"

Alex chuckled. Though a bit work crazy and overprotective of her best friend, Roxie really was sweet.

"Merlot, please."

Quinn had been banished to the backyard so Roxie could apologize. When he heard laughter coming from the kitchen, he figured it was safe to return. Closing the door behind him, he stopped dead in his tracks.

Alex. Leaning against the counter. Swimming in his favorite Seahawks T-shirt, jogging shorts, and socks.

It wasn't an attractive outfit. No woman he knew would willingly be caught dead in that getup.

She should've looked ridiculous.

He bit back a groan.

Should was the operative word.

His mouth turned to dust.

Her still-damp hair cascaded down her back like a black waterfall. Her skin glowed—yeah, fucking *glowed*—and there was a twinkle in her brown eyes as she listened to Roxie tell a story with animated enthusiasm.

Damn. He'd never wanted a woman more.

She caught his eye and smiled.

Holy shit.

His heart thunked. Hard. That smile annihilated him. It made her light up as if someone had turned a spotlight on her. And to know that she was happy to see him was amazing. Humbling. Fucking fantastic.

For a few heartbeats, she held his gaze. Her eyes softened, then . . . heated.

His pulse quickened and something shifted deep in his chest. Whatever it was, it felt right, felt so damn good, and he knew it had been slowly building since he'd met her.

One smile.

That's all it had taken to push him over the edge. This beautiful little slip of a woman had just soured him to all others. With one damn smile.

The air shifted as Quinn stepped into the kitchen, and she became acutely aware of her racing heart.

He wore the same clothes as earlier, but his blue corduroy shirt was now unbuttoned, the sleeves rolled up to his elbows, and his white T-shirt underneath was untucked from his jeans. His dark hair was tousled, and as he watched her, he ran a hand over the stubble covering his jaw.

Edible.

The man was positively edible.

There was an intensity in his misty gray eyes she hadn't seen before, and her fingers ached with the need to touch him.

"Alex?"

She jerked, bringing her attention back to Roxie. She knew her face was flushed, but she somehow resisted the urge to fan herself.

She cleared her throat. "What was that again?"

"Tomorrow. That still works for you, right?"

She struggled to recall what Roxie had been talking about, but all thoughts evaporated as Quinn sauntered toward her, his smoldering eyes locked on hers.

"Sure. Tomorrow's great."

She tried to focus on Roxie. She really did. But no matter how hard she tried, she couldn't pry her eyes from Quinn.

"Roxie," he said, his voice raspy, his gaze never wavering from hers. "I think I hear your landline ringing."

Roxie mumbled a response, then bolted out the back door toward the guesthouse.

Before the door fully shut, Quinn snagged Alex by the waist and hauled her against his chest. His lips crashed down on hers, and fire rushed through her veins.

Closer. She needed to be closer.

In one fluid motion, he set her on the counter and stepped between her knees. Wrapping her arms around his neck, she pressed every inch of her body flush against him. His hands ran reverently up her torso as his tongue explored her mouth. A soft moan escaped her lips when he caressed her breasts, and she sank her fingers into his hair.

Breathless, she pulled her head back and framed his face in her hands. "Wait, we can't," she said. "Roxie . . ."

Resting his forehead against hers, he shot her a sexy grin

that went straight to her heart. And between her thighs. "Yeah, having her walk in on us going at it on the counter probably would be awkward, huh?" He kissed her softly on the nose before helping her down from the counter. Then he adjusted the obvious bulge straining his jeans.

She chuckled. "I think that's a safe bet."

Going on instinct, she rose to her tiptoes and dragged him back down, quickly kissing his lips.

Before her heels could return to the ground, he spun her so her back was to his chest. He held her in his warm embrace, and the rapid beating of his heart soothed her; she wasn't alone in her feelings.

"Holy shit, woman." His chest rumbled as if he was trying to hold in a laugh, then he exhaled loudly. "I think you may kill me."

Roxie burst into the kitchen, her cordless phone in hand.

"Damn," he muttered. "I knew I should have bolted the door."

The other woman paused, head tilted to the side, and gave them an obvious once-over. A mischievous smile grew on her face. "All right, kiddies. Dinner is served."

CHAPTER TWENTY-FIVE

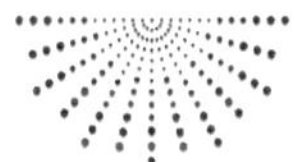

"Thanks for dinner, Roxie. That may go down as the best lasagna I've ever had." Alex relaxed in her chair and sighed in contentment. "Don't worry about cleaning up. I'll take care of it."

Roxie topped off her own glass of wine. "Oh, don't worry there. I don't clean."

Quinn rose and began clearing the table. "She really doesn't."

"I'm a cooker, not a cleaner." Roxie stood, glass in hand, and made a beeline for the back door. "Alex, I'll see you tomorrow. And thanks again for agreeing to come in early. It's our first big catering job, so I really appreciate you helping with the party. Night guys!"

As Roxie pulled the door firmly shut, Alex's mouth dropped open. What had she agreed to?

Her eyes narrowed. She had a sneaking suspicion that she'd been outmaneuvered. Again.

"You're helping Rox with Mayor Green's party tomorrow?"

She brought the remaining dishes from the table to the

sink and took a moment to watch him load the dishwasher. What was it about a gorgeous man doing housework?

"In a bout of distraction, I think I may have agreed to help out." She frowned. "Remember how you said Roxie has a grand master plan for asking you things when you're not exactly paying attention?"

"Yeah?"

Standing next to him, she leaned back against the counter. "I think you may be onto something."

"You know what I think?" He shut off the water, then dried his hands on a towel, a sly grin spreading across his face. "I think the rest of the dishes can wait until tomorrow. What do you think?"

Before she could blink, he hauled her close. His head dipped, and he trailed kisses along her neck.

All thoughts vanished. All she could do was feel.

His soft lips.

His strong hands.

His hard body.

Her eyes drifted shut, and she tilted her head, giving him more access. She ran her hands up his muscular back and laced her fingers behind his neck. Tugging him closer, she enjoyed the sparks his talented mouth detonated along her skin.

Her eyes flew open when he hoisted her onto the counter. She spread her thighs and grabbed a fistful of his shirt, yanking him back to her. When she wrapped her legs around his waist, drawing his hips flush against her, the fire that burned in his gray eyes raged into an inferno.

His lips crashed into hers, and she couldn't help the moan that escaped. Tingles shot from the top of her spine down to her toes as they devoured each other.

When they came up for air, Quinn lifted her from the counter. She locked her ankles at his lower back and glued herself to his chest. His heart thumped hard against hers, its racing beat matching her own.

His hands cradled her ass as he walked them into the living room. He came to a stop in front of the couch, and she drew slightly away. Their breaths were ragged. The evidence of his desire pressed into her, and she rocked her hips against his hard length. His eyes blazed for her. *Her.*

She knew that if she asked him to stop, he would. No questions asked. And he wouldn't be mad. Frustrated, perhaps, but not mad.

Quinn would never hurt her the way Preston had. Ever.

Yes, things were beyond complicated, but she knew without a shadow of a doubt that she could trust him. Her body, her heart, her very soul—all were safe with this man.

With her legs still wrapped around him, she placed her hands on either side of his jaw, caressing the stubble there and running a thumb over his delicious lips. She studied his face, and only one word remained in her brain.

Mine.

Gone was the doubt. Gone was the chaos. Gone was the fear.

All that remained was him.

Quinn.

He was passion, sweetness, and trust. He was hope.

She brought her mouth to his, licking at his lower lip. While their tongues tangled and explored, she tried to show him in one kiss how much he'd come to mean to her.

With a moan, he lowered her onto the couch and lay over her, his arms supporting his weight. His hands roamed her body, setting off tiny explosions everywhere he touched. She pushed off his corduroy shirt and tugged up his T-shirt, the desperation to feel his bare skin on hers overwhelming.

"Quinn, I need you so much," she murmured.

Every touch, every kiss thrilled her. She'd never experienced this kind of hunger before. And yet, she wanted more. She wanted it all.

She wanted him.

Shifting his weight to one arm, he slipped his free hand under her shirt, and she drew in a sharp breath. Her core throbbed with need, desperate for what she hoped was to come. He stroked from the base of her neck to the band of the jogging shorts she wore, caressing and exploring every inch of her skin in between.

She moaned, drowning in pleasure when his fingers traced the underside of her small, firm breasts. He cupped and squeezed them, then rolled her hard nipples between his fingers, and she pulsed. Gasping for air, she arched in anticipation as he pulled up her borrowed shirt and lowered his head to her chest. His mouth closed over her breast, his tongue rolling over her nipple.

"More, Quinn," she begged, burning, rocking against his hard cock. "I need to touch you. Please."

He sat up obligingly and made haste removing both of their shirts.

Her jaw dropped. Sculpted torso, rippling abs, a dusting of hair over a chest that narrowed down and disappeared into his jeans. Jeans that did nothing to hide his straining erection.

The man was exquisite.

The desire to lick him, taste every delicious inch of him, washed over her.

For the first time in forever, she was safe to take what she wanted. So she didn't hesitate. Trailing her lips and tongue over his chest, she smiled when he groaned out her name.

Mine. This man is mine.

Quinn wasn't sure he could control himself much longer. He was seconds away from exploding. And he still had his damn jeans on. Fuck, this woman was phenomenal.

"Holy shit, Alex." He pulled back and tried to catch his breath. She wrapped her arms around his neck, and, unable to resist, he leaned down to taste those kiss-swollen lips.

Their kiss alone had him teetering on the edge. He needed to taste more of this woman before he lost it. He wanted to watch—and feel—her come undone.

Gathering her in his arms, he lifted her off the couch. She weighed next to nothing as she enfolded her legs around his waist and ground against his straining cock. He groaned. He could feel the heat of her pussy through the layers of their clothes. He could smell her arousal, and his mouth watered.

Fuck. He needed her. Now.

Carrying her past the staircase, an image of him taking her on the stairs flickered in his mind. He paused.

No.

Bed first, dammit. Stairs later.

She was feasting on his neck, and his blood sizzled when she gently bit his shoulder. "Hurry, Quinn."

Reaching his bedroom, his eyes nearly rolled to the back of his head at another sensual bite. "You're killing me, baby."

He reclaimed her mouth as he laid her on his bed.

He wanted more. He wanted all of her. Mind. Body. Soul. Everything.

Untangling himself from her, he quickly removed the remainder of his clothes. Turning back to the bed, his mouth went dry. She'd also stripped and now sat naked on top of the blankets. Waiting for him.

The soft moonlight shining through the window fell over her, giving her an ethereal glow. His breath lodged in his chest. She was a fucking goddess.

She was *his* goddess.

Memorizing every delicate curve of her body, every feature of her face, he kneeled before her on the bed, drawing her up to her knees.

Her eyes locked onto his. "I need you, Quinn. And I don't want anything between us. I want you bare. I was tested, and I'm clean." She reached out and so damn slowly slid her hands up his torso, her stomach pressing against his weeping cock. "If you're okay with that—"

His control snapped.

His lips collided with hers and his hands wandered, touching as much of her as he could. She met his frenzied desire touch for touch, kiss for kiss. He leaned her head back to taste her neck, and his hands continued exploring her silky skin. His fingers trailed up her leg. She trembled when he traced circles on the soft skin of her inner thigh, and he smiled.

"Are you wet for me, baby?" he whispered, nipping at her earlobe.

"Please," she moaned.

Satisfaction surged through him when her wetness coated his fingers. Caressing her slick folds, need burned in his chest, in his cock, in his fucking soul.

More than anything, he wanted to bury his face between her legs and lick her until she screamed his name. But first, he wanted her to shatter on his hand.

He stroked and played, strumming and circling her clit while her hips rocked in growing urgency. Without breaking rhythm, he slid two fingers deep into her and moaned when she tightened around him. His cock grew painfully hard. He needed to be inside her.

"Come for me, sweetheart," he growled, working his fingers in and out of her wet pussy.

She gripped his shoulders, and his pleasure swelled when her nails dug into his flesh.

"That's it, baby," he murmured. "Ride my hand."

She jerked, her inner muscles milking his fingers, and screamed out his name. Then she slumped against his chest, dazed and boneless.

Damn, she was perfection.

Letting out a satisfied sigh, she framed his face in her hands and kissed him deeply, pulling him down on top of her.

"More," she whispered into his ear. "I need to feel you inside me." She wrapped her legs around him and closed her eyes.

He nuzzled her neck. "Open your eyes, sweetheart. I want you looking at me when I make you mine."

With their gazes locked, he entered her. Slowly. Her warm, wet pussy welcomed him in. Each inch stretched her, filled her. And he never wanted the moment to end.

There was fucking. There was sex. There was making love. And then there was *this*. The way her whiskey-brown eyes grew hazy with passion was awe-inspiring. The way her lips parted with longing made him want to claim that perfect mouth. And the way her tight body hugged his cock was absolute heaven.

When he was fully seated, her eyes darkened with desire, then lost focus. He moved within her molten core, stroking deep. He felt her inner muscles flutter, and his self-control slipped.

Thrusting harder, he brought his mouth to hers. Within seconds, she groaned his name against his lips, shuddering with her release. He pumped into her, riding out her orgasm, and she quaked again. Desire consumed him, and with a growl, he emptied inside her.

Everything tingled. From the tips of her toes all the way up to the very top of her head. Like a soft electrical current was buzzing through her. She felt freaking magnificent.

She let out a satiated sigh as the dead weight atop her murmured something she couldn't quite make out. She ran her fingers down the length of his muscular back and bottom. "What was that?"

Smiling, he shifted, taking his weight off her. "I said, you're absolutely amazing." He caressed the side of her face before kissing her. Thoroughly. "Am I crushing you?" he asked, his lips against hers.

She blinked. "Uh, what was the question?"

He grinned and kissed her again, and goosebumps erupted over her skin.

Oh, this man . . .

With a sleepy smile, he took her in his arms and rolled so she lay next to him, cradled against his chest.

Lying in the dark, a comfortable silence settled over them. Their heartbeats returned to normal; their breathing evened out.

"Alex?"

"Hmm."

"Where did you get Alex from?"

"What do you mean?" She adjusted her head more comfortably on his shoulder and ran her hand over his sculpted abdomen, her fingers tracing each indentation. "Seriously, Quinn, how do you even get muscles in your stomach like this?"

He chuckled. "There's a big fight gym slash training facility at the other end of the island. Have you met Cade yet?"

She shook her head and continued to trace over his abs. *Eight.* Not six. The man had an honest-to-god eight-pack.

"Well, you will. The man's a sucker for Roxie's pies. He

and his brother own the gym, and he happily kicks my ass every chance he gets. Boxing, jiu-jitsu, MMA—he freaking schools me. But I'm stubborn. Or a glutton for punishment. What can I say?" He kissed the top of her head, and she smiled. "When you decided you weren't going to go by Natalie anymore, what made you decide to pick the name Alexandra Garcia?"

Her chest clenched, but she didn't hesitate. She trusted him with her truth.

"My maiden name was Natalie Marie-Alejandra Stanton. After I got married, I dropped Alejandra and Stanton and went with Natalie Marie Woodsworth. Garcia is my mom's maiden name. When I was growing up, I had a crush on the boy across the street, and he always called me by my middle names. He thought it was funny that I had two.

"After a couple months, he decided Marie-Alejandra was too long, and he shortened it to Mary-Alex. It stuck, and before I knew it, all the neighborhood kids called me that. That name always made me smile, so when I was in the hospital, I decided to go with Alex. I'd always thought it was kind of spunky. I figured I could use all the spunk I could get."

She dipped her hand down to the V of his lower abdomen, smiling when he sucked in a breath.

"Now . . ." She sat up and straddled his thighs. "Are we going to keep talking about all this boring stuff?"

She ran her hands over his chest and ever so slowly moved them closer to where she knew he craved her touch. His abdominal muscles tightened as the tips of her fingers feathered over his stomach. She licked her lips when her hand encircled his hard, hot arousal.

She stroked his erection, and he moaned. "Alex, sweetheart, you don't have to—"

"Shhh." With her free hand, she placed a finger to his lips.

With her other, she pumped his straining cock until he was throbbing. "Just sit back and relax. I want to do this for you."

Replacing the finger she held to his lips with her mouth, she greedily tangled her tongue with his. He tasted of wine and spice and . . . Quinn.

She needed more of him. Much more.

While her fist maintained its rhythm, she blazed a fiery path of wet kisses down his chest. She shifted to kneel between his spread thighs, her lips mere inches away from his arousal. Her mouth watered.

She smiled up at him. When his breath caught, her grin grew. Keeping her gaze locked with his, she closed her lips around the plump head of his cock.

He was salty and delicious. She explored him with her mouth, rolling her tongue down his hard shaft and gently flicking over the sensitive underside.

"Holy shit, baby," he groaned, his gray eyes heavy-lidded with lust.

She loved the feel of his tight, silky flesh against her lips, loved how he filled and stretched her entire mouth. Her lips closed over him again, and she took him as deep in her throat as she could.

Suddenly, he pulled her up, and they were face to face.

"Now, Quinn." She pushed him playfully onto his back. "What'd you do that for? I was having fun. Weren't you?"

"Yeah," he said, his voice hoarse. "But I need to be deep in your pussy when I come, baby."

Her heart skipped, and his erotic words sent a flood of wetness to her core. "Yes, please," she murmured, straddling him once more.

His large hands gripped her hips as she sank onto him. "Ride me, sweetheart."

Sensation after sensation flowed through her. Rapture, elation, passion, love.

Her hips rose and fell with abandon. When Quinn's fingers touched her where their bodies joined, she shattered. He pulled her chest to his and held her tight, pounding into her, taking her back to the edge. Then they climaxed as one.

Breathless, limbs intertwined, she snuggled into his side. No words were spoken, but his comforting warmth enveloped her. She drifted off to sleep, content.

CHAPTER TWENTY-SIX

Getting out of the car, she followed Preston into the house. Exhausted, she set her purse on the kitchen island and climbed the stairs behind him, her feet throbbing with every step.

Once in their master suite, she sat on the edge of their bed and sighed as she removed her shoes. "Whoever invented five-inch stilettos must have been one sick puppy," she grumbled, massaging her aching feet.

"Did you have a good time tonight, darling?" Preston called from the bathroom.

She rolled her eyes but pasted a smile on her face. "Of course. You know I enjoy going to these charity events." She didn't. At all.

With a faucet still running in the bathroom, he emerged dressed only in his silk pajama bottoms. She wanted to question why he'd bothered to put on his sleep clothes when he was going to take them off again in a minute to bathe, but bit her tongue.

"It's no wonder," he said. His eyes raked over her. "You looked fabulous tonight. Truly. That little black dress leaves nothing to the imagination, and those working girl shoes . . ."

The hairs on the back of her neck stood at attention, and her smile wavered. "You bought me this outfit. I thought you liked it."

"Yes, I did." His hand shot out and gripped her chin.

She bit back a gasp, holding herself absolutely still.

"Don't get me wrong, darling. You fill out that dress wonderfully. On other women, it would look beautiful. Elegant, even. But on you . . ." He released her chin and turned away. "Tonight, you looked like a pro. God knows you worked the room like a dockside whore."

Her pulse quickened. What was he talking about?

While she waited for him to say something else, she tried to stay calm. And failed. Fear swelled in her gut.

"His hands were all over you," he finally hissed, his back still to her.

Her mind scrambled for answers. Whose hands?

Spinning, he strode toward her, his fists clenched at his sides. "Did you really think I wouldn't see?"

She sat motionless on the edge of the bed, aching feet forgotten. "I'm sorry, but I don't know what you're—"

"Do you know what the worst part is?"

Her mouth slammed shut, and she fought to keep her expression neutral.

"It isn't that he touched you, darling, because let's face it—you looked hot tonight." He eyed her up and down, and the smirk that grew on his face made her blood run cold. "Just like a good little trophy wife should. I mean, I can hardly blame the man, but the problem . . ."

He grabbed her by the bicep, fingers digging in, and dragged her into the steamy bathroom. "Was you. You clung to him." His spittle sprayed in her face. "You had your arms wrapped around him like a cunt begging for a fuck. And in front of everyone! You fucking humiliated me!"

His fist shot out, and her head exploded with pain. Her vision clouded, and her footing gave way on the slick tiled floor. Catching herself on the edge of the tub, she stopped her fall and slid to the ground. With her knees pulled to her chest, she sat there numbly and waited. He turned off the water to the jetted tub.

He walked by her, and she curled away.

With a dark laugh, his foot struck her ribs. "You stupid whore."

Seizing her upper arms, he hauled her to her feet—and then into the air. Her pounding head screamed in protest.

"Please—I'm sorry! Please don't!" She wasn't sure what she was begging for, but she knew whatever he did next was going to be bad.

Every nerve in her body howled when he dropped her into the scalding tub. Her heart stopped, then kicked back to life, hammering hard. She flailed, arms and legs thrashing, trying to grip the slippery sides of the tub, trying to push herself up, but his hands held her down.

Looking through the reddening water at him, she desperately changed tactics, bucking and clawing at the hands that pinned her. Her lungs burned for air. The painful throbbing at the base of her skull grew stronger.

A glint of metal caught the light above her. She could only struggle helplessly when the knife came crashing down. She opened her mouth to scream, and the scorching water rushed in, boiling her throat. She went numb.

Eyes flying open, a guttural moan escaped Alex's lips. She gasped, desperate for air. Frantic, she tried to sit up, but strong arms held her still. She resisted, jerking against the man's chest, hysterical to be free.

"You're safe, sweetheart. I've got you."

She stilled at the familiar voice, then looked up at Quinn in confusion.

A nightmare. Just another horrible nightmare.

With her lungs still on fire and sweat dripping from her naked body, she focused on his embrace as he softly rocked her. On the quiet, calm words he murmured into her ear.

He pressed and held his lips to her forehead, then tucked her head under his chin. "You're okay, Alex. You were having a nightmare. Relax into me, sweetheart. Just breathe."

Taking in an unsteady breath, she let herself be comforted by his hand rubbing gentle circles along her spine, by his leather and forest scent. With her cheek against his bare chest, the steady thump of his heartbeat beneath her ear brought her pulse back down.

Safe. She was safe.

"He tried to drown me once," she said in a whisper, her voice quivering. "But in my dream, he also had a knife . . ."

"It's okay, sweetheart. You don't have to explain. Not right now. Just concentrate on breathing." He began to massage her scalp. "You've got a big day tomorrow. Just focus on relaxing." He kissed the top of her head. "Get some sleep, Alex. I promise I'll keep you safe."

With each pass of his fingers through her hair, the tension in her body eased. She burrowed deeper into the arms that enveloped her, protected her, soothed her.

"Please don't leave," she murmured.

His grip tightened, and she finally drifted off into a dreamless sleep.

CHAPTER TWENTY-SEVEN

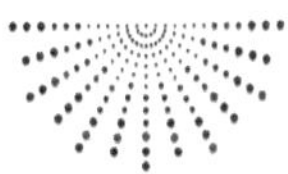

With Aretha Franklin grooving on the café's speakers, Alex put the finishing touches on a quiche and popped it into the oven.

"Look at you. You're such a liar," Roxie said. "Why did you say you were a disaster in the kitchen again?"

"I never said I was a disaster—"

"Yes," Roxie interrupted with a snicker. "You certainly did."

"I may have said I was a little *uncomfortable* in the kitchen, but—"

"Whatever makes you happy, Alex." Roxie rolled her eyes. "So, if you could do eight more quiches, four with the ham and spinach, the other four vegetarian, I'd—"

"Aye-aye, captain." She gave Roxie an exaggerated salute, their squabble from the day before long forgotten.

"You know what?" Roxie said, her tone nonchalant as she kneaded more dough. "I think I liked you better when you were all quiet and shy."

She laughed. "Well, that's too bad for you, I guess." The

spunk she'd once had was returning a little at a time. Baby steps.

Yesterday had been one of the longest days of her life. It had started out so horribly. The early-morning phone call, the flower delivery . . . the horrendous stress of it all. But as the sun had risen this morning, she'd imagined something she hadn't dared to think about in years.

Her future.

She didn't bother suppressing the smile that spread across her face.

When Quinn had kissed her awake this morning, she'd pictured a life that had nothing to do with anger or violence or fear. She now had hope for a future of *normal*. For both her and the baby.

Her heart squeezed, and her smile dimmed. The baby.

As if reading her mind, Roxie asked, "How's the little bambino doing?"

She cleared her suddenly thick throat. "Good. I haven't had any queasiness the last couple of days, so that's a bonus. Doc called this morning to check in. He's concerned about how the stress of . . . well, everything is affecting me and the baby. And he wants me to put on more weight."

Roxie stuck a fork in a freshly baked pie and slid the tin across the workstation to her.

"Thanks," she chuckled, snagging the pie before it went over the edge.

"Seriously, Alex, take a bite." Roxie winked, continuing to put together a fresh bowl of pie filling. "I expect the whole thing to be gone by lunchtime."

Alex shoveled a forkful of blueberry pie into her mouth. Her eyes closed, and she sighed at the wonderful, warm, gooey goodness melting on her tongue. "That will not be a problem." She paused to swallow. "Aside from the weight thing, everything is fine, I guess."

Silence descended. The only sound in the kitchen was Diana Ross and the rest of The Supremes singing "Stop! In the Name of Love." Alex squirmed as Roxie stared at her with an eyebrow raised in question. She was starting to consider the expression a Roxie signature.

"I don't know, Roxie. I know I should be more excited about it—about the baby." She sighed, looking down, her hesitation making her feel like a complete asshole. "But I'm not. I'm just really, really nervous about it."

Steeling herself, she peeked up at Roxie. Bright-green eyes full of understanding and support stared back at her. Her lower lip trembled, and her eyes stung with imminent tears. "I'm so scared, Roxie—"

Before she'd finished her sentence, Roxie was around their workstation and drawing her into a hug.

"Oh, sweetie, of course you're scared. You'd be a complete nut job if you weren't." Roxie pulled away and met her gaze. "We're all here to help you. You know that, right?"

"Thanks, Rox." She swiped away the last stray tears and let out a breath. Straightening her shoulders, she made her way to the sink to re-wash her hands. "So, about this thing tonight," she said when she was back at the workstation. "What do you want me to wear?"

Seeming to understand her desperate need to change the subject, Roxie resumed mixing the bowl of pie filling. "What do you have?"

Her brow furrowed at the thought of her pathetic wardrobe. "Well, that would be the problem. Unless the dress code includes jeans, sweatpants, T-shirts, or sweatshirts, then I'm afraid you're all out of luck."

Roxie paused, setting the bowl aside. "Are you serious? You don't have any dress clothes with you? Not even a skirt?"

"Let's just say that when I started my drive out here,

packing a diverse wardrobe wasn't exactly on the top of my priority list."

"Touché, smart-ass. Touché." Roxie grinned and began rolling out dough. "Let's see . . . It's eight forty-five now. June is taking care of all the regular stuff up front, but we only have her until noon. Nina and Ella should be in any minute. With all hands on deck, the baking and prep work should be done by two. Nina and El are handling the packing and transport. They'll have everything at the party hall's kitchen by four.

"While they handle that, we can run back to the house and get dolled up. You and I will be ready and over to the hall by five thirty at the latest. Nina set up the hall last night, so all we have to do is put stuff out. The shindig officially starts at six thirty, and food only goes until eight thirty. Thankfully, Mrs. Green hired waitstaff, so we don't have to handle that. They're also doing all the cleanup, so I'll only be staying until nine thirty or so. That work for you?"

Wow. Alex blinked. Twice. "It's dizzying, you know that?"

"What is?"

"You. Listening to you hash something out."

"Yeah, I've heard that before." Roxie shrugged. "But does that time frame work for you? Oh!" she exclaimed before Alex could answer. "I have the perfect outfit for you. But in the meantime, after the next round of quiches hit the oven, I need four trays of mini lasagnas prepped. Three meat and one veg."

Alex laughed and looked at her friend in wonder. "It must be exhausting to have all those thoughts racing around in your head. I'm amazed—I truly am."

"Well, you should be." A smug smile lit Roxie's face. "I'm an impressive sort of woman. *But* does the time schedule work for you?"

"Sure. I just need to make one quick pit stop before we

head back to the house." When Roxie gave her a questioning look, she clarified, "Post office. Joe set up a PO Box for me and said he'd mailed some stuff. It won't take long. Promise. I *swear* to you, your precious schedule will not be disrupted."

They went back to baking and prepping, serenaded by another one of Aretha's hits. When the song changed, Alex caught Roxie's eye. "Can I ask you a personal question?"

"Sure." Roxie began attacking a new piece of dough with the rolling pin. "But only if I get to ask one in return."

"Okay . . ."

Roxie smirked. "Hey, you started it."

"True," she said. "What's with you and Joe? You do know he's going to be there tonight, right?"

Roxie's rolling pin paused.

"He left a voicemail this morning," she explained. "Along with the paperwork stuff, he said he decided to fly in later this afternoon. Something about loose ends he has to tie up or something."

Roxie resumed rolling out the dough with what looked like more force than necessary. After a few passes of the pin, she said, "You know, Alex, I'm not really sure what's going on. The three of us grew up together and had a really great relationship. Best freaking friends." Roxie's forehead scrunched. She shrugged again. "But somewhere along the line, something changed between me and Joe."

She set the rolling pin down and turned to grab pie plates. "The three of us always had a really good dynamic. We balanced each other. Of the two guys, Joe was the charmer. Don't get me wrong, Quinn can be just as charming if he puts his mind to it, but he's lazy. For Joe, it's a natural thing. He can talk anyone out of anything. And Quinn? Well, I think he had that strong-but-silent persona perfected by the time he hit third grade. Seriously."

Alex grinned at the thought. It was too easy for her to

picture a mini Quinn and a mini Joe causing mayhem. "And you?"

"I was *the girl*, of course." Roxie chuckled. "It sounds horribly sexist, but that was my job. Since we got into a lot of trouble growing up, I was the decoy. I will egotistically admit that I was an *adorable* kid. Really cute and ridiculously well dressed. My mom's motto was 'if Nordstrom doesn't sell it, then we don't need it.' I truly looked like the poster child for sugar and spice and all that's nice. So, my job was to take the blame for everything, and we'd usually get off scot-free. After all, how could anyone blame such bad pranks on sweet little me?"

The woman flashed an angelic smile, and Alex laughed. Sugar and spice, indeed.

"We all had a good time growing up. It was always fun. We always had each other's backs. We knew each other ridiculously well. Didn't-have-to-speak-whole-sentences-to-get-our-points-across kind of thing. They took off to college a few years ahead of me, but we stayed in contact. They visited often, and everything was great. Then things changed when Joe moved away for good."

"What do you mean, 'for good'?"

"A few years back, he and Quinn were both with the FBI down in California. For my thirtieth birthday—" Roxie paused, her nose wrinkling. "Damn, that was almost four years ago. Anyway, they flew over and surprised me for my thirtieth. It was the sweetest thing . . ."

"I know," Alex said with a sigh, caught up in Roxie's nostalgia. "I've seen the picture." At her friend's confused look, she explained, "Quinn has a picture of the three of you from your birthday party in his bedroom."

Roxie's eyes danced with mischief. "I'm not even going to ask how you know about his bedroom."

Heat rushed over her face. She opened her mouth, but

nothing came out. As hard as she tried, she couldn't hold back the smile that erupted.

"I'm just messing with you, Alex, but from the look on your face, that's a conversation we'll *definitely* have later." She winked and reached for more pie plates. "Anyway, about a year or so later, Quinn's folks were in that horrific car accident and passed away."

Her jaw dropped. She knew Quinn's parents had passed, but she hadn't known any details. Seeing the grief and sadness coloring her friend's face made her soul ache.

"Quinn resigned from the FBI and moved back here to Hudson Island for good," Roxie continued with a sniff. "Before we knew it, he'd been elected sheriff. Joe started coming to visit more. They'd both always talked about moving home, but now that Quinn was here permanently, Joe had been giving it more thought.

"Then one night, we're all hanging out at Monty's Tavern —Quinn, some chick he was seeing, Joe, me, and my then boyfriend Paul—and Joe lost his freaking mind. Just out of the damn blue, he starts yelling at me. I mean, serious, full-on screaming. I'd never, *ever* seen him treat anyone the way he was treating me. He was calling me a slut and a whore and then punched my boyfriend in the face."

Alex's eyes widened in surprise. Joe? For the life of her, she couldn't picture it.

Roxie pointed at her. "Your face right now? *Exactly* how I felt. I was shocked. I had no idea what was going on in Joe's head or why he was acting like a freaking crazy person. It was madness. Quinn's pulling Joe off Paul. I'm throwing stuff at Joe and screaming. Absolute chaos. The next day I go over to Joe's to talk—well, yell—and the guy is *still* a complete jackass. He won't apologize for acting like an asshole and then proceeds *again* to call me a stupid slut! Can you believe that?"

No. She sure as hell couldn't.

"Then he left. Just like that." Roxie snapped her fingers. "Tossed everything in his bag and left. He hasn't been back to Hudson since. When he showed up a couple weeks ago, that was the first time he'd stepped foot on the island since our big blowup. And to this day, the shithead has yet to apologize. Or explain." Her gaze dropped to her hands. "He was one of my best friends. You could safely say Quinn was my left arm and Joe was my right. Now he absolutely hates me. And I have no idea why."

Alex was at a complete loss for words. Roxie always radiated confidence. Always. Hell, she was downright cocky. But now, standing at her workstation with her shoulders slumped, she looked . . . lost. There was a vulnerability in her eyes that Alex hadn't seen before. Yeah, it made Roxie a little more human and a whole lot less intimidating, but still. This was *Roxie*.

"I'm so sorry I brought this up," she said as Nina and Ella walked through Comfort Food's back door. They were chatting a mile a minute.

"Don't worry about it," Roxie said with a soft smile. With a quick exhale, the woman put her no-nonsense boss-face firmly back in place. "Thanks for letting me know he's going to be there tonight. One should always know where the enemy is at all times, right?" The teasing smile she flashed didn't reach her eyes.

As Roxie made her way toward Nina and Ella, no doubt to give them the list of what still needed to be done, Alex's heart hurt for her friend. Behind that über-confident facade, there was a world of pain. And she had a feeling that she'd just unknowingly ripped off the bandage that had been hiding it.

CHAPTER TWENTY-EIGHT

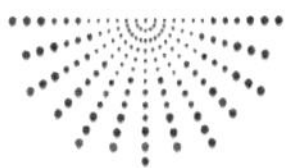

The busy day continued, and dish after dish was put into and pulled out of the ovens. As usual, Comfort Food was filled with decadent aromas, and the workstations were littered with delicious treats.

At two on the dot, the last of the mini chocolate tarts were removed from the oven and placed on the cooling racks. At precisely three, most of the items were packed, and Roxie was steering Alex out the door while calling out final instructions to Nina and Ella.

After a quick stop at the post office, Roxie proceeded to give her a dizzying play-by-play of which items would be at food stations and which would be passed around by the hired waitstaff.

"I've done a detailed diagram on how the girls are setting things. You and I will be there tonight, along with Nina, should anything come up. Not that anything *will*, but you never know, right?" Roxie glanced down at her watch as she pulled into the driveway she shared with Quinn. "It's a good thing we're a bit ahead of schedule. Be at my place by four, and we'll get all dolled up."

Alex only stared. And shook her head.

"What?"

She couldn't tell if Roxie was currently fueled by crazy amounts of nervous energy or if this was simply how she worked. Either way, witnessing her in overdrive was . . . something else.

"In the five minutes it took us to get from the post office to here, I don't think you actually took a breath," she said, marveling. "It was just one. Continuous. Sentence. It was really quite impressive."

Her friend's eyes rolled as she got out of her car. "Alex, my dear, you have been spending *way* too much time with Quinn. You're beginning to sound like him. Not a good quality. Not at all." She turned away with a wink and started toward the guesthouse. Without looking back, she called, "Don't forget, Alex. My place. No later than four."

At precisely four o'clock—because she didn't have a death wish—Alex walked through Roxie's front door freshly showered and dressed in her standard uniform of jeans, a T-shirt, and a zippered sweatshirt.

"Bedroom's in the back," Roxie shouted, her words muffled.

As she followed her friend's voice, she scanned the living room. It was tastefully decorated in dark purples, emerald greens, rich navy blues, and plush burgundies. Furniture and decorative pieces were scattered about in a cluttered yet comforting manner. Through an archway, she saw a small, pristine kitchen that looked as though it had never been used.

When Alex stepped into the bedroom, she smiled. Gone were the lush jewel tones of the living area; soft, peaceful blues and whites reigned here. "Did you do the decorating in this place, or was it already like this?"

Dressed in a fluffy purple robe with a towel atop her head, Roxie laughed. "Are you kidding me? Quinn's idea of decorating is setting up a recliner and a giant TV and calling it done. The man doesn't grasp the idea of painting the walls any color other than white. And actually hanging things up on the walls for decoration? Nope."

Alex chuckled, then frowned. She pictured Quinn's cozy home. Its navy and taupe walls. Off-white accents. Dark mahogany furniture. "But his place is so nice."

"It is, isn't it?" Roxie's smile was smug. "He wouldn't let me go any crazier than that color palette."

She nodded. "Ah, I see. It's all coming together."

Roxie dug through her closet, then held up two outfits, both black. One was a short A-line dress with spaghetti straps, the other a skirt-and-top combo. "Which do you think?"

"They're both gorgeous. But since I'm so short, I'll go with the dress."

"Exactly what I thought." Roxie nodded and handed the dress to her before disappearing into the bathroom with the two-piece outfit. "See if that fits you," she said through the door. "It'll probably be a little big since you're so tiny. What are you? A size zero? Two? But I've got some belts and sashes we can play around with to make it fit."

Changing out of her clothes, she slipped into the dress. As she struggled to pull up the zipper along the back, Roxie emerged from the bathroom. Wearing the long, slim pencil skirt and matching strapless corset top, the woman looked like an Amazonian queen. Even with the towel still wrapped atop her head.

Roxie walked over and zipped up her dress. "What size shoes do you wear?"

"Six. Six and a half."

Roxie pursed her lips as she eyed Alex from head to toe. "Hmm, that could be a problem."

It took all her willpower to not fidget with the skirt of the dress. It was like she was back in middle school, and Roxie was the popular girl sizing her up. "What?"

Frowning, Roxie turned back to the closet and began digging. After a moment, she pulled out a wide silver sash. "Tie this around your waist."

Facing the full-length mirror, she realized why Roxie looked concerned. The dress had transformed her into a giant ink stain. With spaghetti straps.

"I wear a nine, but let me check with the others." Roxie's thumbs flew over her phone. "It'd be a shame to wear sneakers with that dress."

Five minutes later, Alex's wardrobe problems were solved. Nina would bring an extra pair of shoes, and the silver-sashed dress, with a pull here and a fold there, accentuated her small waist and flared at her knees.

She took in her reflection and smiled.

You have nothing to be ashamed of. Nothing. It's time to let go of the guilt and allow yourself to move on.

She allowed herself to admit that she looked nice, and that little progress forward warmed her with happiness. It had been a long time since she'd felt this good about herself. The realization made her smile grow.

Baby steps.

Interrupting her reverie, Roxie pulled her into the bathroom and gestured to the heap of cosmetics on the counter. "Feel free to use whatever you want."

Standing side by side, they began the female ritual of primping.

Roxie opened a bottle of foundation. "It's my turn now."

Alex's brows rose in question.

"For the personal question. You asked me about me and Joe. It's my turn."

"Oh." Trepidation had her forehead crinkling. "Okay. Ask away."

"What's going on with you and Quinn?"

"Oh, um, well . . ." She fumbled, meeting Roxie's curious stare in the mirror. "What do you want to know?"

"Look, Alex. Quinn's like my brother. You know that. So trust me, I *don't* want to know the details." She pretended to gag. "I just want to know what's going on. From your perspective."

"Like a what-are-my-intentions kind of thing?"

Roxie laughed. "Yeah, something like that."

Her thoughts drifted to last night's magic, and her face heated. She cleared her throat as her skin sparked with the memories. "Aside from him being gorgeous, Quinn's different. The more I get to know him, the more intrigued I am to know him even better. I find that there are so many different sides to him. He's like a puzzle I can't quite figure out."

"Do you like puzzles?"

"I do." She really, really did. "I know he has a temper. I can see it in his eyes. They turn dark and flinty, like granite. It should scare me, but it doesn't. He controls it. And I know— deep in my gut—that he'd never, *ever* hurt me. Quinn O'Conner is quite possibly the most genuine and compassionate and fascinating man I've ever met."

Roxie made a circular motion with her hand. "Meaning?"

"Meaning that I've never met anyone like him in my life." She didn't intend to say more, but something about the lack of judgment in her friend's eyes cracked her open. She wanted to be honest with Roxie. And with herself. So, she continued, "Things have been so crazy in my life, but being with him makes me forget the mayhem. Then, when reality hits, I find myself doubting whether I deserve his attention and affection. I mean, I'm trying to enjoy every moment, but honestly . . . I'm scared."

"Alex, give yourself some grace. Allowing yourself to be vulnerable is nauseating. Allowing yourself to be vulnerable after what *you've* been through is beyond scary. Relationships are nerve-racking and dazzling and terrifying all at once. But that's part of the beauty of them, right?"

She nodded. Roxie had nailed it on the head. "This is going to sound horribly cliché, but I've never felt this way about anyone before. I know I've only known him for such a short time—"

"What does time have to do with anything? I mean, no offense, Alex, but do you think if you'd dated your ex-husband six months or even a year longer before tying the knot that it would have turned out any different?"

"No," she said with certainty. "He knew exactly how to play me. Time wouldn't have mattered. But that's the other thing, Roxie. Everything's so damn complicated. Preston's not my *ex*-husband. He *is* my husband. Sure, the divorce papers have been filed, but the last time I checked, I'm still married to him. *And* I'm pregnant with his child."

Roxie shot her a teasing smile. "Well, what relationship isn't complicated?"

"Ahhh, the eternal optimist." She chuckled as she applied a shimmering eye shadow to her lids. "I just don't feel like I'm being fair to Quinn. He deserves more. Really, Roxie, my life is like a bad Lifetime movie."

Roxie recaptured her gaze in the mirror. Waving a mascara wand, she said, "Alex, I know Quinn like the back of my hand, so trust me when I tell you that I've never seen him look at anyone the way he looks at you. God knows I've never seen him *act* the way he does with you. Sure, he's protective of you because that's the kind of guy he is. But he's also tender with you." Roxie made a face. "I've seen Quinn with other women, and the word *tender* comes nowhere into play. Usually, he's an asshole. That's his thing."

Alex's chest squeezed. The third-party confirmation that Quinn's feelings were real helped push the uncertainty away. When she was with him, she was sure he cared about her, but when they were apart, the little voice in the back of her mind screamed that she had rotten instincts. With such an awful track record, how could that voice not exist? But hearing Roxie's take on it all sent a new surge of hope through her.

"And yes, it's complicated," her friend continued. "There's that crazy-husband thing and then there's the pregnant-with-said-crazy-husband's-child thing. But"—Roxie paused until Alex met her gaze—"Quinn knows about these things. He would've *never* made that first move if he had problems with any of these complications. He's a big boy, Alex. He knows what's best for him and what he can handle."

"That's exactly what he said, too." She sighed. "I'm just petrified I'm going to do something that will mess all this up. The last thing I want to do is hurt him. I mean . . ." A smile spread across her face, and she knew it was a sappy one. "Roxie, he is . . . absolutely wonderful. I didn't know it could be like this, *feel* like this. That I could honestly enjoy and really want and look forward to—" She slammed her mouth shut, and a blush spread from her chest to her face.

"Sex?" Roxie finished, her green eyes dancing with mirth.

She hadn't thought it possible for her face to get redder, but there the evidence was, staring right back at her in the mirror.

"Yeah," she mumbled.

"Well, good!" Roxie laughed. "You're *supposed* to enjoy it, you nut!"

"Yeah, but I haven't in a long time." She shrugged, and

Roxie's expression sobered. "It started fine with Preston, but the longer we were married, it became . . . not good."

"Oh, Alex . . ."

She shrugged again. "I didn't realize it at the time, but Preston is one of those guys who only cares about himself. So long as he got off, that's all that mattered. At first, it was just not enjoyable for me. Then, toward the end, it was . . . painful. Literally."

"I'm so sorry," Roxie said. Glowering, she added, "And there's yet another reason to hate that fucker."

"I agree." Alex squared her shoulders and attempted to brush off her mood. No more talk of Preston. He was in her past. And he needed to stay firmly there. "But now, it's different. *Quinn's* different. He's gentle and passionate and the perfect amount of rough." Her smile dimmed. "I worry it's too good to be true, and I'm scared he's going to walk away from me. Then, at the same time, I'm so afraid that I'm going to hurt him."

Roxie shook her head. "The only way you'll hurt Quinn is if you really do care about him, yet you push him away because it's what *you* think is best. Don't insult his intelligence or his need to protect you. That's what makes Quinn who he is. Really, Alex, don't dwell on the what-ifs and over-analyze everything. You'll drive yourself batty. I know you're going to do it anyway because, well, you're a female and frankly, that's what we do. But seriously, try not to. Take the time you have with Quinn and enjoy it. Besides, for all we know, the world will be annihilated tomorrow."

Roxie slicked a final swipe of gloss onto her lips and turned to Alex. "I know three things that are absolute facts. First, you guys care about each other and will face—together—whatever issues come up. Because that's what people who care about each other do. Second, I know that if we don't get out of here in the next fifteen minutes, we will *officially* be behind schedule." Tossing the lip gloss into a tiny clutch, she rose.

"And third?" Alex asked.

The grin Roxie sent her was positively wicked. "Third, I know that Quinn's going to *die* when he sees how freaking hot you look tonight."

CHAPTER TWENTY-NINE

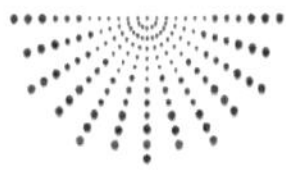

Alex stood behind a banquet table and scanned the displays of hors d'oeuvres, making sure they were full. The last thirty minutes had been a whirlwind, but she'd managed to stay on top of things so far.

She knew Roxie, beneath her shiny and cheerful veneer, was a nervous wreck. Tonight meant a lot to her, and Alex wanted to help in any way she could. It was the least she could do to thank her friend for the unwavering support she had shown her.

A guest asked her a question about one of the delectable bites, and she answered with a smile. When they moved down the table, she shifted on her feet and bit back a groan. The black heels she'd borrowed from Nina were already beginning to pinch.

She glanced around the room, trying to put names to faces, and froze when her eyes locked with Quinn's. Her heart stumbled, then beat in double-time as he approached. She gave him a thorough once-over, and her breath caught. The sheriff was freshly shaved and decked out in his formal olive-green dress uniform. She swallowed.

There were men in uniform . . . and then there was *this* man in uniform.

His brass buttons gleamed, and his broad shoulders and solid frame filled out the suit in a way that was utter perfection. She flushed from head to toe as she remembered what that fabulous body looked like beneath the clothes. And what it was capable of doing to her.

Holy freaking moly. Her blood went from simmer to boil, and she was tempted to fan herself.

***

Quinn's pulse raced as he strode toward Alex. He had to remind himself to slow down—to not march over, lift her into his arms, and carry her away like a caveman. But dammit, one look at her in that little black number had all his blood rushing south. The only thing he could think about was tearing that dress off her and taking her right there on the table, mini quiches and local politicians and business owners be damned.

He rounded the table separating them. When she was an arm's length away, he slid one hand around her waist and drew her close. His other hand caressed her face, tilting her head to the side. He leaned down and laid a soft kiss on her lips. "You look stunning."

Aware of the whispers and stares aimed their way, he pulled slightly back, though he kept one arm firmly around her. Possessive move? Damn straight. He couldn't suppress *all* his caveman tendencies.

She smiled up at him, a saucy look of challenge in her eyes. "You're looking pretty handsome there yourself, Sheriff."

Screw the whispers and stares. He erased the space

between them and brought his lips to her ear. "Do you have any idea what I want to do to you right now?"

Her eyes heated, and a blush tore over her cheeks. He imagined tossing her over his shoulder and finding the first private space available in this damn place. He was two seconds from giving in to the fantasy when Alex elbowed him in the ribs, indicating Mayor Green's approach.

"Sheriff O'Conner, how are you tonight?" the mayor asked with an exaggerated wink at Alex.

He shook the man's hand. "Good, sir. Thank you for having me."

Quinn quickly made the introductions, hoping the mayor would move along. No such luck. Alex, acting as the perfect hostess, initiated a conversation with the man, enthralling him as he loaded his plate with food.

Damn, this was going to be a long night.

Thankfully, it didn't take him more than thirty seconds to spot the mayor's wife, Bonnie. She was hard to miss in her fluorescent lime-green minidress that, unfortunately, was many sizes too small and way, *way* too short. And if the tiny excuse of a dress wasn't awkward enough, she had a giant matching feather thing in her hair. It looked like some poor parrot had crash-landed and died on her head.

He knew jack shit about women's fashion, let alone fashion for the sixty-plus crowd. But no. Just no. She had every guest in the reception hall not knowing where to look.

Quinn waved Bonnie over with a smile and introduced her to Alex. As he'd expected, she chatted with them for only a moment before whisking her husband away to some newly arriving guests.

The second the Greens were out of earshot, he snaked his arm around Alex, hauling her close.

"As I was saying," he murmured, "it involves you. On this table. Minus that lovely dress. Hors d'oeuvres optional."

She elbowed him again, but this time, she laughed. He'd count that as a partial win. "You're incorrigible, Sheriff O'Conner."

"Seriously, though. Do you get a break?"

"The party just started, mister." She shook her head, a grin on her lips. "Besides, Nina's in the kitchen, and Roxie's making her rounds."

As if on cue, Roxie appeared, her eyes dancing with excitement. His friend had impeccable timing.

"Let's switch, Alex. You mingle, and I'll man the tables. Can you believe how well it's going, you guys? I can't believe it! I've already had *four* people request catering services, and it's only the first hour!"

"Are you sure?" Alex's perfect face pinched with concern. "A bunch of people just arrived. If you want to—"

Nope. "I'll have her back in thirty, Rox." He snagged Alex's hand and pulled her toward the door before his friend could comment.

———◆———

"In a rush?" Alex asked as he led her out of the reception hall and hustled her down a quiet, empty corridor. "Quinn, where are we—"

She fell silent when he abruptly turned and tugged her into a tiny room marked Storage. He quickly shut the door, and darkness engulfed them; the closet's small window provided minimal light.

"Quinn, what—"

His lips crashed down on hers.

There was no softness, no seeking of permission. This was raw hunger and demanding passion that had her wanting—no, *begging*—for more.

He backed her to the door, pressing her against it with his

hard body. Her fingers latched behind his neck, and his hands moved over her with a desperation that left her skin tingling and her body throbbing.

Through the thin material of her dress, he kneaded her breasts. She moaned when he captured her nipples between his fingers and squeezed. His answering groan reverberated through her, setting her on fire. She needed him inside her, filling her, stretching her.

She fumbled to unclasp his belt as his hands slipped under her dress, over her trembling thighs, and stopped at her aching center. She was hot, dripping wet, and completely ready for him.

"Fuck, baby. Your pussy's so fucking wet," he growled, rubbing over her clit through her damp panties. "Is this all for me?"

His words thrilled her. No one had ever spoken to her like that. *Ever.* Those words . . . The roughness of his voice . . . *Holy shit.* She needed him. Now. And she wasn't above pleading. "Please, Quinn. More."

He grabbed her panties in his fist and tore them off in one smooth motion.

A shiver tore through her, and her heartbeat became a deafening drum in her ears. She'd never been this turned on in her life.

More.

"I want you to ride my hand, sweetheart," he said between kisses. "Come on my fingers."

Her hands fisted in the lapels of his suit jacket, and she groaned his name when he plunged two fingers deep inside her. Her hips pumped as his hand drove her wild.

She couldn't focus. All she could do was feel. Her release built within her, and he increased the speed, the friction. Then, she burst. He held her in place as she bucked, forcing another explosive orgasm from her. Her legs gave way, and if it hadn't been for the door and Quinn's body, she'd have crumpled in a heap on the ground. Her inner walls continued to spasm around his fingers. She'd never come so hard in her life.

And yet, she wanted more.

***

Her pupils were blown, her eyes more black than whiskey brown. A light sheen of sweat dotted her brow.

She'd never been more fucking beautiful.

With his fingers still deep inside her, working her pussy until she was dripping for him again, he kissed her lips. She was so fucking responsive—he'd never get enough.

"More, Quinn." She was breathless and perfect. "I need you inside me. Now. Please."

Withdrawing his hand, he licked his fingers clean of her sweet and spicy essence. A moan escaped him. He'd never been this desperate for anyone. After making quick work of his belt, he shoved his slacks to the ground and cupped her delicious ass in his hands. He lifted her with ease.

"Wrap your legs around me, sweetheart."

With her back against the door and her legs circling his waist, he lowered her until his cock nudged her slick entrance. Then, in one thrust, he slid into her hot pussy. Their groans filled the room.

"More," she begged. "Harder."

Fuck, yes.

Gripping her hips, he plunged into her. Over and over again. His eyes crossed as she met him thrust for thrust and they drove each other higher. Her gasps of "yes" and "more" spurred him on. He wanted her incoherent.

She cried out again, a guttural moan, and her pussy tightened around his cock, milking him until he groaned and released inside her.

As they came down, the only sounds in the closet were their labored breaths and thudding hearts. Until Alex chuckled.

"Well now, Sheriff, that's my idea of a break."

He laughed. "You have no idea, sweetheart." He placed a tender kiss on her lips and surveyed the dimly lit room. Paper towels, soap, trash bags, and various cleaning supplies lined the shelves. "I can safely say I've never done *that* in a storage closet before."

Pulling out of her warmth, he moaned. Then he set her on her feet and reached down to pull up his slacks, pausing to pick up her torn panties.

"Looks like you're going commando for the rest of the evening, sweetheart. Sorry about that." He wasn't sorry in the least bit. He pocketed her panties and grabbed a roll of paper towels, tearing off a handful for her.

"Souvenir?" She laughed, nodding to his pocket while she cleaned up. "You look like the cat that just ate the canary."

"I kind of feel like it." He took the wadded-up paper towels from her and tossed them into the garbage bin he'd spied in the corner. When she finished straightening her dress, he pulled her into his arms and kissed her again. Because he could. "I was pretty rough. Did I hurt you?"

"No." Her hands framed his face as she drew his lips back to hers. "You could never hurt me, Quinn."

He lost himself in their kiss. His hands wandered over her delicate curves, and his desire stirred yet again. Damn. He truly couldn't get enough of her. By the way she rubbed herself against his hard cock, it seemed the feeling was mutual. Thank fuck.

A loud knock at the door made them both jump.

"Roxie's looking for you guys," a familiar voice said from the other side. "And she looks pissed. Though that probably has nothing to do with you two and everything to do with me."

Alex's face flushed a shade of red deep enough for him to see—an impressive feat, considering it was so damn dark in the storage room. She used both hands to cover her mouth, which had fallen open.

Adorable.

Damn. He was in deep. And he was completely good with it.

"Thanks, Joe. We'll be right out," he said, humor lifting his words. He slung an arm over Alex's shoulders. "Don't worry, sweetheart. He'll be discreet." He dropped a kiss to the top of her head. "Besides, he knows I'll pummel him if he's not."

By nine o'clock, all the food had been cleared, and Comfort Food's inaugural catering event had been deemed an official hit. Alex was beyond impressed by Roxie's accomplishments tonight. Her friend had managed to line up nine new catering jobs, network with the crowd, oversee Mrs. Green's waitstaff, and completely avoid Joe.

"Thanks for all your help, Alex." An exhausted, happy smile shone on Roxie's face. "I truly appreciate it. This was such an important night."

"Such a *successful* night," she corrected. "And thank you for what you said about me and Quinn earlier. Reminding me to enjoy the now and not dwell on the what-ifs. I truly appreciate it."

"We're indebted to each other, then." Roxie nodded toward the reception hall's main door. "I'm going to head out. Are you going to stay for a little bit?"

Alex stacked a couple of empty trays. "No, actually. Quinn

and Joe are stuck in some conversation with the mayor about who knows what, and my feet are killing me. Can I get a ride with you?"

"Absolutely. Why don't you leave those?" Roxie waved at the trays. "Mrs. Green's people will take care of everything."

"Sounds good to me." She rolled her neck from side to side. "I'll meet you out front. Let me just say goodbye."

As she approached the trio of men, she waved to get Quinn's attention. He immediately excused himself from Mayor Green and Joe. "Hey, gorgeous."

"Hey, yourself. I'm going to catch a ride home with Roxie. I'm exhausted." She stifled a yawn.

"I can see that." He tucked a stray hair behind her ear. "Do you want to stay at my place?"

"No, that's okay. I think I'm just going to crash."

"Well, that's probably for the best since Joe will be staying at my place tonight. He didn't want to impose on you."

Her forehead scrunched. "But I'm staying at *his* house."

Quinn shrugged and traced her jawline with his finger. Her insides melted at the gentle touch.

"You know . . ." She toyed with his lapel. "If you don't get home too late, I wouldn't be opposed if you came over to . . . check on me."

"Is that so?" His rumbly voice sent shivers down her spine.

"I mean, if you happened to also stay the night, I wouldn't be opposed. Just sayin'."

He flashed that sexy smile of his, and her stomach fluttered. She still couldn't believe that *she* had made this amazing, mouthwatering man lose control of himself in a freaking storage closet.

She wrapped her arms around his waist. Because she could. "I was thinking that since Roxie gave me the day off tomorrow, and since *you* have the day off tomorrow, perhaps we could have breakfast or brunch with a reprise of the storage closet incident. What do you think?"

He returned her mischievous grin, holding her close. "You don't even have to ask, sweetheart. I'm all yours. You guys drive home safe. We'll probably be a couple more hours." Leaning down, he gave her a quick kiss. "If you're already asleep when I come over tonight, I know a great way to wake you up."

Yes, please. Her tired body hummed in anticipation.

She stepped away with a satisfied sigh. As of this moment, she had no complaints. Sore feet, tired body—none of it mattered. Life was finally looking up.

CHAPTER THIRTY

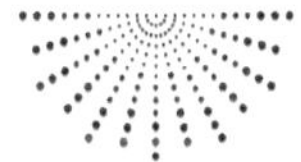

Alex's eyes blinked open. The room was still dark, the only illumination coming from the streetlamp outside. Rolling over, she checked the time. And stilled.

What was that?

She shot up in bed, struggling to listen through the blood rushing in her ears.

She'd heard something. A creak.

Had that woken her?

She eased back down and pulled the duvet up to her chin. It had probably just been the house settling. But a prickle in her belly kept her senses on full alert.

For five long seconds, there was silence.

Another creak. On the stairs.

Her breath locked in her throat. She remained utterly still.

Holy shit, please let it be Quinn. Please.

But she knew it wasn't. The tiny hairs that rose on her arms told her it wasn't.

Her heart threatened to burst from her chest. The doorknob began to turn. Her hands trembled and grew clammy. A bitter, metallic taste filled her mouth.

Fear. It was the taste of pure fear.

The door crept open, and her stomach pitched. A shadow lurked on the other side. It belonged to neither Quinn nor Joe. The intruder's hulking mass filled the entire doorway.

He took a small step into the room. She swallowed a whimper as the light from the window glinted off something in his right hand. A knife.

Beads of sweat broke out over her forehead. A wave of nausea washed over her. Her lips began to go numb, and her vision wavered.

A panic attack was coming. She had to act before it paralyzed her.

He stood at the foot of her bed, his face hidden in the shadows. If he would only move two steps to the right, she could maybe make it to the door. Maybe.

He took one step to the right.

She held her breath. *Just one more. Please!*

As she was about to bolt from the bed, a sound caused her to freeze.

She'd heard it earlier that evening, but under completely different circumstances. Then, it had thrilled her. Now, it filled her entire being with terror.

It was the sound of metal on leather. A belt buckle being undone.

Metal on fabric. A zipper lowering.

Holy shit.

Move, dammit! Move!

Her blood pounded in her veins, but she couldn't move. Not yet.

She lay motionless, her muscles coiled tight, as he edged to the right side of her bed. His left hand stretched out above her. It stilled. Fisted. Then, like a snake, it struck out, hammering down. In the same instant, she threw herself to the left, scrambling off the bed. His fist grazed the back of her head.

On her feet, she made a mad, desperate dash for her bedroom door. She'd barely taken three steps when a sharp pain exploded on the right side of her torso. Before she could cry out, the man collided with her, the heavy weight of him sending her to the ground. Noxious body odor and the coppery scent of blood filled her senses, and she gagged.

He flipped her onto her back and straddled her. Her arms flailed, knocking the sticky knife out of his hand. She wanted to buck like a wild bronco, but he was too damn heavy.

Pinned beneath him and desperate, she struggled, grasping and scratching and punching. *Anything* to get free. Her hands found the flesh of his face and she gripped it, fingers probing. He tried to shake her off. When she felt the squishy give of his eyes, she jammed her fingers in and clawed.

He roared in agony. His meaty fist struck out and connected with the side of her face, stunning her. A black haze threatened to cloud her vision. Another blow struck her jaw, but this time, the icy hot pain shooting through her head brought clarity.

The man wrenched her across the floor. He pulled up her sleep shirt and crouched over her bare thighs. Freed of his weight and fueled by terror, she whipped up her leg and smashed her knee against the underside of his testicles.

He howled in pain and rolled to his side, clutching his crotch.

She surged to her feet, but his arm shot out and tripped her, sending her sprawling across the room. On her hands and knees, she crawled to the dresser and leaned against it. Blood filled her mouth, and her abdomen cramped, stealing her breath.

She was so damn close. The door was *right there.*

The man limped toward her. His face was streaked with blood, his eyes filled with rage. She tried to push herself up, but her knees wobbled and her right arm gave out. Falling back to the floor, her hand brushed against metal. The man's bloody knife.

Get up and run, dammit!

With the knife clenched in her hand, she forced herself off the floor and through the bedroom door. She rushed down the hallway toward the stairs, but her limping stride was no match for his. Her scalp burst into flames when he grabbed her by the hair. She swung out blindly with the knife, striking flesh.

He gasped, then stumbled.

She twisted the knife out and struck him again. And again. He fell backward, down the stairs. But his fist was still locked in her hair, and he yanked her down on top of him.

They tumbled in a heap. Something in her knee popped, and her shoulder exploded in pain. Then everything was in slow motion. Her gaze fixated on the bottom banister post as she hurtled toward it.

There was a deafening crack, then everything went fuzzy and dark.

Sound muted as if she were at the bottom of a swimming pool.

She thought she heard Quinn calling her name. But his voice kept getting farther and farther away until finally, there was only silence.

CHAPTER THIRTY-ONE

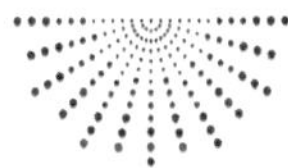

"So, you and Alex, huh?" Joe asked with a grin.

They trudged up the front steps to Alex's house—well, technically Joe's—and Quinn didn't bother trying to hide his big, goofy smile. "Yeah. I know it's been fast." He shrugged, his stupid smile widening. "But she's fucking amazing."

Joe fished his keys out of his pocket. "Had I known you'd swoop in on her when I sent her here, I definitely would have . . ." He frowned, keys seemingly forgotten, as he leaned in to look through the front door's side window.

Quinn reached for the Sig in his ankle holster. "What is it?"

"Fuck!" Joe drew his weapon and kicked at the front door.

Two solid hits, and it came free of its hinges.

Quinn peered inside, and his heart stopped.

Alex was tumbling down the stairs with an unknown man.

He raced toward her. "Alex!"

Her head crashed against the banister post. The loud crack halted both men in their tracks.

She slumped at the base of the stairs, face down, motionless. A pool of blood spread beneath her head. Finding her faint pulse, he crouched next to her, afraid to move her.

"Alex, sweetheart, please . . ." he whispered, unable to breathe. He lay down on the ground next to her and stroked her bruised cheek. "Alex, hang in there, baby. Please stay with me, sweetheart. You've got to stay with me."

When Joe turned on the lights while shouting orders at the 911 dispatcher, Quinn's blood chilled. What he could see of Alex's face was bruised and gashed. Her limbs were lying at awkward angles, and a bloodstain was soaking her shirt. She was barely breathing.

In that moment, any doubt he had about the depths of his feelings for her vanished.

He loved her.

He would give anything—*do* anything—for her to be okay.

His hands trembled as he tried to find the source of the bleeding without moving her. He continued to murmur reassurances, to *beg* her to stay with him, as tears of rage and fear ran down his face.

A hand on his shoulder startled him. Glancing up, he met Joe's somber gaze.

"Ambulance is on their way." He gestured to the motionless man four feet away. "No pulse on the perp."

For the next hour, federal agents and local authorities descended on the Buchanan house. When he was no longer needed at the scene, Quinn walked from Joe's place to his own. He paused at the sight of Joe and Roxie sitting side by side on his front porch steps.

Roxie rose and rushed to him, hugging him hard. "How is she?"

Sinking down onto the step next to Joe, he scrubbed his hands over his face and sighed.

What a fucking night.

"They airlifted her to Jefferson Medical over in Port Townsend. They're not sure if they'll need to fly her over to Seattle or not." He nodded to Joe. "Your dad's with her. EMT said the knife wound to her shoulder was deep but appeared to miss anything vital." He closed his eyes. Anger, frustration, terror, and guilt filled him in equal measure. "She hasn't regained consciousness yet."

Roxie squeezed onto the step between him and Joe. "And the baby?" she whispered, her green eyes glistening.

He looked over at her. "I don't know, Rox."

Alex tumbling down the stairs replayed in his mind. And then the crack. The horrific, loud crack of her head hitting the post. It had sounded so final. Had nearly given him a fucking heart attack. He'd never felt so helpless in his entire life.

"I should have stayed with her." Silent tears streamed down Roxie's face. "I shouldn't have left her by herself."

Joe put his arm around her shoulders and pulled her close. "Don't beat yourself up. There's nothing you could have done." A shadow passed over the man's face. One that looked suspiciously like guilt.

His friend was holding something back. He could feel it in his gut.

Quinn stood, crossing his arms over his chest. "Who the fuck was that guy, Joe?"

Joe gave Roxie's shoulders a final squeeze and stood. He stared at her bent head for a few seconds, an unreadable expression on his face. Then, brusquely, he turned his attention back to Quinn.

"Feds have the body now," his friend said, tone businesslike.

Surprise had Quinn's brows lifting. "That was fast."

Joe shrugged and started pacing. "The guy's name was Jason Fulton. Forty-two years old from Chattanooga, Tennessee. Long record in multiple states. Armed robbery, assault, rape. The works. Turns out he was released from jail a week ago after a stint for simple possession."

Joe met his gaze. Quinn could have sworn he saw disgust flicker in his friend's eyes. He had a sinking suspicion he knew why, but he needed to be certain.

"When he was in the can," Joe said, "Fulton was a cell-block down from Woodsworth."

And now he was certain. *Mother. Fucker.*

Fury raged within him. "So, Woodsworth got to him and told him about Alex." His voice was like gravel, his tone lethal.

"We're not sure right now. Woodsworth was supposed to be isolated from the rest of the inmates. We're looking into it." Joe hurried on as Quinn opened his mouth. "We don't know if this is a random thing. We obviously don't think it is, but we need to talk to Alex first."

Quinn growled and ran a frustrated hand through his hair. He had to do *something*, dammit. "What do you need from me? From my department?"

"Nothing. Our guys will handle it."

He glared at Joe.

His friend held up his hands in surrender. "Look, I'm not going to get into a pissing match with you over who's got jurisdiction, O'Conner. The fact of the matter is that there was an attack in the house of a federal agent. If you take into consideration how Alex is a key player in our investigation of Woodsworth . . ." His hands spread in a helpless gesture. "It's our case. Simple as that."

"Fuck that shit, Buchanan," he hissed. "This is *my* fucking town. And it's *Alex*, dammit!"

His breath left him in a whoosh, as if he'd been sucker punched in the gut. *Fuck!* It was Alex. *His* Alex. His shoulders deflated, and the anger seeped from him. The worry remained.

"Quinn," Joe said, his voice cracking. "I swear to fucking god, I will keep you posted on what's going on. From here on out, *everything* I find out, I will fucking share with you. Even if I'm not supposed to, I swear to you, I will. You know that, right?"

"Yeah," he said, dejected. He collapsed back onto the porch step next to Roxie. "Tell me, Joe, why the hell are you really here? And don't give me some bullshit story about how Mayor Green invited you to his party tonight."

Joe's lips pressed into a grim line. "Woodsworth. He's being released in two weeks. We need Alex to—"

Quinn's cell phone rang.

"Hang on," he said to Joe as he answered the call. After a brief exchange, he hung up and hustled toward his car. "Alex just woke up."

Joe followed. "I'm coming with you."

Quinn hesitated, turning back to Roxie, who was still sitting silently on the step. "Stay in the main house tonight, Roxie, and try to get some rest. I'll check in with you when I can."

"Don't worry about anything, Roxanne," Joe called out. His own phone started ringing, and he fished in his pocket for it as he added, "We'll have a couple men stationed at the house. You'll be completely safe."

CHAPTER THIRTY-TWO

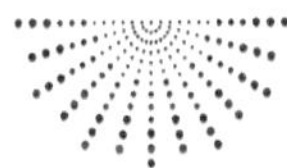

Alex heard someone calling her name. It was faint, and she wished whoever it was would go away. She tried to sink back into the peaceful darkness, but the voice got louder. Though she fought it, her mind gradually cleared, and with lucidity came discomfort. Everything throbbed. Everything burned. Everything hurt.

But she recognized the voice. Quinn. She needed to see him. She needed . . . him.

She blinked. And there he was.

His jaw was covered in stubble, his dark hair mussed and standing on end, as if he'd run his hands through it repeatedly. His gray gaze was full of concern and exhaustion. And love.

Just like that, tears poured from her eyes.

"Hey, gorgeous," he whispered, pulling his chair closer to the side of her bed. He wiped the tears away with his thumb, caressing the side of her tender face.

"Hi," she said. The one word was shaky.

"You and the baby are going to be fine." He brought her hand to his lips. "How are you feeling?"

Alex nodded, then shook her head. Her eyes welled with more tears, and she let out an unsteady breath. She had no idea how she was feeling.

She recalled seeing Doc Buchanan earlier, right after she'd regained consciousness. Things had been fuzzy, but she distinctly remembered that when he'd uttered those three little words—*the baby's okay*—a relief unlike any she'd known had left her sobbing. A deep ache had filled her chest. Gratitude, appreciation, relief.

Doc had hurried on as if she'd misunderstood him, repeatedly reassuring her that the baby had survived the attack and fall down the stairs. At the time, she'd nodded, but still hadn't been completely convinced that she deserved this baby.

Now, with Quinn holding her hand, more than anything, she wanted to prove to herself, to her baby, that she *was* worthy. By some miracle, she'd been given a second chance. *They'd* been given a second chance.

She glanced at the rolling table next to her bed, at the black-and-white sonogram printout. Her eyes misted. Just a little fuzzy blob the size of a blueberry. But it was the most perfect little blueberry.

Her baby should *not* have survived the trauma, nor the blood loss she'd endured. But it had. And she was going to love her child above everything else. Every day, she was going to prove that she was worthy of being its mother.

"I'm okay," she said, swallowing past the lump in her throat. "I was so scared, Quinn."

In a flash, he was on the bed next to her, his arms a soft cocoon. Her head tucked into that perfect spot between his neck and shoulder. She inhaled deeply. His familiar woodsy soap calmed her.

Minutes passed as she simply lay in his arms, taking comfort in his strength and the quiet words of reassurance he whispered in her ear. There was something about this man that settled her, made everything right.

A knock at the door interrupted the quiet.

Joe entered and stood at the foot of her bed, his smile not reaching his gloomy blue eyes. "Hey, doll. How are you?"

"I've been better." She snuggled deeper into Quinn's embrace. "The doctors say we'll be fine, and your dad has been great at explaining all the technical stuff."

"I'm glad to hear that. Truly." He sat in Quinn's vacated seat. "Alex, I know this is shitty timing, but if you're feeling up to it, I'd like to talk to you about what happened."

She hesitated.

Quinn pressed his lips to the top of her head. "I'm right here, sweetheart. I'm not going anywhere."

She nodded at Joe. "Who was that guy?"

"We'll get to that. Let's go through what happened first."

She shifted, wincing as a sharp pain shot up her side.

Quinn tensed. "Are you okay? Do you need the doctor?"

"No." She slowly exhaled. "I'm fine, Quinn. Just no sudden movements." With another breath, she turned her attention back to Joe. "What do you want to know?"

He set his phone on the rolling table and hit record. "Why don't you start from the beginning? When you and Roxie left the party."

"Okay. I caught a ride home with her. We said our good-byes in the driveway." She shrugged. "Roxie headed toward her place, and I went to mine."

"Did you use the front door or back?"

"Front. Why?"

He frowned. "The back door was open."

"Oh." She looked down at her hands. "I didn't check the back door when I got home. I just threw my stuff on the entry table and went upstairs. I guess I should have—"

"It's not your fault, sweetheart," Quinn interrupted.

"He's right," Joe said. "Go on."

"That's pretty much it. I got ready for bed and crashed. I'd been asleep for about an hour when something woke me up. A noise of some sort. I wasn't sure what. Then it happened again, and I think it was the stairs creaking."

Joe rubbed his temples. "Second from the bottom."

"And fourth from the top," Quinn added.

"Those two steps have creaked since we were little kids," Joe explained to Alex. "As we got older, avoiding them became habit so we wouldn't get caught sneaking in and out. Dad's been meaning to get it fixed . . ." He met her gaze. "Good thing he didn't."

She nodded, and a chill skated down her spine. "Good thing."

For a few moments, the only sound in the room was the buzz of the medical machines. Quinn's arms tightened around her ever so slightly.

Lacing her fingers with his, she leaned into him—his warmth, his comfort, his strength. Then she recounted the terrifying events of the night before. When she was done, Quinn ran his hands over her arms, soothing away her goosebumps. His gentle touch was a sharp contrast to the curses he muttered under his breath.

Joe shot Quinn an impatient look. After a moment, Quinn's muttering subsided, though the tension in his arms remained.

"Alex, we believe the intruder entered through the kitchen's back door, and that's where he grabbed the knife."

The memory of Preston doing the same flashed in her mind. She shivered. "Who is he? Did you catch him?"

Joe nodded. "His name was Jason Fulton—"

"Was?" Her stomach clenched. "Does that mean—"

"He didn't make it, Alex."

She gasped, and all the blood rushed from her head. "I *killed* him?"

"It was self-defense, sweetheart," Quinn said.

"He's right." Joe nodded. "It looks like the fall was what caused his death. But know that you're not going to be charged with anything. What happened was a clear case of self-defense."

She opened her mouth, but nothing came out.

"We've been able to trace Fulton's steps. We believe he was the one who placed those calls to you and ordered the flowers."

She shook her head. That didn't add up. "I've never seen that man before in my life. How could he have possibly known about the song and the flowers and the note?" Outside her therapist, no one did.

The two men exchanged a look she didn't understand.

Her brow crinkled in confusion. "What am I missing?"

Joe cleared his throat, rose from the chair, and paced the small hospital room. "Fulton was released from jail a week ago. The same place Woodsworth is in. They were in different cell blocks, so we're still trying to piece together how exactly they had contact, but we're certain that's the connection."

"But how did either of them know where I was staying? Where I was working?" She shook her head again. None of it made sense. "And the flowers were addressed to me—*Alex*. Not Natalie. How could Fulton—or even Preston—have figured that out?"

"The divorce papers?" Quinn asked.

She frowned. "No, I filed those in Boston. I didn't even know Hudson Island existed then."

Quinn's eyes narrowed when he saw a flicker of guilt cross Joe's face again.

Son of a motherfucking bitch.

He carefully unwrapped himself from Alex and stood, making sure not to jar her. He rounded the bed and approached Joe. Fury tinged his vision red. The picture of what had happened was now clear in his mind.

"Quinn?" Alex's voice was filled with worry, but he didn't take his eyes off Joe. "What are you—"

"Back off, O'Conner," Joe muttered. Wariness crawled over his face.

For good fucking reason.

Quinn's fist flew and landed squarely on Joe's jaw. "You motherfucker!"

"Quinn!" Alex screamed, scrambling out of the hospital bed. When her feet hit the floor, she cried out and crumpled to the ground.

His heart stopped. "Alex!"

They both rushed to her side, and he shoved Joe back. Hard. "Get the fuck away from her, Buchanan. You've done enough damage." He lifted Alex into his arms and lightly placed her back on the bed.

"Quinn, I'm fine," she said through gritted teeth.

"Like hell you're fine. I'll get the doctor." He turned to leave, stilling when she grabbed his arm.

"I said I'm fine," she repeated, grimacing. "Just give me a freaking second."

He started to speak, but she held up a hand and glared at him. His mouth snapped shut.

After a few deep breaths, she visibly relaxed. "Do you mind telling me what the hell that was all about?"

With the worst of her pain over, his anger surged back to life. Straightening, he crossed his arms over his chest and turned to Joe. "Care to enlighten her, you fucker?"

"I should have seen that one coming, O'Conner. It was well deserved, though." Joe rubbed his jaw, his shoulders sagging.

Quinn couldn't recall ever seeing his friend look so defeated. But fuck it. The guy had admitted this whole clusterfuck was his fault. He should have hit the dipshit harder.

"I'm really sorry, Alex," Joe said.

Her face clouded with sorrow. "About what, exactly? What did you do?"

Quinn's stomach twisted. When she reached for him, he took her delicate hand. Bringing it to his lips, he pressed a kiss to her palm and settled next to her on the bed, draping an arm around her slim shoulders.

He'd keep her safe, dammit. No matter what, she'd be safe.

Joe stared at the ceiling, his face scrunched in anger. "I know this will sound cold, and I'm sorry. Like I said earlier, we've been investigating Woodsworth, Mayor Downing, and Summerside's city council for years. When he put you in the hospital, we thought we had him for the assault, but so many things got fucked. Then it came out that my partner was fucking Woodsworth, and that shot our investigation to shit. We knew that with his connections, we wouldn't be able to hold him for long for the assault. Once he was out, we needed a way to lure him in."

Quinn felt a shudder run through Alex's frame, and he seethed with fury. He would have done anything to spare her this conversation, especially after everything she'd just endured. But he couldn't. He could only hold her and kiss the top of her head again.

She took in another deep breath, then squared her shoulders. A bit of the tightness in his chest uncoiled. Her strength and resilience left him in awe.

"And I was that lure, right? You told him where I was."

"Yeah." Joe's expression was pure anguish. "We leaked your location and new name to Woodsworth's lawyer."

She shook her head, as if everything was finally becoming clear. By the way her eyes narrowed, she wasn't pleased with any of it. "That's what all that paperwork you wanted me to sign was, wasn't it? That was the catch. I was supposed to be the bait." Her jaw clenched and her hands fisted.

Quinn bit back a sigh of relief. He'd rather have Alex angry than scared any day.

"But I didn't sign any of that paperwork. Hell, I haven't even had the chance to really look at it. Yet you *still* told him where I was. Don't you think some warning would have been helpful? A heads up, maybe?"

Joe scrubbed his hands over his face, tension shooting from him in waves.

Quinn knew the bastard was racked with guilt, and a tiny part of him felt bad for the guy. He knew firsthand what it was like to be stuck in an impossible situation at the hands of the FBI. His friend had been fucked in either direction. If he hadn't followed orders, it would've been career suicide. But following them had screwed over someone he cared about.

"Alex, please believe me when I say I didn't anticipate this happening. I take full responsibility. I should have seen this coming." A haunted expression flashed across his face. "I'm so sorry. For everything."

She eased back, leaning more fully into Quinn's chest, as if she were a slowly deflating balloon.

"What happens now, Buchanan?" he asked.

"The ball's already rolling." Joe's game face returned. "Now we keep Alex safe."

He flinched. "Do you anticipate more attacks on her?"

"No, but . . ." Joe's growl was pure frustration. "All we know for certain is Woodsworth is scheduled to be released in two weeks. It'll get back to him fairly quickly—if it hasn't already—that the attack on you was unsuccessful."

"Why can't you just charge him for hiring that goon to attack me?" Alex asked.

"Because we have nothing solid. It's all circumstantial."

Quinn gave Alex a squeeze, then stood, needing to move. Anticipation and outrage hummed through him like a live wire. "Then what? You're all gonna sit around with your thumbs up your asses and wait until he actually hurts Alex again? Wait until he tries to kill her again before you actually do something?"

He stopped two feet away from Joe. Any closer and he couldn't guarantee he wouldn't deck the guy again. He knew he needed to rein in his anger. The last thing Alex needed right now was for him to lose his goddamn mind. He exhaled slowly, desperate to find calm. "Do you think I'm going to sit around while you wave Alex in his face? Don't you think she's been through enough? She's—"

"I'll do it," her soft voice interrupted.

"What?" both men asked, their heads swinging to her.

"I said I'll do it." Her soft voice gained strength. "Preston's coming regardless, right? Just tell me what you need from me, Joe."

Panic tore through him. "You don't have to do this, sweetheart."

"Yes, Quinn." She looked at him, and the determination on her face terrified him. "I do."

He dropped his head back and stared at the ceiling. But it provided no solutions to his frustration or fear.

"Stop growling and look at me," she ordered.

He counted to ten before glancing her way. When he met her gaze, a vise clamped down on his heart and tightened. Painfully. He couldn't lose her. He couldn't.

"I'm tired, Quinn. I'm tired of being scared of him, of

running from him. For once, I'm not afraid to stand up to him. Not if it means there's a chance he could get put away for good."

Her insistence—her sheer bravery—frightened him beyond belief.

"He's going to try to *kill* you." His voice was gravel. He could barely get the words out over the lump in his throat. "You understand that, right?"

"Of course I do," she snapped, fire lighting her eyes. "But it's a chance I'm willing to take."

A bolt of agony shot through him.

No. Fuck, no. That wasn't an option.

"Quinn, if we're going to have any sort of future together, this is something I *have* to do. It doesn't matter to Preston whether he and I are married or divorced; he'll always think I belong to him. And he'll always blame me for ruining his life. As long as he's walking free, I'll always be looking over my shoulder. That's not a way to live. Not for me. Not for my baby. And I love you too much to have you live like that as well."

His heart tripped and then settled just as quickly. He stared at her in awe.

The woman before him was tiny in her hospital bed. Her hair fell around her in a tangled mess. The dark bruises on the side of her face were angry reminders of the horror she'd suffered. And yet, the look in her eyes was that of a warrior hell-bent on going head to head with a man who wanted her dead.

So she and her baby could have a future—so the three of them could have a future—without fear.

Holy shit. He was humbled by her love and courage . . . and scared beyond words. He *couldn't* lose her. He *wouldn't*. It wasn't an option.

Crossing the room, he placed a finger beneath her chin, tilted her head up, and brought his mouth to hers.

"Alexandra Garcia," he whispered against her lips, "I love you more than you'll ever know. If you need to do this, then I'll be right there with you. Believe me when I say that I'll do *everything* in my power to keep you safe." He would use every tool at his disposal, every bit of manpower that was available to him, every favor he was owed. *Anything* to keep her safe.

A slow smile spread across her lips, and her eyes filled with tears. "I believe you."

He wrapped his arms around her, and a feeling of peace blanketed him. "When this is all over, sweetheart, I promise to spend the rest of my days keeping you happy."

She pulled away and framed his face in her hands. "I don't know what I've done to deserve you." She touched her lips to his. "I love you, Quinn O'Conner."

"Ahem."

The blush that raced up Alex's face was priceless. He kissed her again before turning toward Joe, who stood at the edge of the room, shifting uncomfortably on his feet.

"I hate to break up the party and all, but I'd like to go over the plan of attack with you both."

"Sure." Quinn nodded. "Just go away for a little bit first." He directed his attention back to Alex.

"Excuse me?"

"You heard me, Buchanan," he said, not taking his gaze off her. "Go away."

There was a moment of silence, then Joe cleared his throat. "Uh, yeah . . . Okay then . . ." He mumbled under his breath as he exited the room, pulling the door closed behind him.

"Don't worry, sweetheart. I'm not going to jump you." He grinned at her, and amusement danced in her eyes. "I just wanted to kiss you without an audience."

Pushing her hair away from her face, he brushed his fingers over her bruised cheek. Her wince was barely perceptible. But he saw it. He replaced his fingers with the softest of kisses.

"It kills me that he hurt you," he murmured. "I know we haven't known each other very long, but the time doesn't matter. Because this? You and me? It's right. You've become as vital to me as air. I love you, Alex."

Radiating trust and affection, she watched him with a sweet smile. Everything inside him clicked into place. Taking care to be gentle, he kissed her with everything he had.

So . . . this was love.

CHAPTER THIRTY-THREE

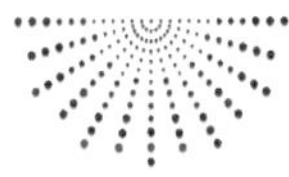

The hum of the machines in the hospital room provided a soothing white noise. Alex pulled the thin, scratchy blanket tighter around her and rolled to burrow deeper into the bed.

A sharp fire blazed along the right side of her body. The air left her lungs in a tormented gasp.

Her eyes darted around the dark room, confusion muddling her mind. The beeping on the machines went wild when she spotted a man in the corner. He stood in the shadows, hidden from the light.

As he stalked toward her, she sprang off the bed. The swift motion ripped the IV from her wrist, but she paid no mind to the sting or the blood trickling down her arm. She raced for the door, and the monitor cords attached to her skin stretched taut. With little pops, the adhesive gave way, and the cords fell to the floor, setting off an unbearable, high-pitched squeal. Before she could yank the handle, the man snagged her by the arm and slammed her face first into the door.

Pinning her against the cold steel, he rubbed his erection against her. Hissing into her ear, he said, "Don't you remember lesson four, darling? Never run from me."

Her skin went ice cold.

Preston slowly turned her to face him.

"I want to show you something. It's another lesson, darling." His tone was conversational now. He pulled her from the door, deeper into the room. "Natalie, you belong to me, and this is what happens when you run."

He released her arm and stepped away, switching on the overhead light.

She recoiled from the sudden brightness, willing her vision to adjust. When it did, when she saw the form lying on the ground at her feet, her stomach heaved. Staggering backward, she whipped her hands to her mouth, revulsion and disbelief numbing her face.

Covered in blood, Quinn stared back at her with dull, lifeless gray eyes.

The room spun, and menacing, hysterical laughter filled her ears. A sob wrenched from her throat as she sank to her knees.

Alex shot up from the bed. She ignored the tears streaming down her cheeks, the aches triggered by her heaving gasps, the sharp pain pinching below her right shoulder. All of it.

Frantically scanning the dark room, she froze when her gaze fell over the silhouette of a man slumped awkwardly in a chair at the foot of her hospital bed. She let out the breath she'd been holding.

Quinn.

She'd recognize him anywhere. Pushing the button that controlled the bedside light, she heaved another sigh of relief. No blood. He was okay. The steady rise and fall of his chest drained the remaining tension from her. It had only been a dream. Another awful, too-real-for-comfort dream.

Pressing another button, she adjusted the hospital bed so she was sitting. Then, watching Quinn, she memorized every feature and angle of his face, every contour of his body. And a serenity settled within her. In such a short period of time, this man had come to mean more to her than she'd ever expected.

After a while, his eyelids fluttered open. Squinting against the light, he sat up and massaged his neck.

"Hey, gorgeous." His voice was raspy from sleep, and he rolled his neck from side to side. "What are you doing up?" He glanced at the clock. "It's only five thirty. Are you in pain? Do you need me to get a nurse or the doctor?"

She shook her head, patting the mattress next to her. He promptly rose and sat on the bed, facing her.

Her hands trembled as his lifeless body flashed in her mind. Her breath hitched, and she laced her fingers with his. "Bad dream. You were dead. He killed you, and it was all my fault. You were all bloody . . ."

Quinn pulled her close, stroking her head and running his fingers through her hair. "Shh. It was just a dream, sweetheart. I'm right here."

As he held her tight, she tried to shut out the grisly images from her mind. The thought of losing this man terrified her.

A tremor racked her body, and she focused on the sound of his heartbeat, on his whispered reassurances. He kissed the top of her head, and she sank into his comforting embrace.

She couldn't lose him . . .

CHAPTER THIRTY-FOUR

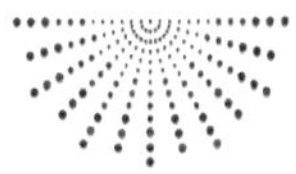

I t had taken a lot of maneuvering on Alex's part to get the doctors to release her from the hospital. However, with a solemn promise to stay off her feet—and Doc Buchanan's assurance that there were numerous people who'd be watching her like a hawk—they had relented, and she'd been released on Sunday morning.

With Quinn's help, she settled into the passenger seat of his SUV. She was happy to be out of the hospital. It had been two nights of noisy machines and people constantly checking on her, poking and prodding. She was beyond exhausted. And sore.

She cradled her stomach. The baby was okay. And *that's* what mattered. She could deal with the exhaustion. She could deal with how every inch of her body hurt. But she wasn't going to lie—the idea of a warm bath and uninterrupted sleep had her nearly weeping with gratitude. Even if both were still a thirty-minute ferry crossing away.

After a mostly silent ride, during which she'd drifted in and out of sleep, they arrived back at Hudson Island and disembarked the ferry.

Clearing her throat, she aimed for a light and casual tone. "Looks like our plans for a Saturday morning breakfast in bed were shot, huh?"

He glanced at her, a concerned expression on his face.

Apparently, her light and casual tone could use some work. "What do you have planned for the rest of the day?"

Keeping his eyes on the road, he reached over and held her hand. "I need to go over some stuff at the station with Joe."

"So, you're taking me back to my place . . ." She frowned as he maneuvered through Hudson's quaint downtown and parked in front of Comfort Food.

"No. The doctors said you need to stay off your feet. I figured if you were at home by yourself, you'd do everything but that. Roxie said she'd watch you."

"'Watch' me?" Her eyebrows hit her hairline. "What do you think I am? An incapable child?"

She was being unreasonable. She knew it. But she was so damn tired, she couldn't make the attitude stop.

He exhaled loudly. "Of course not. And you know it. Now put your eyebrows down."

"Don't mock me, Quinn O'Conner." She crossed her arms over her chest and turned away from him, nose in the air. She might have even huffed.

"Wow, you've got the regal-princess thing nailed." She could hear the smirk in his voice, and she didn't know whether to laugh or punch him. So, she remained silent and told herself to ease the hell up. "Look, Alex. I think you should still be in the hospital, but you were hell-bent on getting out of there. The truth is, I have to meet with Joe, and I don't want to drive myself crazy worrying about whether or not you're okay. I don't want to leave you by yourself."

She sighed. If she were being honest, even though a bath and bed sounded wonderful, she didn't want to be alone, either. Especially at Joe's house. So why was she throwing him attitude? No clue. She was an exhausted mess. Maybe a hormonal one, too.

"Besides," he continued, "I know Roxie's worried about you. When I called to let her know you were being released, she offered to have you come hang out at the café. She wants to keep an eye on you. She's even got the cozy window table reserved for you."

He gave her a brilliant grin, and her eyes narrowed. She'd seen him use that same grin on Roxie. The man was up to something.

"Look. Joe and I have told her otherwise, but she feels guilty about what happened. It will help if she sees you are okay."

Just like that, her annoyance at Quinn's high-handedness was shelved. "Why would she possibly feel guilty? There was nothing she could have done. I mean—"

"I know. We've told her that. But you know Rox. She feels guilty regardless. She just wants to help you out."

"Of course," she said, grabbing the door handle. "I'd—"

Turning back around, she saw him smother a grin. Well, that confirmed the niggling suspicion that she'd been played. But she couldn't be annoyed. Not really.

"Busted, Sheriff," she said, rolling her eyes. "Nice try on the guilt trip, though."

He chuckled. "You're good. Roxie can never spot it." He reached for her hand and brought it to his lips. "Seriously, though, she does feel guilty, and I do worry about you. So please? For my peace of mind, let her babysit you today?"

She nodded, and her eyes filled. She blinked furiously to hold the tears at bay. Gah. She truly was an exhausted, hormonal mess. But this man . . .

"Stay put," he whispered, dropping a kiss to the tip of her nose.

He got out, rounded the hood, and opened her door. Taking her hand in his, he helped her out of the SUV.

"I'm sorry I'm such an emotional basket case right now," she said.

He placed his finger over her lips. "You have nothing to be sorry about, sweetheart. You've been through a lot. The fact that you're still standing amazes me."

Sniffling, she said, "Thank you for saying you worry about me. It means a lot to me."

He tucked a piece of her hair behind her ear and kissed her lips. "*You* mean a lot to me."

With a protective arm around her shoulders, he walked her into Comfort Food. She paused in the entryway, shocked at the number of people crammed at the tables. As the door closed behind them, a hush filled the room.

"Morning, folks." Quinn raised a hand in greeting while he accompanied her to the front counter.

"Hi, guys," Roxie said with a sunny smile as she came out from the back. "I figured you'd shown up by the sudden silence. Alex, come with me to the back first. I'll take it from here, Sheriff."

"Sorry about all that," Roxie said once they were seated in the tiny office.

Alex was behind the desk, and Roxie was perched on a stool next to her.

"It's been a madhouse since we opened. As I'm sure you've deduced, news spreads quickly here on Hudson Island. Everyone's been in asking about what happened and how you're doing. Most are genuinely concerned about you, though there are a couple busybodies snooping." Roxie rolled her eyes. "Quinn's crew and the feds aren't talking, so everyone's dying for any tiny bit of information on what went down."

Apprehension twisted her stomach. "What have you been saying to everyone?"

"The watered-down version that the feds told me to say."

The apprehension grew. "And that would be . . ."

Roxie took hold of her hands and squeezed. "That a burglar broke into Joe's place thinking it was empty. He got spooked when he ran across you, and there was a struggle. You got banged up, and the guy was caught when Joe and Quinn got home."

Watered-down version, indeed. She frowned, little seeds of guilt swirling within her. "But he didn't get caught, Roxie. I stabbed him, and he *died*." She shuddered. "And burglary was the least of his crimes."

"Exactly, Alex. If you hadn't defended yourself, you'd be dead." Roxie's intense gaze held hers, and she took comfort in her friend's strength. "You protected yourself. You protected your baby. You have *nothing* to feel guilty about. Do you hear me?"

She let out an unsteady breath and nodded.

"Like I said," Roxie continued, "I've been giving everyone the version the feds want me to say. I assume they're keeping it quiet that the asshole died for a reason." Her eyes closed. "God, when I think of what could have happened to you . . . I was right there, right across the yard, and I could have helped you. Maybe—"

"No, Rox," she said, wanting to give her friend some sort of reassurance. "There's nothing you could've done."

"I know. This isn't about me. Joe already gave me the lecture this morning."

Alex pursed her lips. She didn't know what that comment meant, but she wasn't going to touch it. "Please don't beat yourself up about this. Really. If you were there, he would have hurt you, too. The man was huge. And scary. I'm lucky to even be alive." Her hands went to her stomach, and her eyes welled. Again. Her emotions were all over the damn place this morning. "I'm so lucky."

Roxie pulled her into a tight hug, and she happily returned the embrace.

"I'm so thankful you and the baby are okay." Releasing her, Roxie swiped away a couple of stray tears. "You're welcome to hang back here if you want some quiet. But if you're feeling up to it, there's a table for you out front. Or I can bring a stool up to the counter so you're not completely in the middle of the chaos."

Alex glanced around the small, claustrophobic room, and her nose wrinkled. "A chair at the front counter sounds good."

They stood and made their way back through the kitchen.

"Good god, woman, don't walk too fast!" Roxie said, catching her hand to slow her down.

"Okay, okay," Alex said, biting back a smile.

Her friend eyed her as they reached the front counter. "Promise me you'll just sit there and not overdo it?"

She laughed. "I promise."

"Seriously. All teasing aside, you *have* to sit. You're not working the register or anything. Just. Sitting." Roxie positioned a padded, high-back stool at the end of the counter, then helped her get situated. "Quinn will kill me. Literally. Not to mention Doc."

She hated to admit it, but if it hadn't been for Roxie, she wasn't sure she would have been able to climb up onto the stool. Every muscle in her body was protesting.

Roxie dropped her voice and leaned in. "Are you really okay?"

"I'm fine. I promise." Yes, she was in pain and her emotions were chaotic, but she needed to be around people.

Not alone, lost in her thoughts, overthinking things and making herself crazy. "This is a good distraction. And I'll stick to the feds' version of what went down."

"And the chair?"

She bit back a chuckle. "Yes, Roxie. I promise I won't move from the chair. Just sitting. I'll even ask your permission before I get up to use the bathroom."

Roxie grinned, throwing her hands up in victory. "Perfect! I'll be up here all day with you, anyway. You just let me know when you need to go."

The next few hours flew past. By eleven thirty, it seemed as though everyone in town had walked through Comfort Food's doors. Even though they closed at eleven on Sundays, the place was still packed. And no one looked like they were in any hurry to leave.

Alex had been intrigued by everyone's curiosity and touched by the concern of the people she'd gotten to know. As she'd promised, she hadn't moved from her chair. And Roxie had never left her side. Once again, she felt forever grateful to the woman for her support, strength, and friendship.

As she finished another telling of the burglar story, this time to Mrs. Abbot and Mrs. Yoshida, Quinn walked in. While the two women fussed over her, he shot her a wink and disappeared into the kitchen. Moments later, he emerged carrying a large paper to-go bag. Roxie was right behind him.

"Ladies," Quinn said, interrupting her conversation with Mrs. Abbot and Mrs. Yoshida, much to their delight. "You're looking lovelier than ever." As per the ritual, he kissed their hands, and they giggled like teenagers. "Would either of you mind if I stole this one away from you?" He draped his arm over her shoulders and treated them to his aw-shucks grin.

Damn. The man was quite the charmer when he wanted to be.

"Of course not, dear," Mrs. Abbot said.

"You take good care of her now," Mrs. Yoshida added.

"You can count on that," he said, helping her down from the stool. "Roxie, we're off."

Her friend turned from the espresso machine and rolled her eyes at Mrs. Abbot and Mrs. Yoshida in dramatic fashion. "Now, if the lug head were only half as nice to me as he is to the two of you . . ." She walked up to Quinn and gave him a fierce bear hug, whispering in his ear.

With a smile that had his gray eyes dancing, he kissed Roxie on her forehead and murmured, "Thank you."

Before Alex could wonder what Roxie had said, the woman wrapped her in a big hug. To her relief, it was much less fierce than the one Quinn had received.

"Relax and enjoy the rest of your day, Alex." She sniffed. "And thanks for letting me watch over you." She pivoted back to the espresso machine. Then, addressing Mrs. Abbot and Mrs. Yoshida, she said, "Your drinks will be right up, ladies."

Alex's brows rose. Were those tears in Roxie's eyes? She started to ask, but Quinn linked his hand with hers and guided her to the door.

Once they had both settled in the SUV, she turned to him. "Is Roxie all right?"

"What do you mean?"

Her friend's parting expression flashed in her mind. "It looked like, I don't know, she was going to cry or something."

"She didn't mention anything. She has allergies. Maybe they were acting up?" He shrugged. Parking a couple of blocks away in front of Ray's Diner, he cut the engine. "Hang tight for a second."

He hopped out of the car and strolled into Ray's. Through the diner's windows, she saw him speaking with Martha behind the counter. He gestured toward the SUV, and Martha waved, grinning ear to ear.

Returning the wave, Alex watched as they talked for a few minutes. Ray appeared, slapping Quinn on the shoulder as his wife shooed him away. Quinn and Martha continued their conversation until Ray returned carrying two bags, and this time, he slapped Quinn on the back of the head. Alex choked on a laugh. With a good-natured shake of her fist at Ray, Martha patted Quinn on the cheek, beaming at him as he walked out of the diner.

Quinn loaded the bags into the back seat, and the food's decadent aromas filled the vehicle.

She inhaled deeply, and her mouth watered. "What was that about? And where are we going?"

"Questions, questions, questions," he murmured, a grin on his lips. "For the second question, home. For the first, what was what about?"

"Martha and Ray? Why did he hit you upside the head?"

"Who knows?" He chuckled. "But probably because he can?" After waving at a young couple crossing the street, he said, "Martha and I were just chatting. She heard about you getting hurt and wanted to make sure you were okay. She's got a big heart."

Minutes later, they pulled into Quinn's driveway. As the SUV came to a stop, he touched her arm, stilling her. "Wait. Please. I'll come around and get your door."

She barely withheld an eye roll. "I can open my own door, Quinn." It was a sweet offer, but unnecessary. Reaching for the handle, she was stilled by his hand again. This time, she succumbed to the eye roll. "When the doctors told me to take it easy, I'm pretty sure they meant to not exercise or do anything strenuous. I'm pretty sure opening my car door is okay."

"I'm sure it's annoying that I'm hovering like you're a fragile piece of glass. Alex, I know you're a strong, capable woman . . ." A shadow crossed his face, as if he was caught in a memory, and she regretted her flippant words. "But, sweetheart, you're so damn precious to me. Anything I can do to make things easier for you, no matter how small, I want to do it."

Her heart melted.

He shot her a roguish grin. "Humor me with the door thing? Maybe for just this week?" He pursed his lips. "Well, maybe until after you've had the baby?"

Her heart melted a little more. "Sure, I'll humor you."

He leaned across the console and kissed her before hurrying out of the driver's seat. After opening her door and helping her out, he snagged the take-out bags and led her to the back door of the house. Once inside, he placed the bags on the kitchen counter. "I have a little surprise for you. Take a seat, and I'll be right back."

She'd been sitting all day, and her back was starting to ache. Well, starting to ache *more*. So instead, she opened the bags and almost drooled.

Golden fried chicken, steaming biscuits, potato salad, and scrumptious mashed potatoes and gravy. Her stomach growled its appreciation. Not thinking it could get any better, she opened the Comfort Food bag and peeked into the box. And groaned. Oh, it got better. A warm, mouthwatering blueberry pie.

"Quinn, have you been talking to Roxie?" she called out as she rummaged for a spoon. "Her blueberry pies are my favorite." She snuck a bite of pie and moaned, the sweet and tart blueberry goodness bursting in her mouth. "Did you know that I can eat an entire pie in under twenty-five minutes? Roxie timed me the other day." She frowned, not quite sure if that was a good or bad thing. "You know, that's actually pretty disgusting when you think about it."

She scooped up another heaping spoonful of pie. One more bite wouldn't hurt.

A quiet laugh caught her attention. She looked up and found Quinn leaning against the kitchen archway, a sexy grin on his face. With a mouthful of pie, she gave him a sheepish smile.

"Twenty-five minutes, you say?"

She nodded, swallowing.

He joined her at the counter. "We'll have to work on that. I clock in at just shy of eleven minutes. And Joe? He's in a class of his own. He can down an entire pie in six minutes flat. It's quite extraordinary, really." He pulled out a serving tray and piled all the food and two bottles of water onto it.

"What are you doing?"

He gently kissed her bruised lips, then picked up the tray. "Come on."

Tossing her spoon in the sink, she followed him into the living room and stopped short.

Her mouth dropped open.

Spread out before the glowing fire was a giant picnic blanket. A huge vase of pink dahlias sat in one corner, and a large picnic basket filled with yellow daisies sat in the oppo-site corner. In the middle, between two enormous floor pillows, Quinn unloaded the tray of food onto the coffee table. Dozens of tea light candles decorated the hearth, and somewhere in the background, Billie Holiday softly sere-naded them.

Seating himself on one pillow, he glanced up at her. "Lunch?"

Speechless. She was speechless.

Knowing tears were imminent, she fought to find the right words.

"Quinn . . . no one's ever . . . Wow." Words failed her, and she let out a watery chuckle. "This is beautiful. Absolutely beautiful."

She lowered herself onto the other floor pillow. Looking up at him, her throat tightened. His dark-brown hair was disheveled, and there was over a day's worth of stubble across his jaw, defining it even more. The light from the window, combined with the light from the fire and candles, cast a soft glow over his face. Gazing into his gray eyes, warmth enveloped her.

A tear spilled down her cheek. Followed by another.

The panic that flashed over Quinn's face as he reached out to wipe her tears away was adorable. If she could have made any sound past the lump in her throat, she would have laughed.

"Alex, sweetheart, please tell me these are happy tears."

Too overwhelmed to speak, she nodded. More tears fell, and after a few moments, she found her voice. "Thank you, Quinn. This means more to me than you could ever imagine." She stood, then joined him on his pillow and held his face in her hands. Running her thumb across his lips, she said, "I know I've been an emotional wreck today, but I meant what I said at the hospital. I love you. With everything that I am, Quinn. I really do love you."

He drew her close and softly kissed her damp cheeks, trailing his mouth down to her lips. "Can I ask you a question?"

She nodded.

"I know I've been an emotional, hovering wreck today." He smiled as he parroted her words back to her. "But I meant what *I* said at the hospital, too. I love you. With everything that I am, Alex. I really do love you. I promise you I'll do everything I can to make you happy—to *keep* you happy—and I will love you forever. Will you marry me?"

For the second time in a matter of minutes, her mouth fell open. Her heart stopped, and she stared at him in shock. When his words at last registered in her brain, she could only blink. Because it was too soon. It was too crazy. It was too complicated.

She waited for the panic.

And waited some more.

But there was none. There was only peace. And excitement. And a feeling of this—of *them*—being completely right.

A smile spread on her face until it hurt. On her next breath, her arms flew around his neck, and she ignored the twinges of pain and discomfort that raced up her sides. She yanked his head toward her and crashed her lips to his, bruises be damned.

With a laugh, he pulled her onto his lap. "Is that a yes?"

"Yes!" she exclaimed, hugging him again.

They lingered in their embrace, and then he pulled slightly away to slip a ring onto her finger. "I hope you like it."

"Quinn," she gasped. The ring—an elegant band with a large, glittery sapphire and small, shimmering diamonds on either side—was stunning. "It's beautiful. I don't know what to say . . ."

"You already said yes. That's all that matters." He pulled her close again. "I know it's a little big on you, but we can get it resized. It was the ring my dad proposed to my mom with. And his dad before him."

"Oh, Quinn." Her heart squeezed as another tear trickled down her face.

She looked at the picnic spread out before her. The food, the flowers, the candles, the ring . . . The thoughtfulness. The love. She caressed his cheek and held his gaze.

"It would be my honor to be your wife, Quinn O'Conner."

Bringing her lips to his again, she made sure to pour every ounce of love she possessed for the man into their kiss.

CHAPTER THIRTY-FIVE

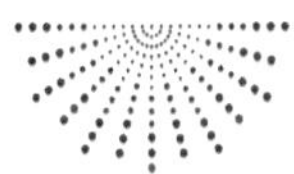

"To Quinn and Alex," Joe toasted, his glass raised high.

"Cheers!" they said, clinking their glasses together.

Alex looked between Quinn, Joe, and Roxie, who were all gathered around Quinn's dining table, and her throat constricted with emotion. "Thank you for this wonderful dinner, Roxie," she said. "And really . . . for everything you've done for me. Your friendship has meant so much."

"Ugh! Stop!" Roxie wailed with an exaggerated shake of her head. "You're going to make me cry again." She pulled Alex into a hug that had her wincing. Upon releasing her, Roxie aimed a finger at Quinn. "And you! What's the deal with telling me you're going to propose when I'm standing five feet away from her? Were you trying to make me break down right then and there?"

Quinn laughed and slung his arm around Roxie's neck, smacking a loud kiss to her forehead.

Joe punched Quinn on the shoulder. "Yeah, and thanks, by the way, for not even telling me. I get to the house expecting peace and quiet, and instead I've got this one"—he gestured at Roxie—"making a racket in my kitchen. I swear—"

"I'm sorry, Joe," Roxie interrupted, "but I didn't hear you complaining about said racket while you were shoveling my lasagna down your throat."

"Yeah, well, it was either that or starve," Joe tossed back.

"You are such a jackass. I didn't—"

"Again, Roxanne." Joe gave her a withering look. "Not everything is about you."

Alex's brows climbed up her forehead. What was going on with these two?

"You're right, Joe." Roxie's green eyes narrowed, and her voice took on a saccharine quality. "Apparently, everything is about *you*." She scoffed, then turned to Quinn and Alex, a genuine smile brightening her face. "Congratulations, you guys. Really." She pulled them into a group hug. "You guys are perfect for each other." With a sniff, she stepped back— and then pulled Alex in for another hug.

"I'm so happy you're okay," Roxie whispered.

She hugged her friend back with everything she had. "Thank you, Roxie."

Blowing out a breath, Roxie gave her a final squeeze before heading for the door. "I'll see you tomorrow."

"What about the dishes?" Joe asked, hands on his hips. "And what about the mess you made in my kitchen? I swear to god, Roxanne, I'm not cleaning all of it up by myself."

"Go to hell, Joe." Roxie's smile was all teeth as she sailed past him.

"Welcome to life with Roxie and Joe," Quinn muttered.

She swallowed a chuckle as Joe stared at the door, fuming.

"What the hell was that?" he asked, facing them. His expression was a mixture of disbelief and annoyance.

Quinn shrugged. "You know the deal. If she cooks, there's

no way in hell she cleans. It's why she started cooking in the first place, remember?"

Joe shook his head and walked to the sink. "Fine. I'll load, O'Conner, and you can do the stuff that doesn't fit. Then you can come over and help me clean up my kitchen."

Quinn cleared his throat. "Oh, would you look at that? It's getting late, and Alex has been on her feet for *way* too long today." He carefully swooped her up into his arms, and she grinned. "I should really get her to bed."

Joe glared at him. "Don't even think about it, Connie."

"I'm an engaged man now, Buchanan." He smirked. "The old ball and chain here is the new boss. And she really is looking tired."

Joe turned his glare to her.

She snorted. "Nope. Don't get me involved in this."

"Fine," Joe grumbled, shaking his head. "I'll take care of all this."

Just as they made it through the kitchen archway, Joe called out, "Oh, hey!"

They paused, looking back at him.

He met Alex's gaze, and his blue eyes softened. "I'm glad you and the baby are okay, doll. And congratulations. Truly. But just so you know, there are no takebacks. You're stuck with that jackass. Forever."

She laughed, catching the wink Joe sent her way before Quinn whisked her down the hall to his room.

CHAPTER THIRTY-SIX

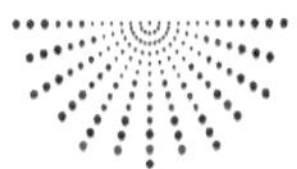

Thirteen days had passed since Alex's attack. Since he'd almost lost the woman who'd come to mean more to him than all others.

She'd officially moved in with him after tearfully admitting she was scared to go back to Joe's house—to where she'd been so violently assaulted. So, over the ten days since she'd been released from the hospital, she'd rested and healed under his watchful gaze.

He winced. Roxie had laughed her ass off when he'd used the word *watchful* with her. She'd said *overprotective* and *hovering* were more accurate terms.

Was he overprotective and hovering when it came to Alex? He sure as fuck was. If he didn't have eyes on her, then someone he trusted did. When Alex wasn't with him, she was with Roxie. And so what if he'd asked Cade, Deputy Chase, and Doc to all swing into Comfort Food during the day to make sure she was okay?

As caveman as it sounded, she was his. Period. That baby? His. Maybe not *technically*, but he didn't care about the semantics. And if he went a little overboard protecting his family, then so be it. Because that's what Alex and the baby were now—his family.

Over the last couple of days, the stitches from her stab wound had been removed, and the bruises over her body had finally started fading. Out of precaution, Doc had recommended she continue to take it easy, so Roxie had kept her relegated to only working the counter at Comfort Food. Aside from making coffee and pulling items from the case, Alex was to remain seated at all times.

The poor thing was about to pull her hair out from boredom. But she didn't want to risk harming the baby. So, while she grumbled about it, according to Roxie, anyway, she did what she was told.

Now, Quinn was doing his own grumbling as he sat at his desk, waiting impatiently for Joe to get off the phone.

It took another five full minutes before the bastard hung up. Fucking feds.

"Jesus, that took long enough." Quinn glared at his friend. "Well?"

"You want the good news or the bad news?"

Goddamn, give him patience. "Does it matter?"

Joe shook his head. "Fuck, not really."

Done with the bullshit, he leaned back and glared some more. "Talk, Buchanan."

"The good news is we know where Woodsworth is. The bad news is that he was released this morning."

His heart tripped. *The fuck?* "He wasn't supposed to be released until tomorrow."

"True." Joe let out a weary sigh. "And like always, I'm the last to fucking know. Nothing's changed in that regard since you left the Bureau, O'Conner. You know how it goes."

"Yeah. I do. All too well." He ran his hands over his face. "Where is he?"

"Woodsworth's still in Summerside. His lawyer picked him up and took him straight back to his house."

"Your team will notify you if he moves?"

"You bet your ass they will."

Quinn got up from his desk and headed for the door. "You better make sure they do."

"Where are you going?" Joe asked. "Woodsworth hasn't left New England. Alex is safe at the café."

He opened his mouth to respond right as Joe's phone rang. His friend held up a finger, then answered and began speaking to the caller.

Quinn paced his office. After what seemed like hours but was probably less than a minute, Joe hung up, a grim expression on his face.

His blood froze over.

"And so it begins," Joe said.

Quinn's jaw clenched at the ominous words, and he braced himself.

"Woodsworth is still at his house, but conveniently, Mayor Downing's private jet has been fired up. Once he's airborne, we'll check the flight plan to get landing coordinates."

"What the fuck, Joe?" Quinn said, his anger spilling over.

He held up his hands. "Look at it this way, O'Conner. If Woodsworth comes out here, it's a six-hour flight. The nearest airfield that can accommodate a jet the size of Downing's is Boeing Field. That's more than an hour away if he takes the fastest route available. Potentially more than two hours, depending on the ferry wait. There are a few different ways for him to get here, but we've got time."

Quinn's skin was on fire. "What do you plan on doing when he gets here?"

"It depends on what he does." Joe pressed his lips into a

flat line. "We'll put a couple agents at Boeing Field. Then we'll have a couple more at the ferry dock."

He nodded. "We've got at least six hours, so let's go over all the possibilities."

Joe sighed. "Ah, the scenario game. I hate this game."

Quinn slammed his hand down on the desk, and heat flashed through his body. "This is *not* a fucking game, Buchanan. This is Alex's *life*. You fucked up once. Do *not* fuck up again. If she gets hurt, I'm holding you personally responsible. And our friendship be damned, I *will* take you down."

Joe's expression hardened. "Don't threaten me, O'Conner."

"Trust me, Buchanan. It's not a threat."

Two and a half hours later, Quinn walked into Comfort Food, leaving Joe on the sidewalk to bark into his cell phone. He caught Alex's eye, and she waved from behind the counter as Mrs. Abbot and Mrs. Yoshida fawned over her ring. He'd heard through the gossip mill that both women had just returned from a cruise to Mexico.

"Ladies," Quinn said, pasting on a grin. "Welcome back. By your tans, I trust you had a good time."

"We did. Now get over here, young man," Mrs. Yoshida said, giving him a hearty hug. "Congratulations, dear boy."

"It's just lovely, Quinn," Mrs. Abbot said, dabbing her eyes. "Your mother would have loved her."

His throat tightened, and for a split second, he could only stare at Mrs. Abbot.

Mom. Damn, how he missed her.

He blinked back the sudden rush of emotion and hugged Mrs. Abbot. "Thank you. That really means a lot."

With a pat to his cheek, Mrs. Abbot turned to Mrs. Yoshida, and they went to their usual table.

Alex squeezed his hand. "I didn't know they were friends of your parents."

He leaned in to kiss her hello.

He loved that he could do that—give her a good-to-see-you kiss without blinking an eye. It reminded him of his folks. They'd had the kind of affection that was so damn natural, so damn right. Deep down, he'd always hoped he would find that kind of love. And looking at Alex, that hope sprouted to life in his chest.

Still, it was bittersweet. What he would give to be in a room with both his parents and Alex . . . Because Mrs. Abbot was right. They would've loved her.

He cleared his throat, and it took him two tries to speak over the lump. He aimed for nonchalant, but knew he'd missed the mark. "You live here all your life, and everyone's friends with everyone. But those two ladies were especially close. If my folks were alive, my mom would be sitting at that table with them, and my dad would be out fishing with their husbands." His throat tightened again. Damn. He scanned the room, desperate for a distraction, and came up empty. "It's pretty quiet in here. Where are Roxie and Nina?"

"Roxie's at the bank, and Nina's doing a catering delivery," she said, a soft smile on her lips. Taking his hand, she placed a kiss on the back and then held it in her lap. His heart settled a tiny bit. "You've never talked about them. What were your parents like?"

"Wonderful," he said, voice thick. "I know death can turn people into saints. My folks weren't perfect by any means, but if you ask anyone who knew them, they'd all say Mom and Dad were wonderful. Good people."

He sighed, lost in fond memories. "They were always really busy with work, charity functions, bowling leagues, and all that typical stuff. But they always made time. Even when I was a surly, obnoxious sixteen-year-old who had the world figured out and only wanted to acknowledge them as my parents every other Tuesday . . . they still made the time."

Not a day went by where he didn't think about his parents. Some days, missing them was a dull ache, and he was unable to comprehend that they'd been gone for so long. Other days, the pain was so fucking fresh, as if he'd just gotten the call they'd been killed.

"For my entire life, there was never a doubt in my mind that they loved me and were proud of me. And it wasn't just me. My mom was especially close with both Joe and Roxie. Joe's mom split right after he was born, but she'd constantly pop in and out of his life when we were kids, and it messed with his head. And Roxie's mom? I suppose she's a nice person, but no one would ever call her *maternal*. So, my mom took Joe and Rox under her wing. When my parents died, it was just as devastating for them as it was for me."

Alex pulled him closer and wrapped her arms around his waist. "How did it happen?"

"Car accident." He dropped a kiss to the top of her head. "They were at an event in Seattle. They were on their way back to the ferry, and a drunk driver got on the freeway going the wrong direction and hit them. Full speed. The first responders said they died instantly. I'm grateful for that. That they didn't suffer, and that they were together."

He took a deep breath in, and Alex's soft floral perfume soothed him. "I honestly don't know what my dad would have done without my mom. And vice versa. That's something, I guess. All their friends came out for their memorial service, friends from all over the world. I never realized how many people they'd touched. Even though there wasn't a dry eye to be found, it really was a true celebration of their lives."

She glanced up at him, and her eyes brimmed with tears.

"Don't be sad, sweetheart," he said, giving her a small smile. "They lived wonderful lives surrounded by tons of people they genuinely loved, and who loved them right back. You would have liked them, and I know they would have adored you."

"What were their names?"

He wiped a runaway tear from her cheek. This woman—*his* woman—had such a big heart. "Liam and Annie O'Conner."

A high-pitched squeal pierced the café. "Oh my word!"

Turning toward the excited cry, he chuckled. Joe had made it maybe three steps through the front door before Mrs. Abbot and Mrs. Yoshida had spotted him. They descended on him with matching ear-to-ear grins.

His chuckle grew into a full-out laugh when Mrs. Yoshida pinched Joe's cheek, causing his friend to flush a bright embarrassed pink.

"My word," Mrs. Yoshida said to Mrs. Abbot. "Now, isn't he just the most handsome thing you've ever seen?"

"You're a doll, Mrs. Y." Joe grinned and wagged his eyebrows, causing both women to titter. "Make sure O'Conner over there doesn't hear you, though. He might get jealous."

"Now, Joe," Mrs. Abbot gently scolded, "why have you stayed away for so long? You know your dad misses you."

"I know, Mrs. A." Joe's blue eyes twinkled. "I actually get to see Dad quite a bit, though. We meet up every few months down in Palm Springs. He *claims* he misses me and that the warm weather does him good, but between the three of us, I personally think it's the wineries, golf, and, of course, all the retired young ladies milling about."

Both women erupted in giggles.

Roxie walked through the front door, arching a brow as she looked for the source of the commotion. When she spotted Joe, she scowled.

Quinn bit back a groan.

"Yikes," Alex muttered.

Roxie completely ignored Joe, giving Quinn and Alex a stiff nod before storming past the counter and into the back.

<hr>

Alex wasn't sure if she should be concerned about Roxie or not. Though she hadn't known the woman for very long, she'd never seen her friend this out of sorts. There were obvious long-standing issues between Roxie and Joe, but something told her that whatever was currently rattling Roxie went deeper than usual.

She reached for Quinn. As if reading her mind, he helped her down from the chair.

Entering the kitchen area, she found Roxie pacing back and forth, her expression flitting between frustration, anger, and sadness.

She could guess at the source of her friend's irritation and anger. But the sadness? She had no clue. That made her heart ache.

"Are you okay, Rox?"

A few moments of silence passed as Roxie's emotions continued to battle one another for dominance. Anger seemed to win out, and Alex let out a sigh of relief. She'd rather see her friend angry than sad.

"He has some nerve, you know that?" Roxie hissed. "After the way he's been treating me these past few years, he has the fucking *nerve* to step foot into my shop?" She came to an abrupt stop in front of the sink. With jerky movements, she snapped on the faucet.

Alex winced as Roxie scoured her hands under the steaming water.

"Then he sits there with Mrs. Abbot and Mrs. Yoshida as they just . . . freaking dote on him and coddle him like he's the best thing since sliced fucking bread. Ugh!" She spun around, dried her hands, and took out a large round of dough from the refrigerator. "I can't even think, I'm so mad. And the fucker just sits there with that smarmy grin—eating it all up, like the world just happily revolves around his stupid ass. He has the nerve to call *me* conceited and self-centered?"

Her eyes widened as Roxie pounded the dough with a rolling pin. Hard. Way too hard. She almost felt bad for the dough. "No, sweetie, you aren't conceited at all."

And Roxie truly wasn't. Yes, her friend was the tiniest bit self-absorbed, but that was because she was so focused on her business. It wasn't malicious. It was just that Comfort Food meant everything to her.

Roxie's face lit up at Alex's affirmation, and she took another whack at the dough.

The poor, poor dough.

"Thank you, Alex. See, that's *exactly* what I'm talking about. The little shit gets on his damn high horse where everything has to be *his* way or not at all. That's it." She slammed down the rolling pin, wiped her floured hands on a towel, and flew past Alex. "He's out of here."

With reflexes she hadn't known she possessed, she seized Roxie's passing arm. "Whoa. What are you going to do? Go out there and yell at him? Scream at him to leave your café? Make a scene in front of your customers? Be *that* hysterical female? Act like a self-absorbed princess and prove him right?" She strengthened her grip on Roxie's arm as the woman tried to pull away. "Take a breather, Rox. Just take a deep, deep breath."

Mouth hanging open, Roxie looked like she wanted to tell Alex to shove it, but she grudgingly obeyed.

Still holding Roxie's arm, she walked her friend into the office and nudged her toward her chair. "Roxie, you need to take the high road on this one. I don't know what Joe's deal is. And neither do you. But guess what? If he hasn't told you by now, chances are he's never going to. Ever."

She paused, taking the seat across from Roxie. "So instead, Joe's just going to be a jerk. What's worse is that he'll continue to be a jerk to you in front of other people—people who care about *both* of you. But no matter how much you may want to, you can't just run out there and yell at him. You're not kids anymore. This is your business. You don't want to do anything to jeopardize it, do you?"

Roxie looked at the ceiling, shoulders tense, and took four deep breaths. She opened her mouth to speak, but quickly closed it. Then took two more breaths. At last, she said, "Of course not, Alex. But he makes me so damn mad. Quinn's pissed me off before, but never like this. Look." She held out her trembling hands. "I've never been this mad at anyone before."

She gave Roxie an understanding nod. "I get it. I really do. But unfortunately for you, Joe's going to be staying in town for the next few days. So, you're just going to have to suck it up and deal with him."

Roxie's mouth dropped open. Again. "Whose side are you on?"

"That's exactly the problem. I don't want to be on a *side*. It's not about you versus him. It's about the two of you needing to get over whatever it is that's bothering you guys and act like adults. Simple as that."

"But it's not my fault!" Roxie huffed.

She couldn't stop the corners of her mouth from tipping up. "Let me guess, he started it?"

Roxie released an angry sigh. "Look, I know it may seem like I'm acting like a child, but I'm really not."

"Have you ever thought that if you stopped reacting to him, he'd stop picking at you?"

"This isn't him just being annoying. Annoying is what Quinn can be. I can handle annoying. But Joe? Joe is *evil*, Alex. Pure evil."

She rolled her eyes. Oh boy . . .

"Okay, fine," Roxie spat. "Maybe *evil* is stretching it. Still, he says mean and hurtful things, and I will not sit quietly while he insults me. I won't do it anymore." Roxie took a breath. When she exhaled, her shoulders sagged. "But you're right. My yelling at him does no good. In some sick, twisted way, it probably just eggs him on. The bastard."

"Roxie!" Quinn called from the front. "Phone. Line one, uh, I think."

"Thanks, Alex. You're a lifesaver. Or a business-saver, in this case." Roxie gave her a quick side hug, then picked up her landline.

Out front, Alex settled back onto her stool. Comfort Food was still quiet, with only Joe, Quinn, Mrs. Abbot, and Mrs. Yoshida occupying a table.

Quinn noticed her return and rose, glancing at his watch. He crossed the room to her. "We need you to come back to Joe's house with us. Roxie, too."

She nodded. "Sure, but good luck getting Roxie out of here before closing time. She won't budge."

"Who won't budge?" Roxie asked, coming out of the kitchen area.

"You," Quinn answered.

Roxie's brow knit in confusion. "Why am I budging?"

"Joe and I need the two of you to come back to the house."

"It's quiet now, so go ahead and take Alex home. I've got a few more hours before I'm out." Roxie turned to answer the ringing phone.

"What'd I tell you?" she said to Quinn, her smile smug.

When Roxie hung up, he caught her attention. "I need you

to head over to Joe's when you're finished here. You're done at four today."

"Probably closer to five thirty," Roxie said while she rearranged the refrigerated display case. "I have inventory."

"You're done at four today," he repeated, his voice low. It wasn't a request.

Roxie's head whipped up.

Alex understood why; there was a definite command in Quinn's tone. She frowned, her nerves tingling with apprehension. She couldn't read the look he was giving Roxie, but whatever message his gray eyes relayed to her worked.

"Okay, Quinn." Roxie nodded. "I'll head out at four."

He helped Alex down from the stool, then ushered her toward the door, pausing at Mrs. Abbot and Mrs. Yoshida's table. "Ladies, I hate to break up the reunion, but I need to steal Joe from you."

She chuckled as the women rose and fluttered about, making one final fuss over both men.

On their way to the door, she saw Roxie and Joe throw glares at each other. She cringed. They were like a couple of middle schoolers, not adults in their mid-freaking-thirties. It took all her effort to not roll her eyes. She had no clue how Quinn hadn't already strangled them both.

CHAPTER THIRTY-SEVEN

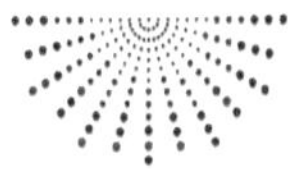

Alex glanced at the clock. Four thirty. They'd been sitting around Joe's kitchen table for the past hour, discussing what-if scenarios and strategies for how to tackle each one.

Well, to be honest, Quinn and Joe were talking. *She* was worrying. And as the minutes ticked by, her anxiety skyrocketed.

The men fell silent as Roxie barged through the back door and into the kitchen, cell phone at her ear, arms loaded with bags.

"Memorial Day weekend?" Roxie said into her phone, setting the bags down on the counter and then rummaging through a drawer. "And Fourth of July?"

Quinn tossed her Joe's notepad and pen, and she shot him a thankful smile as she furiously began scribbling. "*And* the mayor's birthday party . . . Got it."

A few clarifications later, Roxie ended the call and pumped her fist into the air. She spun around and turned on the oven, then unloaded the bags onto the counter. "You won't believe the catering order Bonnie Green just placed with me. *Three* parties!

And earlier today, I had four other people put in catering requests." She turned to the group. "Stroganoff or manicotti?"

"Manicotti," Quinn replied.

At the same time, Joe said, "Stroganoff."

With a slight tilt of her head, Roxie smirked at Joe. "Though the childish part of me says your opinion doesn't count worth a—"

Alex cleared her throat. Loudly.

She appreciated Roxie's distracting chatter, but not when it led to a name-calling match.

Roxie took a deep breath and turned to her. "You're the tiebreaker. What'll it be?"

Petty squabble averted, she eyed the two men. Her gaze settled on Quinn, and she crooked her finger. "Come here."

Without hesitation, he leaned forward. She ran her fingers through his hair, and her insides went gooey when her engagement ring caught the light and twinkled. She pulled his head in for a quick kiss.

"I love you," she told him. Then she pushed him back and looked at Roxie. "Stroganoff, please."

Joe and Roxie burst into laughter.

Quinn stared at her in disbelief. "Damn. That was cold, sweetheart."

"Stroganoff it is." Roxie shoved the dish into the oven and set the timer. "I'll go put this in your freezer," she said to Quinn. Gathering the dish of manicotti under one arm and answering her ringing cell phone with the other, she walked out the back door.

As the aroma of stroganoff began to tease the air, Alex grew restless. She glanced at the clock again and sighed.

Joe had been on the phone for the last ten minutes, and

when he finally hung up, she pounced. "Any updates on where Preston is?"

Joe sat back in his chair. "Downing's jet touched down at Boeing Field. As I mentioned, we put a couple agents there. They said that when Woodsworth arrived, he was met by a car. They're now heading south."

"South?" Quinn asked. "But we're north."

"I don't know, man. The agents have been following him for about twenty. Maybe he's driving around the Sound and taking the Port Townsend ferry over." Joe shrugged, the crease between his brows deepening. "They'll call the second his car changes directions."

Quinn nodded, but uneasiness clouded his expression. "I talked to Gavin. He and his crew are on standby."

"Who's Gavin?" she asked.

"Gavin Frazier. He runs a private security company. They have an office up by Cade's gym. He and his crew are a bunch of retired special ops guys. Good group. They can provide whatever backup's needed."

"Any of your deputies on this?" Joe asked.

"All of them. I've got a couple down at the ferry dock here, and another over at the Whidbey dock with one of Gavin's guys who was already there." He rubbed his neck. "I don't know, Buchanan. Something feels off, and I don't like it. They shouldn't be going south."

"I hear you. Of all the route options, that's the one that takes the longest to get here." Joe rose from the table and began to pace. "My Spidey-senses are in overdrive right now."

Her heart tripped. Great. They both thought something wasn't adding up. Not a good sign.

The thought of coming face to face with Preston made her stomach turn. Saliva pooled in her mouth, and the savory smell of the baking stroganoff triggered a gag. She was going to puke.

Knowing she had to calm herself down, she inhaled, held for four counts, then exhaled slowly.

Picking up on her distress, Quinn closed his hands over hers. "Look at me, sweetheart."

Alex stared at their joined hands for a moment, at the beautiful ring he'd given her, and her breathing evened out.

She could do this. She wasn't alone anymore.

She exhaled again and glanced up at Quinn. His eyes were so full of love and determination that some of the tension inside her eased. She had no idea what she'd done to deserve him, but she was forever thankful he had come into her life.

"He might not come after you right away," Quinn said. "I'm sure he knows that the feds are tailing him, so he may lie low for a while, maybe even for a long while, before coming to find you."

She nodded. "What you're saying is that I shouldn't get my hopes up that this will all end soon. And that I shouldn't let my guard down."

"Exactly." Quinn squeezed her hands. "That applies to all of us."

"That's right," Joe agreed.

"What's with the über-serious mood?" Roxie asked, shutting the back door behind her. "Has something happened?"

"Woodsworth is on the move," Joe said.

She peered into the oven. "How can he be on the move when he's still in jail?"

"Because he was released from jail this morning, Rox," Joe snapped, his shoulders taut with frustration.

She rolled her eyes. "Don't bite my head off, jerk-wad. I just asked one simple question."

"Enough, you two. Roxie, sit," Quinn said. He stood from

the table, and when he passed Joe, he slapped him on the side of the head. Hard.

Despite her fraying nerves and growing worry, she chuckled.

———————————

Quinn placed both hands on Roxie's shoulders and physically steered her—while she grumbled, of course—into his vacated chair. Once she was seated, he glared at Joe in a silent message to shut the fuck up, then began updating her on the most recent developments.

Until her cell phone rang yet again.

"I swear to god, Roxanne," Joe growled as he continued to pace the room. "If that thing rings one more time . . ."

Quinn leaned back against the sink, crossed his arms over his chest, and watched his friends. They were a train wreck. The most irritating fucking train wreck ever.

He could almost see the waves of annoyance radiating off Joe when Roxie disappeared into the living room with her ever-present phone glued to her ear. Of course, it didn't help that she'd waved Joe off with a shooing motion on her way out, as if he were an annoying fly—which, Quinn had to admit, Joe kinda was.

He shook his head as his friend continued to glare at the now-empty space where Roxie had stood. "What the fuck, Buchanan?"

"What do you mean?"

He scoffed. "Come off it, man. You've been busting her balls ever since you got back into town."

"Really? I've been busting Rox's *balls*?"

His eyes rolled. "Yeah, and you know you have. What gives?"

"I don't know."

When Joe wouldn't meet his eyes, his curiosity peaked. "Bullshit."

Joe shrugged. "She's really annoying and—"

"She's *always* annoyed you," he interrupted.

"True. But it's different now."

He frowned. What the hell did *that* mean?

He started to ask, but the words died on his lips when Roxie walked back into the kitchen. Halfway to the table, her cell phone rang again. Joe went rigid.

Quinn cringed, then glanced over at Alex, who was shaking her head.

They both startled when Joe lost his fucking mind.

"Holy fuck, Rox! I'm going to break that fucking thing. Can you please tell your stupid boyfriends to give it a rest? Just for one goddamn night?"

Roxie stormed up to Joe, eyes narrowed, and jabbed her finger into his chest. "This is *work*, you asshole! I don't know if you've noticed, but I run a business. Part of which is catering. Granted, this may be a bit beyond your intellectual grasp, Joe, but try to keep up."

Hoooly shit . . . Quinn grimaced.

Speaking deliberately slow, she continued, "In order to run a catering business, customers have to place an order with me." She jabbed her finger into his chest again. "And that requires people to—that's right, all together now—*call me*." She waved her ringing phone in his face.

Before anyone could blink, Joe snatched the phone out of her hand and threw it against the wall behind her. It shattered.

What. The. Fuck?

Roxie's jaw dropped. Hell, *everyone's* jaw dropped.

Seconds ticked by as silence filled the room.

Quinn could only stare at Joe in dismay. He took a step toward Roxie, pausing when she turned to face Joe. Her usually vibrant green eyes looked like a wounded puppy's, and they brimmed with tears.

"What did I ever do to make you hate me so much?" Roxie asked, her voice barely above a whisper. Alex approached her, but Roxie shook her head, walking to the back door. "I have to go call Mrs. Green. I'll be back in a little bit."

The fury that rolled through Quinn was swift. Apparently, now he was going to have to murder his best fucking friend. But first, he was going to put his fist through said best fucking friend's face.

Nobody made Roxie cry.

He took a menacing step toward Joe, but Alex's hand on his chest brought him to an abrupt halt. When their gazes met, she simply shook her head.

Fuck.

He let out a breath and unclenched the fists he had no memory of forming. He put his arm around Alex's shoulders, and some of his fury dissipated. She was probably right. Smashing Joe's face in wouldn't do anyone any good, especially with so much already going on.

After staring in silence at the closed door for a full minute, Joe raked his hands across his face, then clasped them on top of his head. Looking over at Quinn and Alex, he said, "Sorry about that."

Alex's fists slammed down on her narrow hips. "There's nothing to apologize to *us* for."

"Seriously, man." He shook his head in disappointment. "What the fuck was that?"

"I'm an asshole, okay?" Joe threw his head back and scowled. "Fuck. I'll go apologize to her." He reached for the door right as his cell phone rang. He answered with a heavy sigh.

As Joe listened to the caller, his spine went rigid.

A warning chill raced down Alex's neck. As if someone had flipped a switch, all her senses snapped to full alert. Quinn pulled her close to him, and when she glanced up at his face, his eyes were laser-focused on Joe.

"What the fuck does that mean?" Joe shouted into the phone as he stalked around the kitchen. "Call me when you get your heads out of your goddamn asses!" He disconnected the call, looking about two seconds away from hurling his phone across the room. Composing himself—mildly—he tossed it on the island instead.

"They fucking lost him," he spat.

"Where?" Quinn asked. The one word was so foreboding, it had goosebumps prickling her skin.

She stepped even closer to him, and he pulled her back to his chest, wrapping his arms around her from behind.

Rubbing the back of his neck, Joe let out a sigh. "They tailed the car south from the airfield. About an hour and fifteen in, the car stopped at a gas station. The female driver and a male passenger got out. The agents got a good look at the male passenger and it wasn't Woodsworth. His coloring and height were right, but the guy wasn't big enough.

"The two immediately lawyered up and aren't talking. When the agents checked the car, they found body padding and a fucking face mask that looked like Woodsworth. They're talking high-end, *Mission Impossible*-style shit." He shook his head. "They have no fucking idea where Woodsworth is."

They stood in silence as they absorbed the news. Joe's cell rang again, and he answered immediately.

Nausea swept over her as Joe mumbled into his phone.

The minutes ticked by like hours. Joe went still, and his jaw clenched moments before he hung up.

"What do they know?" Fear made her words curt.

"The person they thought was Woodsworth hopped into the car at Boeing Field, right?"

They nodded, and Joe grabbed a tablet out of his briefcase. Setting it on the table, he pulled up a map of Washington. As they gathered around, he zoomed in on the Puget Sound.

"So, the mystery guy gets in the car here, and they drive south. Our guys tail them for about ninety miles to here." His finger indicated a spot on the map. "Ninety miles, and then they purposely pull off the road and let our guys figure it out. That's about an hour and a half that Woodsworth's unaccounted for . . ."

Her heart raced, and bile climbed up her throat. *Holy crap.* Preston could be anywhere. She hugged her arms around her middle and looked between the two men.

Quinn eyed Joe. "You're thinking Woodsworth hopped a plane at Boeing Field, then?"

"Yeah, but to which airfield?"

Quinn studied the map. "If you look at the three closest airfields to Hudson Island, with a ferry ride or private boat—we shut down helo access aside from medical, so those are your only ways onto the island—they're all about forty-five minutes away, give or take."

"Right." Joe's brow furrowed. "The problem is that according to the agent on the phone, all of those airfields have taken in at least one small plane during the last hour."

"So, we still don't know where he is." Alex's voice trembled, betraying her nerves.

She took in a deep breath, but it didn't calm her. Falling onto a chair, she sat in silence, stomach turning, and listened as they hashed out possible scenarios.

After a while, she grew restless. She had to do something. *Anything.* She couldn't just sit here and wait. She rose from the table.

"I'm going to go check on Roxie," she said.

Walking toward the back door, she slowed when the sound of feet stumbling on the back porch caught her attention.

"Found her," Joe muttered, exasperation dripping from his words. "Sounds like someone snuck into the liquor cabinet and threw back a few."

"And whose fault would that be, Joe?" she tossed back in irritation.

"Touché, Alex," he said. "Touché."

Seconds later, the back door exploded. Splintered wood and shattered glass flew through the air.

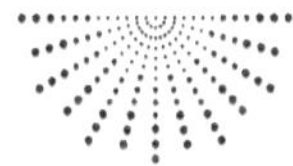

CHAPTER THIRTY-EIGHT

Quinn's heart stopped. He lunged for Alex. Grabbing her, he used his body as a shield and quickly moved them backward through the kitchen archway into the living room.

"Stay," he commanded. He ran to the side table, retrieving the holster and Glock he'd placed there earlier. "Joe?"

"Clear," Joe called out.

"I'm serious, Alex. Stay behind this wall. Do *not* move from this spot." He kissed her quickly on the lips as she nodded. He sprang to his feet, peering around the corner.

Cautiously, he re-entered the kitchen, weapon drawn. Joe was to his right, crouched behind the kitchen island with his own weapon aimed at the empty doorway. Quinn joined him behind the island.

Seconds ticked by before a movement beyond the splintered door caught his attention. A figure gradually came into view.

On either side of the island, both men froze.

"Fuck," he muttered. His rage took a dangerous turn.

Preston Woodsworth stood in the doorway. In front of

him was Roxie. Blood streamed down her face, and one of her shoulders fell at an unnatural angle. Woodsworth had an arm locked against her neck, holding her in place, while his other jammed a gun into the side of her head.

"Evening, gentlemen." Woodsworth's voice was smooth and conversational. "You may want to lower your weapons."

No way in hell. "Let her go, Woodsworth," Quinn said, rising. In his peripheral, Joe did the same.

"Natalie! I know you can hear me. Come see what surprise I have for you." His arm visibly tightened around Roxie's throat, making her whimper.

Motherfucker. He was going to destroy this asshole at the first opportunity.

"Natalie," Preston called out again. "I can either choke her to death or blow her brains out. Which would you prefer, darling? Either one sounds like a good time to me."

Upon hearing Preston's voice, Alex peeked around the corner. Her breath caught at the sight before her. Quinn and Joe, guns drawn, stood opposite Preston as he held Roxie captive. Her friend's eyes were wide, her skin flushed and covered in blood.

"Let her go, Preston," she demanded, sounding stronger than she felt. She inched into the kitchen, hands outstretched before her to show she was unarmed.

"Natalie, darling, what have you done with your hair? You know I hate your natural color." Though his volume rose with every word, his hold around Roxie's throat relaxed. "How many times have I told you that, you stupid bitch?!"

Her heart broke at the terror in Roxie's eyes.

"Let her go, Preston," she repeated.

Ignoring her, he looked back at Quinn and Joe. "This is

the last time I'm going to tell you boys." He smiled, tightening his grip around Roxie's neck. "Drop your guns. Or it'll be my pleasure to put a hole in this hot little number's head."

She walked deeper into the kitchen.

"Alex, stay back," Quinn barked.

"Alex?" Preston asked with a raise of his eyebrow. "That's right, you're using that ridiculous name now. So provincial. Really, what the hell kind of name is that, *Natalie* darling?"

"Please, Preston." She didn't dare make eye contact with Quinn. "Let her go. Please."

"Boys?" Preston pushed the muzzle of his gun harder against Roxie's head, and when she cried out, both men lowered their weapons.

Preston smiled. "Put the guns down and kick them to me. You know how this goes."

Quinn and Joe placed their weapons on the floor and then kicked them in opposite directions. Away from Preston.

Preston's eyes narrowed, and he tsked, redirecting his attention to Alex. "Natalie, darling, you have ten seconds to bring those guns over to me."

She nodded. As quick as she could, she retrieved the guns. Then hesitated.

Preston pinned her with his malicious blue eyes. "It's very simple, Natalie. If you want your friend to not have a hole in her fucking head, you'll toss the guns out the door, and we'll make a little swap. You come with me. End of story. If you want to play hero and shoot me, that's fine, too. But I'm taking your little friend here out with me. Can you live with that?"

She stole a glance at Quinn, and her heart sank. His attention was bouncing between her and Roxie. Anguish and fury warred in his eyes. And tore at her heart.

There was no other choice.

"Okay," she whispered. "Please don't hurt her."

Warily, she moved past Preston and heaved the guns through the remains of the back door. As she turned around, her gaze locked with Quinn's.

I love you, she mouthed, her chest clutching painfully.

Goodbye, she thought with her breath locked in her throat.

She glanced down at the sapphire and diamond ring on her finger. And her heart shattered. She'd been so close. So damn close to her happily ever after.

Lifting her chin and squaring her shoulders, she faced Preston. She had no doubt that he would kill her. Just like she had no doubt he'd make her suffer first.

Well, if she had to die, she was taking him with her.

"Let. Her. Go."

With a smile, Preston loosened his hold on Roxie, leaning her slightly forward. Then, like a flash, his hand swung out. The butt of his gun struck the back of Roxie's head. The crack was deafening in the silent room.

Roxie crumpled at his feet, blood rapidly pooling beneath her head.

"Roxie!" She reached for her friend but was yanked back by the hair. Flames licked her scalp.

"Don't even think about it, boys," Preston said, trapping her in the same headlock he'd just relinquished. He pointed his gun at Roxie's unconscious body. "Don't think I won't do it. Because I will if you make me. Now, face down on the ground you go."

Quinn and Joe lowered to the floor as Preston dragged Alex out the mangled door.

"Hang on, Alex," Quinn murmured.

Hatred. Anger. Terror. Helplessness. He felt all of it.

He'd seen the hopelessness in Alex's eyes. He'd known

when she'd mouthed *I love you* to him that she thought she was walking to her death.

There was no way in hell he was going to let that happen.

The second Preston was out of sight, they crawled to Roxie.

"Hold on, baby," Joe whispered to Roxie while dialing his cell phone. "Gun safe, Quinn."

Nodding, he ran to the living room closet, keyed in the safe's code, and returned to Joe in under a minute.

"I'll go around the back. You take the front," he said in a hushed voice. He handed Joe a revolver and added the Sig to his holster. His gaze shifted to Roxie. "How is she?"

"Breathing. Her pulse is strong right now, but I don't know. Backup and paramedics are on their way. I don't want to move her."

"Then don't. Let's go."

Both men laid a soft kiss on Roxie's lifeless, bleeding head, then stood.

As they were about to part ways, he put a hand on Joe's arm. "I'm shooting to kill, Buchanan. I don't care if you all want Woodsworth alive or not. When he gets in my line of sight, the fucker's a dead man."

"No—" Joe glanced back at Roxie. His eyes filled with pain.

Despite whatever shit the two of them had going on, Joe was just as devastated as he was to see the third member of their best-friend trio lying unconscious in a pool of her own blood.

"Yeah. If you've got a shot, O'Conner, take the mother-fucker out."

CHAPTER THIRTY-NINE

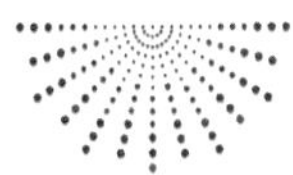

Preston towed Alex down the steps and into the yard before finally relaxing his grip around her neck. She gasped, sucking in a desperate breath.

"You fucked him, didn't you?" he hissed. "I can see it in the way he looks at you. You're fucking him, aren't you, you stupid whoring cunt?!" Spit dribbled down his chin as he shouted.

Still gripping the gun, he swung out his hand and crashed the barrel into the side of her head. She dropped to her knees, and bright flashing stars consumed her vision. He grabbed her by the hair again and dragged her farther across the yard. Her teeth rattled in her head.

She gripped his wrist with both hands and struggled to get her feet under her. Losing her balance, she flung out her arms to brace her fall.

Her heart stuttered when her left hand touched metal. A gun. One of the guns she'd thrown out the door. She clamped her fingers around it. Before she could do anything more, Preston's foot connected with her chest, and her breath left in an agonizing rush. She heard a loud pop, and she gasped for air while white-hot fire blazed across her torso.

Wrenching her hair harder, Preston pressed the muzzle of his gun to her forehead.

"You're going to beg, Natalie," he spat, eyes demonic. "Then I'm going to beat that bastard baby out of you, you cheating whore! You're going to *beg* me for your life."

"Never," she said, her fingers tightening around the cold handle of the gun. Summoning the last of her energy, she raised the gun, aimed it blindly in Preston's direction, and pulled the trigger. Then again. And again.

Preston cried out and released her, staggering backward.

She dropped to the ground, every part of her on fire. Desperate to get away from him, she managed to push to her knees.

Something connected with her head, and a flash of light exploded across her vision. A split second later, she was on her back. Preston loomed over her, blood oozing from his shoulder and chest. She groaned when his foot landed on her stomach, holding her down.

He pointed his gun at her head. A victorious smile cut across his face. "I'll see you in hell, bitch."

She raised her gun once more, her arms trembling uncontrollably. "You first."

They both pulled their triggers, and the sound of fire-crackers filled her head. Throughout her body, nerves deto-nated. The gun fell from her hands.

Like a slow-motion movie, Preston's eyes widened with shock, and he dropped to the ground.

In the distance, she heard voices shouting. Seconds later —or it could have been minutes, hours, days, she wasn't sure —Quinn's face hovered over her. He was speaking to her, but she couldn't make out his words.

"I love you," she tried to whisper, but it felt like she was drowning.

She attempted to lift her hand to his face, but a shocking, fierce pain answered the movement.

And then her world went dark.

CHAPTER FORTY

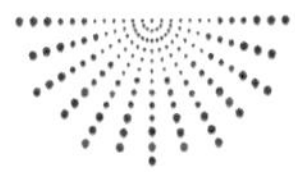

"Hey, gorgeous."

Alex blinked away the haze, and Quinn's face came into focus.

"Hi," she croaked.

"You know, Doc says he's pretty tired of coming to the hospital to visit you and that tough little baby." Quinn's gray eyes shone bright with emotion. "Stitches, knife wounds, bullet wounds . . . Said it's getting to be a bit much, sweetheart." He kissed her gently on the lips, relief evident on his face. "And frankly, I'm in agreement. No more playing with bad guys for you and the little one."

"How're you feeling, doll?" Joe called from the doorway with a smile.

She grimaced as she took in the unfamiliar hospital room. "Like I've been run over by a train." She exhaled slowly. She knew that she was probably on some sort of pain medication, but man, everything hurt.

"Close," Quinn said. "You got shot." A shadow passed over his face. Then, just like that, it was gone, and his charming smile was back in place. As if she'd imagined it. "And banged up pretty good. Similar aftereffect."

She had no idea what this sweet man had been through while she'd been in and out of consciousness, but from the dark circles beneath his eyes, it had been a lot. "How's Roxie?" she asked.

"She's fine," Joe said, walking to the foot of her bed. "She's already ordering everyone around. Driving everyone mad. Which means she's pretty much back to normal." He chuckled, flashing her a grin that didn't quite reach his eyes.

Quinn ran a reverent hand over her, as if he couldn't quite believe she was truly okay. "So, about this hospital stay, do you want the good news or the bad news?"

"Annie," she blurted out.

He paused, confusion on his face. "I'm sorry, what?"

She took his hand and held it, letting out a breath. She had honestly thought Preston was going to kill her. She'd thought her chance to be with Quinn—to have a life of love —was over. And yet here they were, sitting together, clearly exhausted but never more grateful.

She squeezed his hand, and her heart filled. She was taking this second—no, *third* chance the universe had given her, and she was running with it. "Annie. If this baby's a girl, I want to name her Annie. After your mom. Or Liam, if it's a boy. After your dad."

"Sweetheart," he whispered, bringing both of her hands to his lips. "You humble me."

"I love you." She tugged him toward her. "And I didn't think I'd ever get the chance to tell you so again."

Warmth and peace settled over her soul as his lips met hers. The pain melted away, and it was just them.

"Ahem," Joe interrupted, grinning like a loon from the foot of her bed.

She blushed. Apparently, it wasn't *just them*, after all. "Sorry, Joe. I forgot you were there."

He chuckled. "So it would appear."

Quinn sat on the bed next to her. "So, sweetheart, good news or bad news about this hospital stay?"

She groaned, shifting on the bed, needing to be as close to him as possible. "Surprise me."

"The good news is you can be out of here in a couple days. The bad news is the doctors won't—"

"Wait." She narrowed her eyes. "Where am I?"

"Seattle."

Her lips parted in shock.

"Yeah, sweetheart. They airlifted you over, and you've been here for four days."

"Holy crap, Quinn . . ." *Four* days?

"Exactly, sweetheart." He dropped a kiss to the top of her head, then laced his fingers with hers. "So, the doctors here were hesitant to release you. But our Doc has been here from the start—"

"You are my dad's favorite patient," Joe said with a wink.

"And Doc negotiated with them that if you went on full bed rest for at least the next month, then they'd spring you. The gunshot wound in your shoulder was miraculously a through-and-through, but it's the two bruised ribs that have everyone concerned. Bed rest is nonnegotiable. You okay with that?"

That explained the fire that consumed her with each breath. "I do feel pretty awful, so bed rest doesn't sound bad at all. But bed rest at *home*. With you. Not here."

Quinn brought her hand to his lips. "As for the other stuff, you want to hear both the good and bad news?"

She nodded. "Please."

"The good news is that Preston Woodsworth—"

"The third," Joe chimed in with an eye roll.

"—will never bother you again. You can call me a cold-hearted, vindictive bastard, but I'll happily admit that I did a little dance of joy when the son of a bitch died on the operating table."

She leaned her head back, meeting Quinn's gaze. Silence filled the room as she absorbed what he'd said.

Dead. Preston was dead.

She'd thought she would have conflicting feelings. She'd imagined that guilt, grief, and happiness would war with each other. But as the news of Preston's death reverberated in her head, she was left with only one emotion.

"Does it make me a horrible person if I'm relieved?"

Quinn shook his head. "No. Not one bit, Alex."

Seconds ticked by as the reality of it all began to sink in. The enormity of the relief she felt was breathtaking. Staggering, really.

It was over. Truly over. Preston was gone.

A smile lit up her face. She shook her head, not fully believing it yet. "Wait, you said there was bad news?"

Joe cleared his throat, then patted her foot tucked under the bed covers. "I'm going to go check on Roxanne." He placed a kiss on Alex's forehead, and as he walked by Quinn, he gave him a brotherly slap on the shoulder.

She frowned. Worry began to simmer. "What is it? What's the bad news?"

"Well . . ." He tucked a stray hair behind her ear. "You know, that's my favorite piece."

Perhaps it was the drugs, or maybe it was all the chaos of everything crashing down on her, but she was thoroughly confused. "What?"

"That's my favorite part of your hair," he murmured. "It always falls in your face, and it gives me a reason to touch you."

"Quinn . . ." When he kissed her, the butterflies in her stomach took flight.

"I hate to break it to you, but the bad news is . . . well . . . you're stuck with me, sweetheart." His charming grin returned, and he pressed a kiss to both her palms. "Forever. Even if you want to shake me, I'm afraid it's too late. I just can't let you go."

She chuckled. "You know what, Quinn O'Conner? I can think of worse things than that. And if you want to shake *me*, it's too late for you, too. Because I'm not letting you go, either."

"Good. Because I love you and I need you to marry me. Soon." He slid the sapphire and diamond ring back onto her finger. "Alexandra Garcia, I promise you that no one will make you happier or drive you crazier or love you and this baby more than I will. If I have to spend the rest of my life proving that to you, then I'm looking forward to every minute of it."

Her eyes welled with tears. Could he be any more perfect? "How long is my bed rest for?"

His forehead knit, the crease between his brows popping. "Sorry?"

A tear slid down her cheek. "How long am I on bed rest for?"

He wiped away the lone tear, concern flickering across his handsome face. "Happy tears, right?"

She laughed, nodding as more fell. "You better believe they're happy tears, Sheriff."

With the pad of his thumb, he wiped the others away. "One month of bed rest. Up to six weeks, depending on how your ribs heal."

"Great." She knew she was smiling like a fool, but she didn't care. "Let's get married then."

With a matching grin, Quinn brought his lips down onto hers. "Absolutely, sweetheart."

EPILOGUE

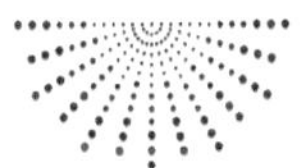

It had been five weeks of bed rest. The first couple had been a blur. She'd been so exhausted and in pain. Every time she'd moved, breathed too deep, or twisted the wrong way, it had been agony. But with Quinn by her side, everything had been fine. She'd slept, and she'd healed. Slowly.

The last three weeks had been another story entirely. The pain in her ribs had subsided, but Doc had still insisted she stay on bed rest to be safe. She'd been anemic, and her blood pressure had fluctuated too much for his liking.

She'd binge-watched countless shows but gotten restless after a few days. Her attention span had been nonexistent, so reading—one of her favorite things—hadn't been an option. While Quinn had gone to work, her saving grace had been the flood of visitors. Doc had stopped by to check on her every day. Over the course of the entire ordeal, he'd become more than just a doctor. More than just her friend's dad. He'd taken on the role of her surrogate father figure, and she treasured each and every one of his visits.

The Comfort Food crew—Nina, June, and Ella—had stopped by regularly. Mrs. Abbot, Mrs. Yoshida, Ray, and

Martha had sat with her as well, keeping her abreast of the latest and greatest Hudson Island gossip. Even Quinn's friend, Cade de la Rosa, had stopped by with an offer for free self-defense classes when she was feeling better. He'd also spilled embarrassing stories about Quinn that had put her in stitches.

Then, of course, there'd been Roxie. Her friend spent time with her every day after work. Though Roxie insisted she was fine—she'd suffered a concussion, a dislocated shoulder, and numerous bumps and bruises—shadows remained. While her friend was still chipper—and still a drill sergeant at work, as reported by the crew—Alex felt like something was off.

She couldn't quite put her finger on what exactly was wrong, but it was something. And it hurt her heart because she had no clue how to help her friend. But she'd give Roxie time and hope her friend would confide in her eventually.

Now here she was. She'd been officially taken off bed rest three days earlier.

She'd wanted to make good on her deal with Quinn—get married once she'd gotten the all-clear—but to her surprise, he'd hesitated.

He'd promised it wasn't because he didn't want to get married, because he did. He just wanted to hold off a few days. Apparently, he had a surprise for her first. She couldn't say she was a fan of surprises, but the excitement that had sparkled in his gray eyes had persuaded her to relent.

Which had led her to the present moment.

For the first time in weeks, she was dressed. In real clothes. Not sweatpants or leggings or baggy T-shirts. But an actual dress. With sandals. She'd even shaved her legs and put on mascara.

It was her first non-medical outing since all the craziness with Preston.

Placing her hands over her growing baby bump, happiness filled her. While she had so many conflicting feelings about Preston—feelings she was working with a therapist to sort out—regret was no longer one of them. Her little avocado wouldn't be here if it hadn't been for him. And while she was still reconciling her emotions, she'd come to find peace with that.

Large, calloused hands covered hers, and she smiled.

"You ready, sweetheart," Quinn murmured.

She leaned back into his chest and glanced up.

This wonderful man, who'd been her rock . . . he wouldn't be in her life if it hadn't been for her ex, either.

Life was crazy and mysterious like that. It truly was.

She squeezed his hands. "Yup. Let's see what this big surprise you have is."

Lacing their fingers together, Quinn pulled her toward the entrance to Monty's Tavern, a bar and grill a street over from Comfort Food and five doors up from Ray's Diner. While she'd yet to dine there, she'd met the owner, Four, numerous times since he was good friends with Quinn and Roxie and a Comfort Food regular.

Stepping through the door, it took a moment for her eyes to adjust. Though the tavern had a full wall of sliding glass doors, it was considerably dimmer than outside. The décor was a charming old-world nautical theme and—

Her heart stopped.

She wavered on her feet.

But strong arms settled at her waist, holding her up.

"Breathe, sweetheart," Quinn's loving voice whispered.

"Surprise," the woman before her said.

Tears sprang to her eyes and spilled down her cheeks. Then she was in motion.

"Mom," she sobbed, launching herself into the open arms awaiting her.

The scent of Old Spice hit her nose, and another sob tore from her throat. Lifting her head, she met her father's shimmering whiskey-brown eyes. "Dad."

She wept with joy and shock as she hugged her parents for the first time in over five years. When she came up for air, another figure stepped into her line of sight, and a fresh wave of tears engulfed her.

"Kayla," she said, her throat thick.

Then she was in her big sister's arms, with their parents hugging them both.

After what felt like the world's longest and most joyous hug, she released her family. Taking a moment to sop up her damp face, she knew her makeup was wrecked. But she didn't care. Not one bit.

A hand settled at the small of her back, and her heart threatened to burst. Gazing up at Quinn, her lower lip quivered. He'd done this. For her.

"I love you so much, Quinn. Thank you."

Wiping away a tear with his thumb, he dropped a kiss to her lips. "Happy tears?"

She nodded, her vision growing misty again. "Can I ask you for one more thing?"

His eyes crinkled at the corners. "Anything, sweetheart."

"Can we get married now?"

He threw his head back and laughed. Pulling her tight against him, he lifted her off her feet. "Absolutely, Alex Garcia. Absolutely."

Then his lips claimed hers. Hoots and whistles sounded around them. And everything was perfect.

ENJOY THIS BOOK?

Reviews & ratings encourage other readers to try out a book. They're so important to getting the word out about a book and mean the world to every author.

I'd love your help in spreading the word. If you could take a quick moment to rate and/or leave a review for Shattered Vows on your favorite book site, I would be forever grateful! You can do that on Amazon, Goodreads and/or Bookbub. Thank you!

ABOUT THE AUTHOR

Christina Sol is an award-winning author who writes what she loves to read—romance books filled with heart, heat, and suspense.

An avid reader from the get-go, Christina was obsessed with The Babysitters Club, Sweet Valley Twins, Sweet Valley High, Christopher Pike, and all things V. C. Andrews. Her love for romance started with the Sunfire books, a YA historical romance series. Caroline by Willo Davis Roberts was her favorite of the series, and a copy of the 1984 novel is one of her most treasured possessions. Then she discovered Danielle Steele and Nora Roberts. And never looked back. She's still a voracious reader and enjoys all genres of romance but leans toward romantic suspense and dark romance.

She lives in the inland Pacific Northwest with her husband and two kids. When she's not writing, reading, or knitting, she's watching football or fueling her planner, sticker, and washi-tape obsession.

To find out more, visit: www.christinasol.com

ACKNOWLEDGMENTS

My wonderful readers: time is precious & I know there are so many entertainment options to choose from. From the bottom of my heart, thank you so much for choosing to spend your valuable time reading Alex & Quinn's story.

Heather G, Jen C, Danielle R, Megan S & Lynne P: thank you all for your comments, feedback, and honesty. It means so, so much!

LJ at Mayhem Cover Creations: your covers are breathtaking—thank you!

Todd, Lucy & Jackson: you three are my world. None of this would be possible without you.

My family & friends: thank you *so* much for all your support! It truly means the world to me.